Dan Pinckney is a retired military NCO with a combined service of 20 years of active service and another ten years as a military contractor working with inner-city youth in different schools. While on active duty, he attended college taking classes at different colleges in different states, until he was able to graduate with honors from Stonehill College in Easton, MA. After retiring, he obtained a teaching certificate in history, then applied and was selected to perform as a Junior ROTC instructor and assigned to a city high school.

While there, he used his skill and experience to encourage students to remain in school and even become interested in subjects like history and English, encouraging all his students to achieve what they thought was impossible, staying in school and graduating. Many, in fact, became interested in English and several are now teachers in different states.

However, it was while he was involved with the Air Force that he fell in love with stories and putting those ideas on paper. To date, he has had one self-published novel, *Journey to the Catskills* which is receiving more interest from publishing houses for possible remarketing, and is currently in negotiations to create a website to advertise his current and future works.

Dan Pinckney lives with his wife and kids in Rhode Island.

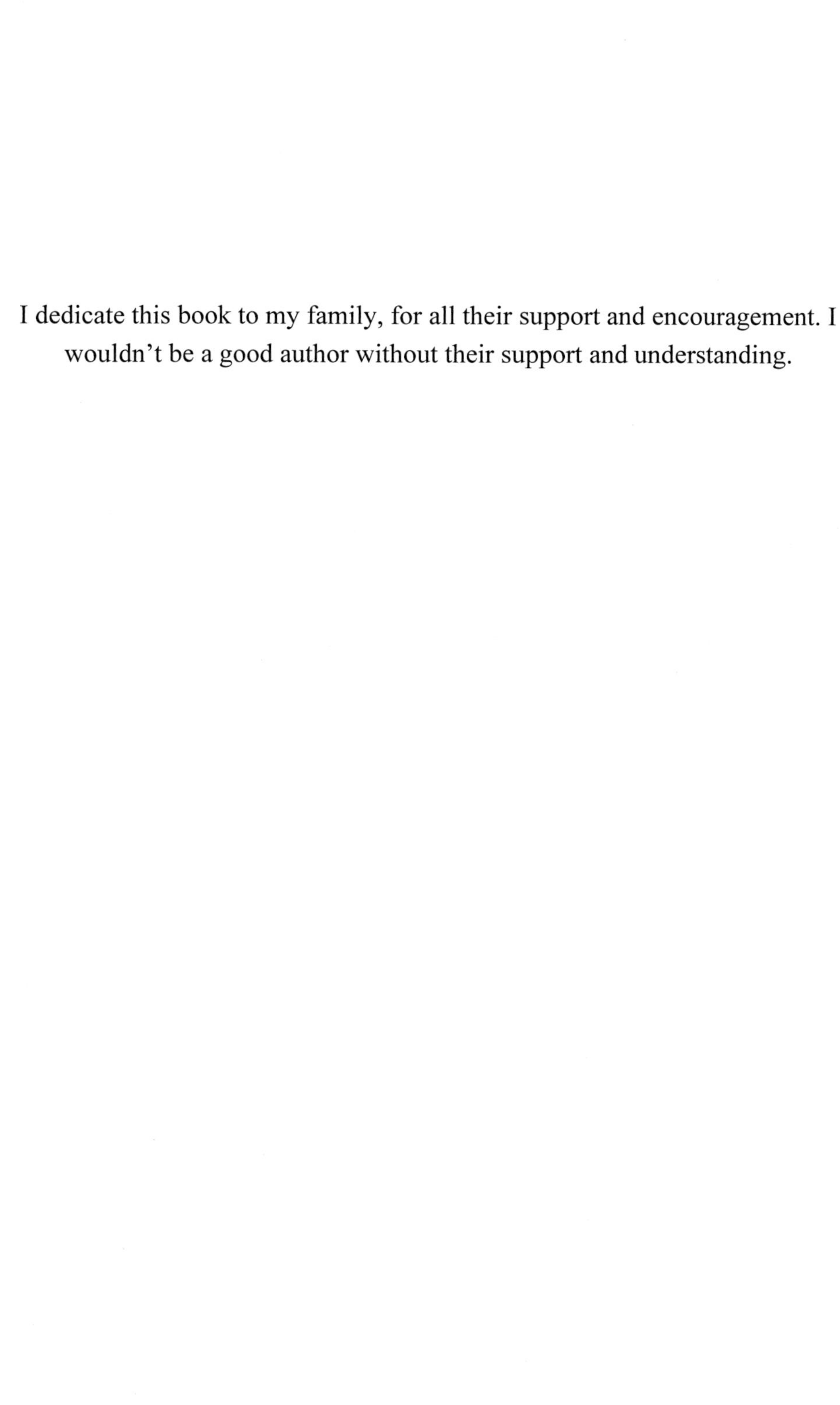

I dedicate this book to my family, for all their support and encouragement. I wouldn't be a good author without their support and understanding.

Dan Pinckney

HURRICANE RESCUE

Turmoil

AUSTIN MACAULEY PUBLISHERS™

LONDON * CAMBRIDGE * NEW YORK * SHARJAH

Ordering Information
Quantity sales: Special discounts are available on quantity purchases by corporations, associations, and others. For details, contact the publisher at the address below.

Publisher's Cataloging-in-Publication data
Pinckney, Dan
Hurricane Rescue

ISBN 9798889103790 (Paperback)
ISBN 9798889103806 (ePub e-book)

Library of Congress Control Number: 2023920490

www.austinmacauley.com/us

First Published 2024
Austin Macauley Publishers LLC
40 Wall Street, 33rd Floor, Suite 3302
New York, NY 10005
USA

mail-usa@austinmacauley.com
+1 (646) 5125767

To my wife for helping me understand the world around me, and to my friends who reviewed my writing and helped me work through the rough areas, to make the story more enjoyable.

Table of Contents

Chapter One
School

Even the youngest of us may be wrong sometimes—George Bernard Shaw

Andy Thompson walked slowly toward school, looking through the windows that lined the school at the sunlight trying to spear through the cloud cover. It was late October, near the end of hurricane season and his thoughts were taken by the upcoming event, Halloween. This year, his father had agreed to allow him to dress as the Devil; well, his father had agreed only because his mother had taken his side and helped to convince his father, a devout Catholic, that it was a good choice. Yesterday, Andy had gone to church, as he did almost every Sunday and realized how his father felt. He called it a what? Oh yeah, a sacrilege or something. He was smart enough to realize that a sacrilege was bad, but finally his mom convinced him it was only for the night and was harmless.

Andy didn't think it was such a bad thing. Last year, his best friend, Nathan Harp, had described how he had 'cleaned up' during the night and his costume looked great. Andy had dressed as a cop and as the two walked from house to house in their neighborhood, they played a form of 'Good and Bad'. They both had a good night, though it was at one house where an older woman made a comment about how Nathan's costume was handmade, versus his costume that he had bought at a store.

Andy was a bit jealous of Nathan; he was an only child and when his father left for weeks at a time to work on an oil rig in the Gulf of Mexico, Nathan's mom would dote on him, doing what she could to fill in for his father while he was away, which meant making his Devil costume from scratch. Andy had to admit, it was good, so he wanted the same thing this year and asked his mom to help him make it. She did the best she could; after all, she had a full-time job and though she put some time into it, the costume wasn't as good as

Nathan's. Andy hid his disappointment, knowing his mom stayed up late to make the costume, so he pretended to love it and wore it to school the day of Halloween. As he walked into their homeroom, he spied Nathan sitting there in a cop costume. Andy was just about to tease him when he saw a new girl sitting three seats over from his friend looking uncomfortable and nervous, her eyes darting from kid to kid. She wasn't wearing a costume, only a flowered dress, but since she was new, she probably didn't know that this day Andy felt bad for her and walked over. "Hi, I'm Andy Thompson." Out of the corner of his eye, he could see Nathan making faces at him, but Andy ignored him.

The girl looked up at him, she flashed a nice smile back, something Andy would always remember. "Hi, Andy, I'm Millicent Richards, but my friends at my old school called me Milly," she replied. She looked around the classroom as more students came in for attendance. "No one told me I should wear a costume today," she spoke quietly, the smile fading as she said this.

"Ah, don't worry. You look good in that dress. You can say you're Dorothy," he responded, then added, "you know, from the Wizard of Oz."

Milly smiled at this. "Thanks. I like that idea. I will."

Then the teacher came in and Andy headed to his seat which was behind Nathan. The teacher introduced Milly to the class and asked where she came from, to which Milly explained that she had moved from a town in South Carolina to Aurora, but she had been born in Italy when her father lived there and then moved to the United States when she was only two years old. This allowed the teacher to start asking students some geography questions about where Italy was. Andy didn't really care. He already knew a lot about geography but didn't like the other subjects as much except history and stories about pirates on the high seas.

But Milly had a chance to shine as she was normally shy and was worried about making friends in her new town. This type of questioning was something she excelled at and took pride in answering the questions, even throwing in some Italian, something her family spoke fluently. This surprised the other kids greatly and secretly she relished the opportunity of some of the other girls talking to her and asking questions during a break.

When she went home after school that first day, her spirits had lifted considerably and when her mother, Mary, asked her if she had made any new friends, she listed several girls and one boy. Mary took notice of this; she had been raised in Italy and only moved to the United States to attend college at the University of South Carolina where she had met and fell in love with her husband and Milly's father, Ned Richards. Mary and Ned spent a lot of time together during breaks in class; however, it was a great surprise to her when Ned asked her one day to marry him, after arranging a special day with her being surrounded by her friends as Ned got on one knee and proposed.

Ned returned to Italy with her after they were married and they tried living in her home country, but a recession and problems with the common market, convinced them both to head back to the United States after some rough financial times, especially after the birth of Milly. Mary followed Ned several weeks later to their new home in North Carolina where he had found a good job as manager in a large shipping firm. For Milly, the move had been almost terrifying, heading to a new country with new customs and things like dressing up for a special day made her feel confused and so shy, she hardly spoke to anyone, let alone strange males. But now, just two weeks back in the United States and she now had a young male friend on her first day of school. That was something she thought was of great interest and made a mental note to pass this information on to her husband, Ned.

When Halloween finally passed and school continued, Andy went right back to what he had done before Milly showed up, being the class clown. He didn't care much for schoolwork and found math to be boring and tedious. He enjoyed sporting events and would often accept challenges from his classmates. He could run faster than any other boy in his class and his favorite challenge was Dodgeball. Then one unusually warm day in early November, the class was told they could go outside for recess. Andy was really perked up for this and was hoping they could go outside and play.

As the kids lined up for recess, he noticed Milly standing there quietly. It was still her first week of school and she didn't know many people yet, so Andy decided he would talk to her a bit. As he stood beside her, Milly smiled at him as they stood there not talking. She hadn't had the chance to get to know most of the kids and they didn't have recess in her old school; only two long gym classes where they were encouraged to join in and exercise. She hadn't told anyone, but she was good at sports and enjoyed the classes. Unlike Andy, she also enjoyed her educational classes, especially art and science.

Once they were outside, Andy headed off with his friends and a race was on for the slides, they were always popular with the fourth graders. Usually, they would climb up them rather than slide down and it was always a race to see who could be first up. Normally, it was Andy, but even as he climbed the steep slide, he could see Milly on the monkey bars. She was moving up faster than he could, though he would never admit that and then he saw her do something he never would try, hanging upside down from the top by her legs. Another boy saw her as well and his shout alerted the others to what she was doing.

Instantly, Nathan was beside Andy, challenging him to show up that new girl. Then the other boys were calling on him to do the same, as Andy looked on. He never told anyone, but the reason he never played on the top rungs of the monkey bars was that he was a bit afraid of heights and only his cheering friends made him walk over to the bars and look up at Milly.

She smiled down at him. "Hi, Andy, you coming up here?"

Andy smiled back before looking over at his friends and giving them the thumbs up sign. "Yeah, I can do that," was how he replied. Before he would let his fear overcome him, he charged up the monkey bars, calling out how boys were better at sports than girls.

Milly, meanwhile, smiled down at him, though she could see the hesitancy in his face as he made his way up. "Andy, you don't have to do this. I'll come down if you want," she said with concern.

Andy just waved her concern away. If she could do it, so could he. When he reached the top, he didn't look down, just straddled the top for a moment as he took a couple of gulps of air before he swung his body through the bars, but he made a mistake even as Milly tried to warn him. He hadn't put his legs over the bars like she did, and when he dropped his torso though the top bars, he attempted to put his legs over the bars then, but it was too late. He managed to get one leg up, but his moment made him lose control and even as he tried to reach up and grab the bars, he plummeted to the ground over ten feet below, landing on his head, getting knocked out cold.

When Millicent saw what had happened, she quickly scrambled down and hovered over Andy, grabbing his hand and talking to him as another student ran to get a teacher. Several teachers were standing in a group keeping an eye on the kids from a distance and only when they saw several of the children hovering near the monkey bars and then a student running toward them in a panic, were they aware that something bad had happened.

Years of training in emergency situations spurred them into action. While one teacher called on her phone to the office, another called the nurse as the remainder ran toward the commotion. Their first order to get to the injured child and learn the extent of his injuries, while a few others corralled the children around the monkey bars and hustled them inside. Instead of heading to individual rooms, the kids were taken to the gym, mainly because several of their teachers were still outside and no one wanted to leave the children unsupervised.

Within four minutes of the accident, the nurse was racing outside, followed by the principal and an aide who was talking on the phone to the town fire department which was already in the process of dispatching an ambulance and truck to the school. The nurse saw that only two children were still hovering over Andy, the boy she knew was his good friend, Nathan, but there was also a girl she didn't know and with her knowledge of the school and how the children usually acted, she suspected that this girl was the cause of the accident.

By now, Andy was awake and trying to sit up, but one of the teachers was telling him to lie on the ground and not move. Thankfully, she saw that Andy was talking, not to the teacher, but to the girl who was crying and holding one of his hands. That reinforced her suspicions and judging where they were, she instinctively knew that Andy had fallen, but how and why was still a mystery. She climbed through the monkey bars and kneeled next to where Andy was laying. Before saying anything, she asked one of the two remaining teachers to escort the children to their class, before she began talking to Andy. At the same time, she uttered a silent prayer that he wasn't paralyzed, but when he moved his arms and started to move his legs, she let her breath out and offered another prayer of thanks to the Lord.

When Andy came to, he looked up to see the face of what appeared to be an angel, the sun behind her had finally broken through the sparse clouds and her face was framed in an aura of the sun, almost like she was glowing. It took Andy a few seconds to realize where he was and a small rock was poking him in the back, but when he tried to move his arm to push the stone out, the angel grabbed it. Andy did go to church on Sundays with his family and through all the years of Sunday school, he knew enough to wonder if he was dead and the angel was trying to take him up to heaven, but then he looked closer and saw the tears and made out that the angel was Milly, and she was crying.

He didn't know why, but he smiled at her. Without thinking about the pain in his neck and head, he reached up with his other hand and attempted to wipe the tears from her face, but suddenly the nurse ordered him to lie still. He looked around, a bit embarrassed at all the concerned faces staring back at him and he got really scared when he heard the emergency vehicles coming in. He moved his head a little and saw not only an ambulance, but a police car and a fire truck.

In a short while, Andy was placed on a stretcher as the EMT's attempted to get him to explain what had happened. It was embarrassing for him, admitting he could not do what Milly could. He looked back at her as they started wheeling him toward the ambulance and he smiled again, then gave her a thumbs up. He felt a lot better when Milly smiled back at him and waved. Just before they pushed him onto the ambulance, Milly was allowed to see him off, while the teachers and other staff hung back.

"You're going to have to teach me how you do that hanging thing," he said to her.

"I will, and I'm glad you're not mad at me. How do you feel now?"

"Well, my neck and head really hurt, but these ambulance guys say I'll be okay," he replied.

"I'll try and come to see you later," Milly said, and Andy smiled back just as they closed the doors to the rear of the ambulance and sped off.

Chapter Two
Finn

*Be slow to fall into friendship; but when thou art in, continue firm
and constant*—Socrates

Andy was only at the hospital for a short while when his mother walked in the door, followed not long afterwards by his father and finally the school principal. Other than the tests and review by a doctor, it was kind of boring; there wasn't even a TV in the room, just two beds with curtains around them and the other bed was occupied by an older person with tattoos on his arms. As his parents and the doctor walked to the other side of the cloth screen, Andy clearly heard the doctor tell them that he should stay overnight for observation, which meant he couldn't join Nathan for some video games, not that his mother would let him on a school night, but after this injury, he thought she might give in this time. Well, that wouldn't happen while he was here.

Both his parents came back in and said they would have to leave, but his mother was going to come back and spend the night with him, and she promised to come back with some of his comic books and a portable radio so he could listen to the news. Unlike his friends, he liked to hear the news, especially the closing prices of the stock market. That surprised his parents when he expressed an interest, and on a whim, they invested a small amount of money in stocks. Andy liked learning how much his stock had gone up or down each evening.

He was bored as he waited for his mother to return and ended up chatting a bit with his roommate, the older man with a lot of tattoos. The man fell asleep easily and talked in his sleep, mentioning something about sailing, and the occasional 'Aye Aye, Sir'. It was funny at first, but Andy soon lost interest and as he sat there, he heard a familiar voice outside his door, and when it opened, there was Millicent with an older woman, probably her mom, Andy guessed.

Milly was holding some comic books and a paper bag filled with baseball cards. As they came into the room, Milly introduced her mom, Mary, when suddenly, Andy's mom, Samantha, showed up as well. Milly's mother wanted to see how the boy who fell was doing and to make sure no one tried to put the blame on her daughter. That's what things were like lately, an accident happened, and someone was always there talking about legal repercussions and getting a lawyer. It wasn't anything like Italy where she grew up, but her husband had that great job offer and she also enjoyed America when she had been in college and felt that Milly should be allowed to go to school here as well.

As the adults talked, Milly gave him the things she had bought for him. Andy was all smiles as he took the paper bag from Milly and saw the baseball cards, he asked her how she knew he liked them, to which he got that funny 'know-it-all' look from her. "Gee Andy, daddy said all boys like baseball cards," she replied to which Andy smiled and agreed. "But mommy, says, he's just a big kid because he still collects them himself."

"So, how are you feeling now?" She asked him.

Andy shrugged. "My neck is still a little sore, but my head feels better. I really just want to go home, but the doctor told my parents that they want to keep me here for tonight."

"You won't be able to go to school tomorrow," Milly said, like it was a terrible thing.

Andy beamed at this. "Hey, that's right. I'll bet my mom asks someone to bring my homework to me."

"I can do it," Milly said, excitedly. Then she spoke more quietly when she realized that Andy might want Nathan to do it. They lived only two houses away from each other and she lived almost four streets away. "That is if you want me to."

"Yeah! I mean, if you want to. Don't you have to ask your mom first?"

Milly looked to where both parents were chatting. "Let me find out," she said, resolve in her voice.

Andy watched as Milly slipped gently off his bed. Unlike Nathan, she did it so quietly, almost daintily. That wasn't Nathan's style; he would have just jumped off and hit the ground with both feet. Then he noticed how she walked slowly toward their parents, almost like she was waiting for just the right moment and when she finally broached the idea to her mother, she spoke quietly, so quietly that Andy couldn't quite hear what was said and could only watch quietly, waiting for the answer. At one point, both parents turned and looked at him, Milly's mom looking quizzically, his own mother with a look of suspicion. Then Milly turned around and gave him a quick smile. Andy wasn't sure what to think, so he just waved and sat there wondering what was being said. There was a quiet giggle between the mothers, but with Milly now facing their parents once more, Andy couldn't see if she giggled as well.

Suddenly, Milly was nodding quickly, then she turned and raced back to Andy, a look of joy on her face. He looked up suddenly to see his mother, a strange smile on her face. Milly was then in front of him. "Guess what? Both of our moms said I could bring the homework to your house, and your mom invited my family over for dinner."

"You're all coming to my house? I thought you were just bringing my homework," Andy said, a bit confused. He had the feeling that there was more to this, but Milly quickly said her family wanted to meet his and her little sister and brother were coming as well.

"My sister is nice, but my little brother is a brat," she said. "Hey, who is that man?" She asked, pointing to Andy's roommate.

"I don't know his name, but he's okay. He didn't say much, just that he was talking about sailing. I think he's a sailor," Andy replied.

After this, Milly's mother mentioned that it was time to head home and get supper ready for her father and the rest of the family. Milly grabbed her jacket and smiled at Andy in such a way that his insides felt weird, though he didn't know why. She was gone only a few minutes, when his mother asked him if he liked her.

Andy looked at her, confusion on his face. Honestly, he didn't know how he felt. In a way, it was like being with Nathan, but with her there was something else, something he couldn't say how he felt. His mother just smiled at him and handed him some more comics, then she left the room to talk to the nurse. While he was waiting, his roommate awoke and looked at him with one eye. By this time, Andy's mom had returned and was sitting in the visitor chair with a magazine.

"Who's the woman?" The guy asked Andy quietly, seeing that she was busy reading.

"That's my mom. Why?"

"I know her," he said.

While this quiet exchange was occurring, Samantha overheard the whispering and looked up. "Andy, who are you talking to?"

Andy didn't get the chance to respond before the old sailor spoke. "It's me, Sam, Phinnius Gropper," he said, as Andy tried to stifle a snort of laughter. "You think my name's funny, boy?"

Samantha was instantly on her feet, moving between her son and the sailor her focus no longer on Andy, but the old sailor, as she stepped up to his bed. "Finn, is it really you?"

The old man looked up at her, "Samantha. Of all the people I could bump into here," he replied then looked at Andy, "And this little monkey must be? Wait, don't tell me, Addy, or Andy. Right?"

Andy was totally confused. What he thought was going to lead to problems, ended up with his mom bending down and giving the old salt, he heard her say though he had no idea of why, a tight hug. They started chatting a lot and Andy just sat there, totally confused. To make matters more confusing, the door to his room opened and his brother came in the room, followed quickly by his dad who was carrying a lot of take-out food. They both stopped short when they saw Samantha lean over and hug the old sailor again.

Mark Thompson was especially confused watching as his wife of nine years gave a really deep hug to an older man covered with tattoos in the next bed. Mark had seen him before, but only briefly when Andy was first told he would have to stay overnight. The man had been sleeping then and was easily dismissed from the mind. Not now though.

Mark said hello to his wife, who turned around to face him, even though the old sailor still had part of his arm around her middle. "Oh Mark, hi. Hey, you don't know this man, but he's a friend of my family from when I was a child. This is Phinnius, Finn for short. He and my father were old friends from his Navy days. Isn't that right, Finn?" She stopped there, like she was going to add something but didn't.

The old man smiled and nodded. "Sam was the prettiest girl in her neighborhood," Finn replied, seeming to enjoy the blush she displayed. "Oh, Samantha, I'm so glad I have the chance to see you. Lost track of you over the years," he said.

Samantha beamed as she looked around the room at her family, then focused on Finn. "You were away so long. We moved, a couple of times. I grew up and life continued. So strange to find you here in this hospital. Now that brings me to why are you here?"

"I guess I overdid things a bit," he replied. "Suffered a hernia and now I'm getting some surgery," he said, shaking his head. He looked over at Andy and pointed at him. "What's my mate in for?"

Samantha explained how he was injured, and they talked about how he was a lot like her brother. Finn had to decline the invite to share their supper since he was scheduled for surgery the next day and was restricted. The evening ended with Samantha and Finn talking about getting together and Andy thinking about Milly.

Chapter Three
Friends

Youth is happy because it has the ability to see beauty. Anyone who keeps the ability to see beauty never grows old—Franz Kafka

The dinner went well except when the dog knocked over a punch bowl and Andy saw how it spread over his mother's favorite table cover. He only stopped laughing when his mother gave him a look that he knew, stop laughing or else. After this, the meal was a bit subdued, but Andy noticed his dad and Milly's seemed to connect when they began discussing jobs and the best places in their town to live. Mark convinced Ned that his family should think about purchasing a home on their block, since they were only renting their current home. Then it was time to leave and for both Andy and Milly, the following weeks passed in a blur, everyone concentrating on the upcoming Christmas season which was so different here from how it occurred in Italy, Milly told him. There, people concentrated more on religion and the birth of Jesus, and she wasn't sure how she liked this new life.

After Christmas break, school started up once more and Andy and Milly saw each other every day, their conversations centered on recent movies or video games. He was really excited when a snowstorm, unusual for this part of the state, closed school once cold February day, though he wasn't as thrilled when his father sent him to Milly's house to shovel out their driveway since Milly's father had taken sick with the flu and Mark had volunteered Andy to shovel.

Andy was angry that he hadn't been asked and was told not to ask for money, but he felt better on his way over to Milly's house when Nathan came walking out of his house and joined him, a shovel on his shoulder as well. "Hey, Andy," Nathan started off, "you know your dad called my mom and suggested I help you shovel out Milly's house. Why'd he do that?"

Andy shrugged, "I don't know. He told me to shovel her out, but I'm glad you're coming along. We can knock this out quick. Their driveway isn't that big."

The two walked in silence for a moment. "So, what's with this girl, anyway? You act like she's cool and you spend a lot of time with her," Nathan mentioned, not looking at him.

Andy was shocked at the statement. "I hang out with you all the time," he answered defensively.

"Not like you used to, especially at school," Nathan retorted, the jealousy obvious to Andy.

Andy didn't know what to say. He felt he was still spending most of his free time with Nathan, though as he thought about it, realized he was spending time with Milly as well. However, that wasn't entirely his doing as his mother would often suggest they go over to her house and Andy would be dragged along. He knew his mom and Mary were becoming friends, but it went a little crazy when Milly told him several days ago that her mom was going to have another baby. She hoped it was a girl, as her little brother, who was almost five, always teased her about hanging out with Andy.

When they arrived at Milly's house, they just started to shovel when Milly came outside. Nathan looked over at Andy when he stopped shoveling for a moment. Normally, he wouldn't have minded her joining them, but often Milly would just stand around and watch them, well, watch Andy, and he started to realize that they liked each other. He would watch as Andy would stop working and chat about different things, mostly about what it was like waiting for the new baby girl. Her mom had been tested and they knew the baby's gender. Milly was excited since she wanted another sister and not another brat like her brother.

Andy didn't stop to chat with Milly this time, instead he helped Nathan shovel as she stood, once more, off the side chatting with both. All Andy really wanted to do was to shovel this driveway and get home to play one of the newest games on his Play Station that he and Nathan had gotten over Christmas and Milly trying to chat just slowed them both down. Finally, after her third question to him, Andy stopped and looked at her. "Milly, I know we always chat, but can you stop talking so we can finish this? Nathan and I want to get done so we can get back home. We want to play a neat game…"

That was it, he never got the chance to finish, as Milly made some a strange noise with her mouth, like quickly expelling air and let her lips flap a little, before turning and storming back into the house, slamming the door behind her. To which Nathan said, "About time," as he kept shoveling.

Andy stopped a moment. He wanted to finish, but realized he had said something that upset Milly, he didn't know exactly what it was, rethinking what he had told her as he kept shoveling. Each time, as he played the words back in his mind, he didn't think anything was bad and he didn't know what to do or say, to make things better, and Nathan didn't help things. He just kept saying things like, 'she's finally gone', or 'they could finish much faster now', showing off a bit by shoveling fast a couple of times to prove his point. As they kept shoveling, Andy grew more upset as time went on and pushing himself to shovel faster as well. It worked. They were done in about an hour and when they finished, the two looked around like there had to be something they missed, or that there was more to do. Andy said, "Let's do the sidewalk too."

"What? My mom said to shovel out the driveway. Not anything else," Nathan replied.

"Yeah, but Milly's dad is sick, and her mom is pregnant, so how will they get out to their cars, okay?" Andy replied. "We should do it."

"Darn it, Andy, you're gonna make us do more work," Nathan stated.

"Well, I kind' a thought, since Mr. Richards is sick, that we should help," Andy responded defensively.

"You can, but I'm not," Nathan almost shouted.

"Come on, Nate," Andy said, using his short name, which he did when he was upset, like now. "If you don't help me, it'll take me a lot longer to reach their door."

Nathan placed his shovel on his shoulder. "No. We don't have to. Maybe you should ask your girlfriend to give you a hand. I'm leaving," he replied, then turned and headed back home.

Andy just stood there, thinking. Now, he had two people mad at him. Knowing he couldn't leave without finishing the job, he got back to shoveling. The snow had drifted here and though not heavy, there was a lot of it. He kept shoveling, having to take longer and longer breaks. He stopped one time and looked back, seeing that he was only about halfway done, when he heard the door open and looked up to see Milly coming out, this time she was carrying a mug of something.

"Probably hot chocolate," he said to himself, but as he looked, Milly walked right up to him and handed him the mug.

"Here, my mom says this is for you," she said, then grabbed his shovel.

Andy didn't know what was going on. First, she was mad at him, then Nathan was, now Milly was nice to him again and he hadn't done anything more. He took the mug and started to sip it. It was hot chocolate, and it was good, really good. He sipped the brew and watched as Milly started shoveling. She could shovel! As he stood there, sipping his drink, Milly started shoveling the sidewalk faster than he had. Of course, he had already shoveled their driveway as well and was tired; Milly hadn't shoveled earlier and was fresh.

Andy stood there sipping the cocoa and just as he finished, Milly reached the steps to her house. She stood back and wiped her brow. "That was hard," she said, and Andy noticed she was smiling now. "How did you finish the driveway so quickly?"

He stood there, so many questions in his mind. She was angry and left, then Nathan had left as well. Now, she was back, and it was like their previous talk hadn't happened. He took a few seconds, thinking about his answer. "It was me and Nathan. It wasn't hard," he responded, still totally confused.

"Okay, mom said to invite you in so you can warm up before you go home. You want to come in?"

"Yeah, sure," he replied, though he really wanted to leave and play that game. Still, he followed Milly inside. Milly had been to his home, but he'd never been inside hers, so he was curious as to what it would be like. As the door closed and his eyes became accustomed to the light, Andy saw Mrs. Richards sitting at the table, a book in her hand. She looked over at him and smiled. "Did Milly help you finish the shoveling?"

Andy nodded. "Yes, she did. And thank you for the hot cocoa," he remembered to add.

"You're most welcome. Milly said it was cold out there and she wanted you to warm up, so please come in and take off your coat," she told him.

Andy looked at her then; *it was Milly's idea. That girl is so weird*, he thought. He looked around the room and Milly invited him into their living room where he saw her father napping on the couch. Milly put her finger up to her lips and warned him to be quiet, even though her little brother was throwing some plastic blocks off to one side and making a racket. Yeah, she was right, he was a brat.

Milly walked down a short hallway and into a room. There were two beds here, much like his room at home which he shared with his brother. For some reason, he expected there to be canopies over both, but the beds were simple. Instead of models or trucks around the room, the place had doll houses, a few board games, and stuffed animals. There was no TV in her room like he had but other than that, the rooms had similar furniture and various toys scattered around.

The two of them sat around, Milly showing off some of her possessions, much like he had the day she had come over for supper, but his mother had left them alone mostly. Milly's mom was constantly stopping in and checking on them. Then they talked about school and their classmates. Andy did ask her what she remembered of Italy, a place he told her he wanted to visit one day. Milly listened aptly as he talked about what he wanted to do when he was an adult, which was not what she had in mind.

When Milly spoke, she didn't mention what she wanted to do, simply saying she didn't know what she wanted, she was just glad Andy was there. When Andy asked her why she got angry earlier, she looked at him and just shook her head, but she smiled when he said he was sorry. That seemed to do the trick and it seemed to him that she was over whatever upset her earlier. What he did notice was her smile, it beamed like no other smile he had seen before and didn't know why, but he liked it when she was happy.

They had been talking for almost an hour when Milly's mom came back into the room and told Andy that his mother had called, and he had to go home. Andy didn't know how much time had passed and quickly retrieved his coat and boots as he headed for the door. Before he left, he received some money from Milly's mom, thanking him for shoveling and spending time with Milly. He was about to ask her why Milly had gotten mad but left the question unasked when he saw her standing there, just a few feet away. Mrs. Richards did thank him as well for being a gentleman, which he figured had something to do with his talking with Milly, but it was a mystery as to what exactly.

Walking back home, he noticed the sky had cleared but it had gotten colder, so he didn't slow down, just walked faster. He passed two of his classmates pulling a sled and heading in the opposite direction. He knew they were heading for Pickle Hill, a favorite sledding spot for kids his age and he wanted to join them, but Milly's mom said his mother wanted him home, and he kept walking.

When he got home, his mother met him at the door, wondering where Nathan was. Andy told her that he had shoveled and how Nathan had left, then how Milly had come out to help finish the sidewalk and how he was invited in for hot cocoa and had spent most of the time chatting with Milly. Yes, he was a gentleman he mentioned before his mother asked.

After supper, Andy was tired, so he headed for bed. While there, he picked up his walkie talkie and contacted Nathan who came on in less than a minute. "Just got home a little while ago," he said to Nathan. "You still mad?"

"Nah," Nathan responded, "I just didn't want to shovel anymore."

"After you left, Milly came out and she finished shoveling."

"No way. She did the shoveling?"

"Yes, and she did it while I drank a cup of hot cocoa," Andy stated, then added, "and it was good."

"Well, your girlfriend must really like you," Nathan stated with a little laugh.

"She's not my girlfriend," Andy retorted.

"I think she is," Nathan responded, totally unfazed by Andy's comment.

"I'm signing off. Goodnight," Andy said, then spent the next hour or so thinking about Milly before finally drifting off to sleep.

Chapter Four
"Munck"

The sea, once it casts its spell, holds one in its net of wonder forever—
Jacques Yves Cousteau

The months passed quickly, and Andy continued his 'friendship' with Milly, ignoring comments from Nathan and his other friends about how they were now a couple. The comments began to fade as they got older and began to mature. There were little changes, he noticed, like how some of his friends began to talk more with the girls. Then in May, Andy received a birthday invitation from Milly. He was a little nervous about letting the others know that he had been invited until he learned a couple of the other boys had received the invite as well, including Nathan.

Having spent a couple of days visiting Milly's family and her family with his, Andy had a good idea of what to buy, something he didn't bother to share with Nathan or his other friends. He went to a toy store with his mother and purchased the game 'Life', which he thought was a way of letting Milly see there were more things to look forward to as they got older, that the world was filled with adventure. It didn't have the effect he wanted.

Andy and Nathan were the first to arrive and while waiting for the others, the boys were treated to a tour of the rest of Milly's family home. Her father, Ned, invited the boys to view his sports memorabilia in his study and Nathan was fascinated by the number of items her father had collected. Most fascinating for Nathan were Ned's collectibles, like an autographed photo of the Florida Marlins baseball team, that and the other collectibles from teams like the Atlanta Braves. There were even a few autographed balls, one from a former Boston Pitcher, Kurt Schilling, and another from former Yankee infielder, Alex Rodriguez. To Nathan, these were worth their weight in gold. Then Ned pulled out the final item, an autographed glove he stored in a safe in the closet, which was signed by Hank Aaron. They were not allowed to touch the glove or the photos, but both boys were fascinated and asked Ned questions about how he obtained the items, until it was time to put them away as the other kids arrived.

At the party, there were the usual kid games, jumping on a bouncy castle, but a different collection of foods. There were pastries, and foods covered with sauce mostly from Italy, Milly told them. Toward the end, they competed with team sports, one of which was tying a cloth around the eyes of one kid in a team and the other had to guide them around obstacles without touching them. It all ended with a three-legged race, one boy attached to a girl, and of course, as the birthday girl, Milly got to choose and she chose Andy, with many non-verbal gestures from his friends, but oohs and ahs from the girls.

Nathan was attached to Maria; another classmate and the race came down to them and Andy with Milly. It was a close race, and though Andy and Milly didn't win, they both had a good time with each other. Milly was a good companion, but so were Nathan and Maria and there was a lot of good-natured kidding when Nathan and Maria won pennants. Andy didn't mind, he liked how Milly did her best, but Maria and Nathan had longer legs and both teams ended up in a pile at the end, quickly joined by other teams in a huge pile after they all finally crossed the finish line.

Just before everyone left, Milly opened her gifts, getting a lot of clothing from the girls, and some gift cards and dolls from the boys, but when Milly opened Andy's gift, she was excited and gave him a hug. She invited him over to play the game one night and regardless of what his friends would say, he accepted the invite. Then it was time to head home as their parents arrived.

The next school day, Andy and Milly sat together at lunch, but the surprise was that Nathan and Maria joined them. It was a trend that would continue through the rest of the school year and Nathan admitted to Andy later, that the party was a blast and he enjoyed hanging with Maria. Those were the good days as all the kids looked forward to the summer and made plans for what they would do.

It was during the start of summer that Nathan's father returned from the oil rig one day and both Andy and Nathan were there to meet him. Andy was excited that Nathan got to see his father and knew how badly he had missed him. As Nathan hugged his father for a long time, Andy felt like he was intruding and quietly went home to allow them privacy. Right away, Nathan and his father began doing all the things that Nathan had wanted to do, like see a baseball game, and go fishing. Andy felt a little left out but was glad that Nathan was happy and hid his feelings.

A month later, Andy was moping around the house since Nathan was still spending time with his father before he left once more, when his mother announced that her old friend Finn was coming to visit. She pushed them all hard to 'make the house presentable' she said and clearly Andy knew this was more important to her than anyone else. His mother seemed flushed a bit when questioned about Finn and Andy noticed his father wasn't that thrilled, especially when Finn arrived and his mother spent more time with him, almost ignoring the rest of them as she fussed about making Finn feel welcomed. Andy's father clearly didn't enjoy this outing and turned a shade of red when Finn suggested the family join him on his boat.

Andy's father mentioned that he was busy with work, though Andy kind of wondered if it was because his father didn't like Finn for some reason, but his mother would go, so he felt it would be okay. He had never been on a boat, or sailed on the ocean, so he was both nervous and excited. Then he asked if he could invite Nathan. Finn didn't care and his mom said it was probably a good idea. Andy immediately called Nathan and was thrilled when Nathan's dad said he could go. Andy let his mother and Finn know and he spent the remainder of the visit making plans for the boat trip with them.

That next Friday, Nathan joined Andy and his mother for the trip. His little brother was staying with a sitter while their father worked a rare weekend shift. The three of them drove to the Aurora Marina along the South Creek waterway, a tributary of the Pamlico River which emptied into the Atlantic. His mom parked in a small lot with only a few cars and led Andy and Nathan down to the dock, like it was an everyday event, explaining to them that her father had docked here as well when she was a little girl.

"Mom?" Andy asked. "If you've been here a lot, how did you lose track of where Finn lives?"

"Oh, he was a free spirit when I was younger, bouncing from port to port. When I graduated from high school, he was somewhere in California, and I didn't know if he would ever return here. He was your grandfather's friend, and they would sail together a lot," she responded. "I miss those days."

Andy explained that his grandparents had both died when he was little and he knew that his mom missed them terribly, which was why he said it quietly, so only Nathan could hear. Then he heard his mother get excited. "There's his boat. Isn't it beautiful?"

The boys looked at the small sailboat attached to the dock, yet so many other boats near it were much larger, yet it was like those boats didn't exist when his mom saw Finn's. He figured she was remembering her younger days and neither boy said anything about the small size of the boat they were approaching. Then they saw Finn come up on deck and wave. Samantha hurried both boys along and when they reached the boat, Finn jumped onto the dock and gave her a big hug.

"So glad you could come and see her again," he said, waving his arm along his boat which was named 'Munck'.

"Oh, Finn, this reminds me so much of when I was a young girl," she replied, as Nathan gave Andy a strange look. Andy could only shrug. His mother was acting strangely, and he didn't know why. She had told him the boat was large, it wasn't, at least compared to the others around it, and she was acting like a kid around Finn, something she never did with others, at least not that Andy could remember.

As soon as they were aboard, Finn pushed off the dock and they were on South Creek and from there merged onto the Pamlico River. The water was a bit choppy, but not bad. Andy watched in fascination as his mom held the tiller and Finn hoisted the sail, turning off the small electric motor which had propelled them onto the river. In no time, they were out into more open water where the sail caught and the 'Munck' was able to pick up speed.

Andy caught Finn's attention. "What does Munck, mean, Mr. Finn?" Nathan looked at Finn then, obviously interested in what the name meant as well.

Finn chuckled a bit, then pointed at Samantha. "That was what I used to call your mom. Well, I called her Munchkin. I knew she would get mad if I named the boat that, so I shortened her nickname. And told her it's a Finnish word, meaning sleek, but that's a load of horseshit. Oops, I mean, horse manure."

Nathan replied, "That's okay, Mr. Finn, you don't have to protect us, we're not little kids. You can say shit." Andy turned to look at him so quickly, he almost lost his balance. Never had he heard Nathan swear before. But Nathan just looked at him and smiled. "It's okay to swear, we're at sea."

If Finn noticed Andy's look, he didn't let on. He kept looking back at Samantha, giving her suggestions on the tiller as he moved about the boat, pulling on lines by hand or cranking what looked like an oversize fishing reel. The little boat responded with each action, like it was gaining speed which was a thrill for Andy. He stood on the small bow ramp, hanging over the water and letting the wind rip at his face and clothing. His mother had insisted that he and Nathan wear swimsuits with only a thin shirt and it was the right move.

The little craft tore over the water like a gazelle over land, even small swells, Finn called them crests, were nothing and the course the boat took made Andy realize how much fun it was. They had the wind now and zipped by other craft, especially some of the big tankers like they were standing still. Andy looked over at Nathan, who seemed to be enjoying the cruise as much as he was, then he looked back at his mother. She was sitting in front of Finn, who had one arm around her and was holding her hand on the tiller. His mom was smiling, but when she saw Andy looking back at her, she pushed Finn's arm off her chest, though she laughed about it. For some reason, it bothered Andy, though he didn't know why and just dismissed the feeling, guessing it was nothing. Still the feeling it was wrong stayed with him.

It seemed like a lot of things were not making sense to him lately. First Milly, then Nathan, and now his own mother. He was turning ten in just a couple of weeks and worried a little that he was missing things. When the boat began to slow down a bit, Finn suggested they get ready to go swimming.

Nathan was excited now. "Come on, I've never swam this far out before, let's go!"

Finn lowered the sail and coasted closer to the north side of the river where he dropped the sea anchor and the boys quickly scrambled to the stern and jumped off. Andy hit the water first and came up to splash Nathan who had jumped in a second behind him. The boys tasted the salty water as they played with the swells. Andy then called for his mother to join them, but she said she wanted to remain on board and catch up with Finn. He called down to them to remain in sight of the boat, even though they were close to the river side. Finn watched them for a moment before throwing over a safety float which the boys caught and tossed around on the water. Finn explained to Samantha that the float was tied off to the side of the boat and the kids could enjoy it while they chatted.

As they began swimming, neither noticed that the incoming tide was slowing, moving them away from the boat, they were having so much fun that it seemed they had had the water to themselves. It was only when something bumped into Nathan that he let out a cry. "I think a shark just hit me!"

They both scoured the water, seeing no sign that anything was lurking below them. "Are you sure it was a shark?" Andy asked.

"Well what else could it be?" Nathan replied, doing his best to tread water and keep an eye out at the same time. "I'm getting tired, let's head to the float."

Andy agreed and they both started for the float which was only a short distance away. When they reached it, Andy was laughing when something suddenly hit his legs as well. It was like a gentle bump, and he started looking around. He told Nathan and they both looked up to the boat to ask what it might be in the water. Not seeing anyone on the deck, Nathan began to yell, but when no one came into sight, Andy started to swim there to find out what was going on, when Nathan stopped him.

"Wait, Andy, we don't have to swim, we can pull ourselves back," he responded, holding up the tie down rope.

"Good idea," Andy shouted and together the boys pulled themselves quickly back to the rear of the boat where they reached a small ladder extending into the water. Nathan was first up almost bumping into Finn who was on the deck, shirtless and wearing ragged cutoff shorts. His mother was nowhere to be seen.

Finn asked them what was going on and as Nathan explained, Andy noticed his mother was now standing on the deck off to the side, listening. "What was it in the water?" She asked.

"We don't know. Nathan thought it might be a shark," Andy said.

"I should have gone out with you," Samantha replied, her hands over her mouth.

"Where were you when we were calling?" Nathan asked.

"Finn was just showing me around the galley while we made some coffee. We were only gone a couple of minutes," his mother said defensively, but Finn jumped in quickly, trying to stifle a laugh.

"Ain't no sharks in these waters. They're too fresh. Sharks don't like swimming in fresh water. Probably a Catfish. They can get big here and they push stuff out of the way when they swim."

The boys looked at each other, the relief washing over their faces when they realized Finn was probably right. It was just so surprising they panicked a little. Then he thought about where his mom was and asked, "What's a galley?"

Samantha was surprised by the question but recovered quickly. "It's a little kitchen down below. You saw it when we first got on board. Do you want to go down and take a look at it?"

Andy didn't miss the look Finn gave her. It was quizzical and it sparked his interest. "Sure, I'd love to see it," he replied, as Nathan shook his head.

"Who cares about a kitchen?" Nathan asked quietly as they walked over to some steps that led to the interior of the boat, which they began climbing down after grabbing their towels.

Finn led the way to the galley just a couple of steps from where they climbed out of the water. Inside, Andy saw the smallest kitchen he had ever seen, really just a hot pad stuck to a cabinet top and a small microwave, which he was told was powered by car batteries, which in turn were charged by a small windmill device attached to the top of the mast. Andy had seen that little device at the top of the mast earlier, before the sail had been put up, and watched as it spun in a counterclockwise rotation. Around the room were couches which turned into beds and a small privy behind a curtain, really a small plastic pail under a toilet seat and cover. Finn saw him looking at it and laughed. "Hey, with your mother aboard, I had to make sure there was a place for her to go. If it were just us boys, well we'd use the water," he said as he kept laughing.

"That's terrible," Samantha said, giving him a playful slap.

Andy looked around a bit more, trying to find the answer to a question that made him want to visit the galley. He knew the term from a book he had read, it's just that he had that question, which really wasn't answered, but he was determined to question his mother later and get the truth.

As the group now filed up to the deck, Finn looked up and said they needed to get going. Andy looked up as well and saw the advancing clouds. "Mr. Finn? Are those storm clouds?" He asked.

"They are at that, matey. I was distracted by you two," he said, pointing at each boy, "and your mom, or I would have picked up on it sooner." There was a flash of lighting in the distance followed a short while later by the rumble of thunder. "It's a way off but coming our way fast," Finn said.

The group retreated into the galley section as the rain let loose and poured onto the boat. While it continued, Finn went outside and began turning on the navigational lights, making sure other boats could see them. The boys joined him, ignoring the rain. "Hey, we're wearing our bathing suits," Nathan told Finn. They asked if they could swim some more, their previous fear abated now, and when Finn saw Sam nod, he agreed, but told them not to go far, to stay right by the boat. The heavy rain only lasted a few minutes and when it let up, the boys stopped swimming and headed onto the boat once more, finding Finn and Andy's mom sitting next to each other looking at photos. Sam was drinking wine while Finn had a beer, and they greeted the boys warmly.

"I thought you'd be scared of swimming in the rain especially with that Catfish out there, but you sure are made of some tough stuff," Finn said, as he raised his beer in salute. Andy's mom smiled at him and tipped her glass of wine as well. Then after a short lunch, the heavy rain slowed, and Finn said it was time to head back since he had seen that the swell had increased.

Following Finn's instructions, the boys helped him raise the sea anchor and stow the sail. With this done, Finn started the electric motor and manned the tiller, instructing the boys to man the bow plank and keep a sharp lookout for obstacles. As the boat moved back up the river, the swells made standing harder, but Andy loved it. He and Nathan held on as they alternately climbed and dipped over the swells, both boys laughing. Andy looked back one time and saw his mother was once again sitting in front of Finn holding her glass of wine. As the boat would dip or climb, she would alternately fall back into him, or he would use his arm to keep her from falling off the seat. Andy didn't like that much for reasons he couldn't determine, but he was having fun with Nathan and loved it when the water was more active like this.

When the rain suddenly slowed to a drizzle, Finn increased the speed a bit, seeing even darker clouds approaching from the distance with more lightning. Checking a device in the galley, he told Samantha it looked like a nasty weather front was moving it and it would be best to get docked. He said something else that made his mom laugh and hit him again, before he opened the throttle wide. Andy spent the entire return voyage on the bow, basically ignoring comments from his mother to come in. He was simply having too much fun, the wind and spray in his face, the feel of the water cascading over his body, it was amazing. He loved it. An hour later, they passed Hickory Point and Andy knew they were entering South Creek. The wind let up for a bit as Finn navigated closer to the western shore and soon, they were pulling into the private dock they had left from, just as the lighting started again.

Andy's mom and Nathan hurried along the path to where the car was parked while Andy helped Finn tie off the boat.

"You'll make a hell of a sailor someday," Finn said to him.

"Thanks, Mr. Finn. Can I ask you one thing before I leave?" Andy said.

"Sure," Finn replied, taking out a can of tobacco and putting in in his lip. "Don't tell your mother I'm using tobacco again. She thinks I gave it up," he said quietly.

"I won't, but my mom said, 'You both were in the galley making coffee when we were swimming'."

"Yeah, so?"

"Well, when we went downstairs, there was no coffee pot," Andy replied.

"You're one smart kid. Don't mention that to your mom, and I'll take you out again. I know you liked sailing."

"Okay, I promise. Why?"

"Your mom and I were talking about the old days with your grandpa. I guess she didn't want to bring it up. Just let her have good memories," he responded, looking off into the mist.

Andy nodded, then said goodbye and headed to the car to join his mom and Nathan, with even more questions in his head than before. He ran quickly toward the car where his mother and Nathan were waiting, then climbed in the back with Nathan. Seeing his face, Sam asked if he was okay.

Still young, but wise enough to know he couldn't ask her questions about his thoughts, he put on a brave smile and just nodded. As they were getting ready to pull away, Samantha looked back at the boat and smiled. "You know, the name of that boat is Finnish," she said.

Both boys had to hold back their smiles as they nodded, "Yeah, it means sleek," Nathan said, biting his tongue to keep from laughing.

Sam saw this and smiled back. "I know it isn't," she said carefully. When she saw the looks on the boys' faces, she knew her hunch was right. "Did Finn tell you it is really short for Munchkin?"

The surprise on their faces was evident. "You know?" They asked in unison.

"Of course, I know. I wasn't born yesterday. Besides, I looked it up on the internet a few days ago when I saw Finn in the hospital. He kind of gave it away when he called me Munchkin, and then when he started talking about his boat, I suddenly realized the similarity in the name and when I got home, I looked it up, just to make sure. There is no Finnish word for Munck. Don't tell him that I know," she added quickly.

Both boys looked down sullen at this. It was a secret that they liked and now she knew the truth. *Mom is smarter than I realized*, Andy thought.

The ride home seemed a lot quicker than the drive up. When they arrived, Nathan quickly headed home, and Andy helped his mother empty their car and carry the things inside. They found his father and little brother already there.

"How was the sailing trip?" Mark asked his wife.

"We all had a good time. The kids went swimming and Finn and I just chatted on his boat," she mentioned.

"What did you talk about?" He pressed a little.

Samantha looked at him, sensing that the question was more involved than she had expected, and she answered carefully. "Just about our lives, what you're doing and what I'm doing now. Stuff like that."

"Uh huh. Well, we had rain here," he said, looking at her.

"So did we," Andy said, not noticing the relief on his mom's face when he did.

Samantha got up. "I'll get dinner ready," she said and hurried into the kitchen.

When she was gone, Mark turned to Andy. "Anything interesting happen?"

Andy wasn't sure what to say and just shrugged. That seemed to please his father as Andy went to his room to change.

Chapter Five
Carnival

Life's tragedy is that we get old too soon and wise too late—Benjamin Franklin

The remainder of the summer passed too quickly for Andy, especially when his birthday arrived. Of course, Nathan showed, but so did Milly and a couple of other kids. Milly brought him a telescope, and Andy really liked it, his second love. He told her all about the sailing trip and mentioned how they thought they'd seen a shark and had to make their way back to the boat alone. Andy's dad listened to this exchange as he was flipping burgers, though Andy thought the burgers looked like he was making them well done, something he didn't like and he caught his father's attention, pointing to the now 'well done' burgers.

Mark jumped at the grill, quickly pulling the burgers off before they burned and muttering a silent, 'sorry', to Andy, as he put a few new burgers on the grill.

Andy didn't notice as he now saw Milly grab his mom and say thank you, though he didn't have time to think about this as his friends left the picnic table when they were told it would take a bit longer to get them ready. Unlike Milly's party, his family stayed with the usual hot dogs and burgers and there were no challenge games, just a lot of water balloons and squirt guns. After the party, Andy noticed that his parents had gone into their bedroom, and it sounded like they were arguing as he heard their voices raise. That was typical in his home; however, by the morning, things had returned to normal, and his parents seemed to be happier like they usually were.

Then the summer and Andy made ready for school once more, this time it would be middle school and he was excited. They had a new school and as luck would have it, he ended up being assigned a seat behind Milly, Nathan was seated halfway across the room, but only three seats from Maria, and so he seemed happy with his seat as well.

Then something bad happened the third week at school. Nathan wasn't at the usual place where they met and when Andy knocked on Nathan's door, all he could hear was a lot of yelling and crying. He headed back home immediately and told his mother, who raced over to the house leaving Andy at home with his little brother and he could only watch from their porch. He saw Nathan's mom open the door and invite his mother inside. He decided he wasn't going to school until he knew what was happening. His mom came outside a few minutes later with tears in her eyes. Andy raced to meet her as she approached knowing it was bad news. His mother saw him and led him into the living room. Looking out the windows on the way, he saw Nathan's dad leave their house as Nathan and his mother stood holding onto each other.

Andy didn't know that Nathan's dad was back already, he wasn't supposed to return for three weeks, and yet now he was leaving in a hurry. Samantha closed the shades and sat Andy down on the couch as she went to get his father. Andy kept looking out the window and when his parents came back, they told him the bad news. Nathan's dad had come home early to end his marriage and was moving away. Apparently, he had met and fallen in love with a woman who worked on the oil rig with him. Because Nathan's dad paid the mortgage, Nathan and his mother would have to move back to his grandparents' home in Florida.

Nathan did not return to school after that and he ended up moving with his mom only a week later. It affected Andy a lot, he saw the hurt that Nathan felt, like he was betrayed. Nathan's mom looked the same and Andy's mom spent a lot of time helping them pack. For some reason, Nathan didn't want to hang with Andy much and when he finally moved away, Andy felt the loss, but his mother insisted he went to school that day and when the tears came later in the morning, some of his classmates teased him.

That was the first time that Andy felt anger, real anger. The next time one of his classmates teased him about him being a crybaby, Andy punched him in the gut. A second classmate tried to stop this, but Andy turned and punched him as well before the teacher was able to step in and end the fighting. She ordered Andy to the hallway to await the principal as she assisted the boys whom Andy had struck.

While the teacher attempted to restore order amid the chaos from the fight, Milly slipped into the hallway and walked over to Andy and looked him in the face. Andy didn't understand what she wanted and at first thought she was there to see what he was doing and report it back to the others, but she simply placed her arms around him and gave him a deep hug. Andy was reluctant and started to pull away, but when Milly hugged him harder, he relaxed, letting go of some of his tears and his anger. He couldn't describe it, the feeling of Milly hugging him was like when his mother's hug, only this time was better and as they stood there, he hugged her back until the principal and school therapist arrived. They sent Milly back to class and before she left, she kissed her fingers and waved at Andy, making him smile for the first time in weeks.

The principal and therapists talked with Andy and after warning him of future consequences for fighting, his mother was called, and he was suspended for two days. It was the first time in his life that he'd been suspended from school, and it was traumatic. He also expected to hear a lot from his parents, but even after they got home, neither of them scolded him, they just told him they understood, of course they said this must never happen again to which Andy agreed.

The rest of the year passed slowly for Andy, missing his best friend as he did. One time he got a phone call from Nathan, but as time passed, his loss diminished, and he felt a little better. Of course, having Milly there made the year more bearable and the two grew closer. They started spending more together and sometimes Andy would go over to her house. Of course, they would play board games, one of their favorites being the game of Life.

While playing, Andy hoped Milly would notice the cool things she could do once they grew up and graduated, but Milly always chose the path of marriage and over the years, she made little stickers with her name and his that she would put on her car and even would question Andy as to what they would name their kids. Other times, she would do things that he enjoyed and when he brought his telescope over, they would look at the stars as Andy told her the names of each one. However, even though he enjoyed spending time with her, the image of Nathan's father leaving kept coming back and he grew to believe it was best not to get too close to anyone, the idea of marriage and having kids could end in a flash if one of them decided to end it. He never spoke of this, but it was something he thought of when he was alone. He even had nightmares about it, and though he felt he would never do something like this, Nathan's parents had seemed happy when he was home and Andy hadn't seen the warning signs that hinted there was trouble, even Nathan was taken by surprise. Andy heard his parents talk about it when they thought they were alone and he would sometimes eavesdrop when they spoke of how they felt things weren't well and why, but even they had been surprised.

When the school year ended and when the carnival came to town, her parents rewarded her passing with tickets to it for her and one friend. Of course, she asked Andy to accompany her, which she said carefully, since this would be their first real 'date'. She pulled back to gauge his reaction, but instead of smiling, or refusing, Andy just laughed a bit, which bothered her. He agreed to go and seemed excited, but she had hoped he would hug her or something. She wanted to know how he felt about her.

The carnival was fun, even with both their parents shadowing them as they moved around the different events and rides. They said they were there only to have fun, but when Milly noticed her mother standing nearby at a ring toss game, she realized they wouldn't be alone and kept looking for a place they could be alone, but it seemed like the whole town was there, so their options were limited. Then she spied one booth where she knew he could do well, the 'Balloon Boom'. Here, people used water pistols to shoot water into a figure's mouth and the person who filled the water balloon and popped it won. The place was popular as there was always a winner. Both tried their hand at the game and after a bit, they finally won a small stuffed animal, which Andy graciously gave to Milly. There were a lot of laughs and then Andy spied another booth, one that offered better prizes, 'Spiral Flip'. Andy used his own money and Milly watched as he was given three wooden rings, which had to land around a wooden dowel. The dowels were arranged with thin ones at the bottom of a circular pyramid and the higher the pyramid went up, the thicker the dowels became.

Milly tried her hand as well and going first, managed to put a ring around a low peg and won a plastic whistle. Andy had tried this sort of thing the year before and learned something important. People usually threw the ring like a disc, but he watched one man then throw the ring in an arc and it landed on a higher dowel. Taking care, his first flip hit a dowel near the top and tumbled off. The second try hit and landed on a dowel three levels up, winning another stuffed animal. His third throw was a good one and landed on a dowel near the top.

The woman standing there pointed to several other prizes, all trinkets; however, one shiny item caught his eye, a leather necklace with a nice quartz stone in it. He chose that prize and gave it to Milly, who instantly removed the necklace from the plastic pack and wore it. There was also a button, when pressed, which caused the necklace to sparkle brightly. Milly loved it.

As they left this booth, Milly spied her father nearby and she still wanted to hang with Andy alone. As they moved through the place, hoping to lose their parents, she spied the large Ferris Wheel located in the center of the carnival. Quickly, she pulled at Andy's arm as she pointed at the Ferris Wheel towering over them.

Andy didn't fear much, except high places, and though he was reluctant to ride the wheel, he didn't resist as Milly pulled him up to the rear of the short line and through the gate where they were locked into the wheel's chair. As the chair went backward, he almost jumped out, but the car kept moving and in seconds, it was too high to safely jump. All Andy could do was grip the safety bar with both hands and keep his eyes closed. Not wanting to appear scared in front of Milly, he started thinking about the ride, remembering what the ride attendant said about it lasting only five minutes. He figured if he could just hold on and keep his eyes closed for that amount of time, it would end and he could get off.

The ride came to a sudden stop and the car rocked. Andy finally looked down and saw it had stopped letting people off and new people on. He hadn't counted on that. The ride continued for a bit and would stop occasionally, and the swinging would begin once more as the cars were unloaded or loaded again. After a bit, he realized the ride should be ending soon and he began to relax. Then a mechanical noise and the ride came to a jarring stop as the car swung wildly. There was shouting below, and Andy knew there was a problem. It was obvious with all the people gathering below and pointing at the ride. He tried to stare at the stars above, but they were of no hope and then he realized he hadn't said anything.

Milly looked over the bar, then at Andy. She had seen him start to relax a little, but now he was holding onto the safety bar once more and she could see his breathing increase quickly. She had hoped they could talk a bit, but now she knew Andy was starting to panic. Taking the initiative, she grabbed his arm that was closest to her and pulled it to her side. At this, Andy looked right at her, not saying a word. When she smiled and grabbed his other hand, he didn't know why, but his face moved closer to hers and for a second, they kissed. Both kids had seen their parents kiss, but this was different. Milly broke free from him for a second, looking at him, not realizing her breathing was coming as quickly as Andy's. Then she moved in, and they kissed again, this time longer and a bit more intense.

Milly was in a different world at this moment; it was like nothing she had ever felt before, the intensity, the yearning. She had always felt something for him before, now she felt love. The kiss continued and Andy's hands moved around her back. She could feel this, feel how his touch made her skin tingle. They were still young, she knew, but at that moment she knew for sure, he was the one she wanted to be her husband.

For Andy, it was something so different, something he never imagined he would feel. No, that wasn't right. It was something he never knew existed. Yeah, that was more like it. How could someone he had known for a couple years suddenly make him feel like his stomach churn like it was filled with worms? He squeezed her tightly after that kiss and listened as she whispered to him, things like she was there for him now and not to be scared that it was going to be alright. He kind of realized this, but it was enjoyable to simply hold her.

When they finally broke their hug, Andy grabbed her hand in his as they smiled at each other. They felt so good, until first Milly and then Andy looked down at the number of people who had gathered near the Ferris Wheel. Instantly, Milly could see her parents among the throng, and they were looking right up at her. She didn't know if they'd seen anything that had happened between her and Andy, and she didn't care. This was her night, and it was everything she had hoped it would be.

Almost an hour later, Andy and Milly were once again on the ground, via the help of the Aurora Fire Department bucket truck. The Ferris Wheel had stopped working and since the threat of thunderstorms made getting the riders down a priority, the local fire department was called in and each car was unloaded with the bucket. Their car was almost halfway up, and the fire department had started at the top and it took some time to get everyone down. And even though he was still afraid of heights, he had to admit Milly had made their time stuck together bearable, something he told his parents about as they headed home that night. He never told them about the kiss, and Milly didn't tell her parents either, afraid they might overreact and prevent them from seeing each other over the remainder of the summer.

Chapter Six
Royalty

Time forks perpetually toward innumerable futures—Jorge Luis Borges

The school years passed quickly for both of them, Milly and Andy seeing each other a lot, doing homework together at each other's houses, or going on dates into town. It was awkward going to the movies with her, Andy admitted to himself. Rather than being able to spend time alone, their parents would often attend, and he just knew they were watching whatever they did. The one-time Milly kissed him at the end of a date, Andy opened his eyes to see her mother standing in the window with a disapproving scowl on her face.

Then a change occurred that affected each of them, when both sets of parents brought new life into the world; Andy becoming a big brother again to a sister, Sarah, born when he was in seventh grade and in Milly's case, her mother bore another sister, Monic, born when she was in eighth grade. Then, a year later, when her parents announced the family was moving, Milly went into a panic. When she asked why, her parents simply explained that they had outgrown their home and they needed the space. They did say they found a new place and Milly would have her own room, which made it a little easier for her to accept, but when she asked where it was, her parents vaguely said it was in a nice neighborhood and they had taken the Thompson's advice, purchasing a new home in the town.

Milly was really feeling down when the big day came to see their new home. She sat in the rear of the car, seeing a lot of familiar neighborhoods and it was only when her family drove them to the new house that she realized it was only four houses away from Andy. The relief that washed over her face was 'priceless', her mother said, as they pulled into the driveway. Of course, Andy had learned about the move the week before and was sworn to secrecy.

He was standing in the driveway as the family pulled into the yard and she realized where they were, having walked by this very house hundreds of times.

Milly was the first one out of the car and flew into Andy's arms where he gave her a big hug. His family was there as well and invited her family to a prepared cookout, to celebrate the move. Only four houses away, the two spent almost every day together. When they finally entered high school, they became a real couple, which surprised neither of their families and it was common for them both to attend family events. They even joined Karate together, moving up the belts at the same time and gaining confidence in themselves and each other, and both achieving Black Belt status in their junior year. They also continued to excel at sports and with Milly's help, Andy's grades improved, and they appeared to be a happy couple.

Milly was first to receive her driver's license and offered to help Andy learn to drive, but he refused, insisting that he could drive as well, if not better than her, and when he too received his driver's license, he tried to show her, accidentally putting the minivan in reverse and then bumping into a tree, a mistake which caused him some embarrassment and ribbing from his family when there was no damage. Milly, however, didn't tease him, as was her way, but warned him she wouldn't put up with any reckless driving. Andy accepted her commands, but the moment he was free of her influence, he would tear out of that spot following his own rules. This upset Milly at first, until she realized she couldn't control his antics when he was alone, instead she insisted he drive carefully when she was in the car. Andy's parents appreciated her influence and hoped she would continue to as they grew older. There was even talk among the parents about how they expected their kids to marry, since they made such a great couple and seemed to be happy with each other. They even debated when Andy would 'pop' the question.

It was in their senior year though that their relationship began to wear thin and eventually ended.

Milly had become very popular with a large circle of friends, while Andy was happy with a small close group of friends whom he had grown up with, others though, were jealous of their relationship and often tried to disrupt it, mostly by playing jokes on Andy, or doing what they could to undermine his status with her. The biggest problem however, occurred in their senior year, when they eagerly awaited the news of who would be crowned as this year's, Homecoming King and Queen which was held the night before the big football game just before Thanksgiving. As usual, Milly spent several days after school with her friends, decorating the gym, the school colors displayed prominently, while Andy spent time cleaning up the leftovers and doing odd jobs.

Though the school wasn't large by any means, the two of them stopped when they were finished to admire the work Milly and her friends had accomplished. The place really looked great and not like a gymnasium/auditorium. Then they hurried out to get ready for the dance.

Andy was certain he would win, but when the votes were counted his worst rival, Matthew Grimes, one of a handful of boys Andy felt was a jerk, won the contest by only two votes. Matthew sauntered up to the awards table throwing a cocky look at Andy as he moved by him and then placed the crown on his head. Andy held his disappointment in check until it was announced that Milly had been elected queen. He looked over at his rival and saw the evil smile Matthew had since tradition dictated the Homecoming King would be the one to place the crown on the Queen.

Matthew made a big deal of this, shaking his butt to those around him as Milly approached. She was so excited, she didn't notice his antics, but Andy, in his anger, felt she was enjoying it and his blood began to boil, especially as Matt began to lower the crown slowly, trying to stretch it out the moment until he felt it touch her head. Then he reached and pulled her hand to his mouth, giving it a gentle kiss. As he did this, many girls laughed or expressed joy in what they thought was a rehearsed moment. Milly didn't like it and quietly told him to stop or else, but Andy, now pushed back by the swarm of girls advancing on the couple, didn't hear what she had told Matthew.

Most of Andy's buddies crowded around, telling him it didn't matter, that the election was rigged, but his humiliation at not being elected king was a crushing blow. He quietly watched Matt's antics when it came time for the traditional dance of king and queen, which made his blood boil. Milly looked at Andy and though his face held a small smile, she noticed his hands closing into fists and releasing, a Karate move designed to allow the owner to disperse anger. She raised her shoulders in a sort of sympathetic shrug, then before Matthew put his arm around her and escorted her to small stage for the dance. Matthew felt this was a chance to cause more of a rift between the happy couple and as they danced, he gave a smug look to Andy. When the first dance was almost over, he did the unthinkable, grabbing Milly's face between his hands and placing a gentle kiss on her lips. Milly was surprised by this, but from where Andy was standing, it appeared that she seemed to accept, if not actually enjoying it.

When Matthew asked her to dance again, she declined, and Matt made a comment about how great she was and what a loser Andy was, listing things that he knew, or simply made up. He lied about how Andy had been flirting with another girl and that he didn't deserve her. Milly finally took this moment to tell Matt off and to leave her alone. She was Andy's girl and that was that. She also told him that she hadn't stopped his kiss because she didn't want to make a scene on the dance floor, but if he ever tried that again, she would kick his ass. Then she grabbed the arm of her friend Maria and walked away. Andy didn't see or hear this exchange, opting to leave when they kissed.

Later that evening, as Matt left the school, Andy was there to greet him and the two got into a fight that was only stopped by some of the teachers who had been at the dance and because they saw Andy throw the first punch, he who was suspended for three days and prohibited from playing as a tight end in the homecoming game the next day and without his rival there to steal the show, Matt Grimes, in his position as a defensive end, was able to cause the other team to fumble and grabbing the loose ball, scrambled through the defensive line for the game winning touchdown.

Andy was there, having driven in alone to watch and support his team, but when Grimes won the game, he saw the cheer leaders, Milly among them, crowding around Grimes. All Andy could do was watch as Grimes became the hero and when Milly gave him a hug, he disgustedly got in his car and drove away. That afternoon, when Milly attempted to call him to tell him the news, he refused to talk to listen, just told her that he had seen the end of the game and hung up.

Weeks passed with an uneasy tension between the two until the holidays started and Andy decided to invite her to spend the night at his house and watch a holiday movie, but Milly had a difficult day and was angry, so she declined and said she needed to spend time at home. This was a big letdown for Andy, he had been ready to let go of his anger and spend more time over the holidays with her. That didn't appear likely now and he let her know it. They argued until Andy slammed the phone down. Upset at what had occurred, he decided to join his friends at a popular hang-out spot near the river, drinking beer one of his buddies had swiped from his father. As they were sitting on their cars near the river, Andy felt better. The weather was cool, and he noticed the grass was beginning to turn from the lusty green to tan, a sure sign that the season was changing, but not cold enough to prevent them from enjoying the night until they noticed two cars driving down toward them.

When the first car came to a stop, Matt Grimms got out of his car. "Oh shit," Andy said.

Grimes hopped out of his convertible, a car his father had bought for him after the last game and Andy was bummed. It was cherry red and had a big engine, which made everyone, including Andy, jealous, especially when Grimes would peal out of the parking lot after school. Now, all Andy and his friends could do was stand there, staring. His friend George told Grimes to get lost, that this was their spot for the night.

Matt just laughed at this as he walked around to the passenger side of his car and opened the door. To Andy's shock, Milly climbed out looking like she wanted to be anywhere else before pulling the seat forward and letting her friend Maria out along with Brian, a good friend of Matt, who joined Maria and put his arm around her. Where Matt was tall and lean with light blonde hair short hair; Brian was almost the complete opposite, with long brown hair and a squat muscular body, which complemented his position on the football team as a defensive tackle.

Milly stared at Andy, her mind spinning. She had gone to Maria's after her argument with him and then Brian showed up with Matt and they convinced her to come along. Of course, Matt was outside, and she accepted a ride with him when Maria begged her to come. She agreed only because she didn't like Maria going alone and had no idea where they were going. Now, she stood at a loss of words and was surprised when Matt suddenly put his arm around her, seeing the look of anger on Andy's face.

Quickly, Milly slipped out of Matt's arm and tried to make a joke of this, saying quietly to him that she appreciated his help, but was uncomfortable with him doing this. Andy didn't hear this exchange, his eyes boring into Matt, ignoring the other car also filled with Matt's friends; instantly, Milly realized that things were going to get serious, and she turned and headed toward Andy, but was stopped when Matt grabbed her arm.

"Hey, where are you going?" Matt asked. "If you want to leave, I brought you here and I will be the one to take you home."

Then Maria was beside her. "Mill don't bail on me. You told me you needed a break from Andy. Just hang with me and we'll go somewhere else."

Milly nodded, then looked and saw Andy approaching. Matt saw him as well and stepped beside Milly, putting his hand out as Andy got close. "This doesn't concern you, Andy. She's with us tonight."

At least Matt didn't say she was with him, and she tried to inject calm into the situation, but Matt's friends were starting to have words with Andy's friends and when she saw a friend of Andy suddenly push a friend of Matt, she knew it was too late.

Matt didn't back down, but decided to goad Andy a bit, pointing at the minivan Andy was driving and the old truck Andy's friend George had brought. "See," Matt said to his friends, "these are the kind of crap-cars losers drive." That got a snicker from his buddies. "Hey, Andy, you should hear what Milly thinks of my car."

Milly just cringed, remembering what she said when she climbed in, but she was just being nice when she said she liked how great it looked, though she did decline Matt's offer to try drive and simply took a seat in the front after Maria had climbed in the back with Brian.

Andy saw the cringe and knew that she had liked it, but his parents told him they couldn't afford a new car for him, and he opted for the minivan which made it easier to collect his friends, it also held a bit of importance for him since it was the vehicle where they first made out. Funny, but as he looked at Milly, all he could remember was how beautiful she had looked and the perfume she had been wearing. He shook that image out of his mind, it wasn't the place to remember that day.

Andy hopped off his car and approached Matt. "She's not interested in a glory hound like you. Milly, why don't you dump this ass and join me?"

"Hey, she came with me, and I'll be taking her home," Matt responded. Then he looked at Milly with a questioning look. "It's up to you."

Milly was torn, she had accepted the ride from Matt, and he had been nice to her the entire way over, even letting her choose the music and she could tell, he was doing his best to make her comfortable. Then there was Andy, her boyfriend up to recently, the guy she thought she was in love with, the first person who had loved her. But now, well, he was acting unusual and even from a distance, she could see the beer in his hands. He had been drinking and she didn't know how intoxicated he was.

"Andy, I'm sorry, but you've been drinking, and Matt did bring me, so I guess I need to stay with him."

That infuriated Andy. He felt fine and didn't like Milly hanging with his arch nemesis, but when Matt put his arm around her and she didn't resist, he got angry. "He's a piece of trash, Milly. You just want to hang with the hero. That's stupid, Mil, you're not thinking clearly,"

With that, he threw his almost empty can at Matt, but his aim was off, and he ended up missing quite a bit. Matt just laughed and told him to go home before he got in trouble, but Andy flipped him off and walked back to his vehicle.

Milly wanted to go to him, but Matt held her there. "Mill, you're right, he's drunk. Please just stay with me and I'll take you home right now if you want. Just don't get in his car, it's too dangerous."

Milly looked up at Matt, tears now streaming from her eyes. "He's been my boyfriend since the third grade, I just can't leave him," she stated, crying.

Brian and Maria came over to her then, and Maria gave her a hug. "He's being an ass, Mil. Just let him go and stay with us. Matt's a good driver and we'll go right home. If you go with him now as drunk as he is, he might get in an accident."

"Maria's right," Brian added. "Let's just go. He's drunk and you're going with him won't end well."

From a distance, Milly watched as Andy hopped on the minivan and opened another beer, the look of anger on his face, highlighted by the vehicle lights made her scared of him then. "Alright, please just take me home."

The four of them got in their car, the other girls followed them and both cars left the area. Milly looked back and saw Andy peg them off and she burst our crying.

Andy just watched the cars leave and debated with himself whether to get in the minivan and follow them, but his friends stopped him. "Andy, forget her, she's not worth it," George said. "Let's just call it a night and you can call her tomorrow, when you're sober."

Andy looked at George in a rage. "What does that mean?"

His friend just looked at him. "Dude, we've been friends a long time. You've had too much to drink. Billy can drive your car," George stated, referring to another of their group. "The night's ruined."

Andy was going to argue, but when Billy put his hands out for the keys, Andy surrendered them and soon they were on their way as well.

Andy was only home a few minutes when the phone rang and as Samantha answered, Andy saw her face harden as she looked directly at him. She spoke a moment more, apologizing to the caller before she hung up. Immediately, she pointed at Andy. "You've been drinking?"

Caught red handed, he couldn't think of a good answer and just lowered his head.

"Did you get into a fight with Matt?" Samantha asked, as his father stopped watching the game and turned toward him.

Andy shook his head. "We had words is all. My friends and I were just sitting there talking, when he showed up with Milly."

"I know. That was Milly's father. He said she came home crying and told him everything and he's mad at you and said you owe her an apology. And it better be sincere."

"That isn't all," Mark added. "I want to know where you get off thinking you can do what you damn well please. You drove your mother's van. You went drinking and we didn't know where you were. And mostly you did something that upset your girlfriend, a girl your mother and I both adore. What the hell happened?"

Andy noticed his father using cuss words, something he only did when he was really upset. "We had an argument. It was small, but it was why I went out with my friends. I didn't know there would be alcohol, but I didn't object. I think everything between Milly and me is falling apart. Then she showed up with Matt Grimes and I guess I lost it. I'll go apologize to Milly now."

"No, you won't," Samantha said.

Both Andy and Mark looked at her. "Why not now?" Andy asked, his father looking like he was confused as well but not saying anything. Over the years, he had learned when not to question his wife. This was one of those times.

"You were too vague. I want to know exactly what happened, everything." Both his parents looked at him, searching his face for any clue as to whether this was true or not. It was something they had done in the past, but to Andy, their intensity was different, and he felt the squiggles in his stomach, when he realized this scrutiny meant it was serious, really serious. He knew he had to tell them everything and he did. When he was finished, his father shook his head.

"You betrayed our trust and because of this, you're grounded. No going out alone. No using the car unless it's a chore your mother or I give you. And your brother will accompany you. And no more drinking, period. Is this understood?"

Andy nodded. He knew he messed up and he also knew, he had to apologize to Milly. "Do I have your permission to go over to Milly's to see her?" He asked contritely.

Mark and Sam looked at each other. Mark was about to say yes, but his wife shook her head. "I believe," he said slowly, trying to get the gist of what his wife was thinking, "that you're still grounded, so you'll spend the evening here, without television, and apologize tomorrow."

Andy saw the look on his parents' faces. There would be no arguing his case, not that he had one, so he asked to go to his room. And once there, lay on his bed staring at the ceiling and reliving the night. He was interrupted when his brother came up and sat on his own bed, since they shared a room.

"Dude, what the heck were you thinking?" Robert asked him. As usual, Robert lay on his bed throwing a single die in the air and catching it, one of the things he often did before going to sleep.

For some reason, Andy was mesmerized by the die, watching it turn in the air only to drop quickly into Robert's waiting hand. Each time the die came down with a different number and he felt it related to his night. There were so many different variations of what might have happened earlier. If only Matt hadn't shown up, if Milly hadn't been with him and if he hadn't drunk beer. So many different outcomes other than what had occurred. He was thinking about this when he fell asleep.

The next morning, Andy slipped out of the house before his parents woke. That was probably because Andy heard them arguing most of the night. He wasn't sure if one of them took his side, or if they were both so upset at what he had done and he worried they might try to stop him from seeing Milly. He also felt he had to do this, attempt to repair any damage he could.

He slipped through the trees, avoiding lawn decorations of the holidays. Staring, as he walked, at a large Minora of one neighbor. The next house had no decorations at all. The house before Milly's had a small train set which he didn't notice until his foot knocked over the locomotive. Instantly, he bent to righten it as a car pulled into Milly's drive. He'd seen this car before but couldn't place it. This changed when Maria exited the passenger door and Brian, the driver's side. He thanked God that Matt wasn't with them as the two walked to Milly's front door. Already partially hidden by a medium-sized evergreen which had some bulbs and lights on it, Andy remained on one knee as he watched as the door opened and Milly emerged with some skates.

She looked around, then shook her head before walking to Brian's car and the three left. It was then that he remembered he was supposed to take Milly skating today and now he'd messed that up as well, which didn't matter really, since he was grounded and his parents wouldn't have let him go, but he should have called and explained. Dejectedly, he turned and headed home before his parents woke.

Chapter Seven
Spiraling

Sometimes good things fall apart so better things can fall together—Marilyn Monroe

The next few months for Andy were the loneliest of his life. His friend Nate was gone and now Milly wasn't speaking to him, and he tried to ignore the stares from many in the school when he walked by. One day, he stopped at his school locker to switch books for his next class. As was the case in most schools, the locker was small and crammed full of his books and jacket, and as he attempted to change the texts, the stack of books came tumbling out. That had not happened before, and he was befuddled as to why this happened. That's when he spotted the fishing wire entwined around his stuff.

He realized someone had managed to open his locker earlier and wrap all the books together, so whichever book he chose, all of them came tumbling out, his jacket included. The books landed on the floor with a loud thud and several of the kids stopped to look, which embarrassed him. Andy began to unwind the line when he spied George and Matt in the background laughing at him, but what upset him most was the line had ripped his jacket when it was pulled out and he knew that one of both had something to do with this.

A couple of junior girls stopped nearby, looking, and whispering. And he tried to spin this event in his favor. He grabbed his books, doing his best to untangle them as he stood and as he looked at the girls standing nearby, when he got an idea. He flashed a smile, making it seem like it was nothing and laughed it off. This made the girls smile and they came closer, asking what happened. Andy simply said it was nothing, then asked them about their most recent science exam, which he found difficult. Some of the girls agreed and the incident was quickly forgotten as they chatted amicably. That was when Milly came around the corner and saw him chatting with them. Andy saw her in the background but felt he had to chat with these girls first and ignored Milly's stare.

As Milly stopped and tried to discern what was going on, she didn't notice Matt coming up behind her, making a comment about how Andy was up to his old self, flirting and probably saying bad things about him. Milly didn't want to believe this, but she saw the way Andy looked at Matt when he saw him, and she had to wonder if Matt was telling the truth.

Then one of the girls laughed at Andy's holding the fishing line on the books when he showed them how they were tied together and made the statement that some fisherman really had a bad aim. To Milly, it seemed like one of the girls looked at Matt as she was laughing, not realizing she was simply laughing at the joke Andy said, which was unrelated to Matt and she had just looked in his direction as she laughed, making Milly think Andy had said something bad about him.

Milly simply told Matt to 'Hang in there' and walked toward her next class without waiting for Andy.

Andy noticed her leave and excusing himself, hurriedly shoved his books in his locker, before heading to talk to Milly, but couldn't reach her before she entered class. He stood there a moment, debating what to do when the bell rang and he had to run to his own class, arriving late, his teacher telling him he had detention after school. Andy didn't argue and just took his seat dejectedly, knowing he wouldn't be able to talk to Milly and it tore him up.

Two days later as he was sitting in the cafeteria after school studying math, Milly suddenly sat down at his table. Before he was able to speak, she told him to listen to her, explaining why she was with Matt that night. When she was finished, she looked at him. "So, do you have anything to say to me?"

Andy took a deep gulp of air first. "I'm so sorry. I shouldn't have been drinking and lost my temper and I should have given you the chance to explain why you were with Matt. I just didn't listen to you. Again, I am very sorry. Do you forgive me?"

Milly looked at him carefully, seeing that he looked sincere. "Yes, I do, but it better not happen again. I won't put up with that sort of thing in the future," she stated, doing her best to control her own anger at the remembrance of what occurred flashed through her mind.

Instead of feeling relief at what Milly said, the way she said it, so demanding, Andy got a bit angry himself, that he turned back toward his math.

"Yes, it won't happen again. Now, if you don't mind, I need time to get this math down. We have a big test tomorrow and I need to do well."

Milly nodded, her own thoughts a jumble as well, and she debated whether to offer her help, or just let him be. She wasn't sure why, but she decided to leave to let him cool down. "Alright, I'll leave you alone," she responded, as she stood and walked away.

Andy sat there stewing and was about to go after her, when he saw Matt in the hallway watching what had occurred and felt it might be best to let Milly leave since he would have to pass by Matt, who now sported a huge smirk. Already in trouble with his parents and Milly, he realized if he got into an argument with Matt now, it wouldn't end well and he just buried his head in his work and let it go, doing small exercises with his hands to burn off the anger.

A week later, after things had calmed down, Andy learned that Milly had been accepted to several colleges, he had applied only to one, a community college in Greenville, but hadn't heard anything yet, which was fine by him. His only good times lately were when he sailed on the Munck with Finn. He even invited Milly to come along one day to show her how exciting and fun sailing can be. Still, it did nothing to help his predicament and the end of high school hung over his head like the Sword of Damocles and Milly seemed even more distant than before and worse yet, they didn't spend much time together.

Then it was time for Prom. Andy debated about going and his parents kept pressuring him to do it, asking if he was taking Milly. They knew something was wrong but didn't want to pry into his life. Then the big surprise, when he learned that Milly was going to the Prom with Matt. That hurt Andy more than anything else, but he put on a brave face and went to the school alone, which was where Prom was being held, in the same gymnasium where this all started, the day of Home Coming.

After school for several weeks, faculty and students worked hard to convert their gymnasium into a dance floor, only finishing that night. As with other Proms, most of the boys wore suits or tuxedos, while the girls were adorned in expensive gowns and dresses, added to that were the hours they spent grooming, making them appear much older which many felt was part of their heritage, a rite of passage, so to speak, and which gave the dance more importance than any other event they had experienced.

Inside, he saw Milly and all that happened came back to him when he saw her. She was beautiful, wearing a soft rose-colored dress that dropped to her feet. All he could do was stand there and stare at her beauty, something that Matt noticed, and he made a point of putting his arm around her, before trying to get her to kiss him, saying it loud enough that others could hear.

Milly was uncomfortable with this and told Matt, "Remove your arm. And yes, I came to the Prom with you, but I don't appreciate you trying to act like we're a couple."

Matt was upset with this, saying he expected her to act like his date and loosen up a bit. After all, he had asked her to come along when no one else had, and he expected her to appreciate him. "I'm the king and you're my queen, so act like it." When Milly gave him a look that told him she was angry, he just replied. "Fine, why don't you find Andy and share his misery?"

Totally shocked at this exchange, Milly walked off the dance floor, wondering if all boys were jerks. She had hoped Andy would ask her, even though they were in a bad place lately, she hoped that maybe they might be able to repair their relationship and had only accepted Matt's request when the Prom got closer. She wasn't even sure he would come but when she spied him staring at her, she realized why Matt was putting on a show. Both boys disliked each other, she understood that, but Andy was her first love, and it was hard to think their long relationship was now over. The problem was, Matt was her date and had been nice at first but now was only acting like a fool just to bug Andy.

Another of Milly's friends came up and grabbed her by the arm. "Come on. They're announcing the trophies," the girl said, as she pulled Milly toward the dance floor. Milly looked around for Andy, hoping he would join her and their friends as the trophy titles were called but she didn't see him.

All the seniors were called up to the DJ table and awarded small plastic trophies, which had been voted on by the entire senior class, with labels on them like, 'Best Dancer', or 'Most likely to become a doctor'. There were also 'couples' trophies and this is where Andy and Milly were chosen, as 'Most likely to be married'.

Milly laughed as she looked around for Andy before heading up alone, to collect the trophy, now a bit embarrassed since she expected Andy to join her. Her friend Maria however, had found him and was now pushing him into the room and toward the trophy table. Milly accepted the trophy and showed it to him when he arrived as the others in the room clapped or hooted. Then she grabbed his hand doing her best to get him into the spirit of the award.

"Well, it looks like everyone thinks we're going to be married. What do you think about that? We are going to get married, someday?" She added that last word hoping it would spark something in him. He had been acting like an ass lately, but she so wanted to put the past behind them and take up where they had been since it affected both their futures.

Andy grabbed her gently by the arm and led her away from the others before attempting to answer. "Honestly, I don't know anymore. You're here with Matt and you seem to be having a good time. Why don't you go back to your date?"

"Seriously, Andy? What about us?"

"Right now, I can't lie. I don't see an *us*," he paused for a moment, trying to think of the right words. "You know, you look fantastic tonight and I miss you, but we're looking at different dreams. I've tried, Milly, I've really tried to move into your dream, find a school, and find a job. The problem is, I can't. I don't want to get just any job, but something I can enjoy, and I especially don't want to go to school. Those are your dreams. I just don't see how I fit in. With time, maybe we'll find a dream we both agree on, but until them, I don't see how we can continue."

When he finished, he saw the look of hurt on her face, like her dreams had just been destroyed and realized he had crossed a line, one that they might not be able to repair. With that, he kissed her gently, before breaking the kiss and turning to leave. "I need time to find my own dreams," he said, not stopping.

Milly watched him walk away and called out, "Don't do this, please."

Andy just kept walking.

Chapter Eight
Graduation

A friend is one that knows you as you are, understands where you have been, accepts what you have become, and still, gently allows you to grow—William Shakespeare

Andy's parents didn't know what was going on with their son, but when he arrived home early on the night of the Prom and went straight to his room, not saying a word to them, it made them unsure of how to react. Sam decided to call Milly's parents who told them Milly hadn't come home yet but had phoned saying she would be home later. After a quick conversation, they decided to adopt a 'wait and see' posture, hoping he would tell them what had happened and why he had returned home so early, and more importantly, what had happened with Milly.

The next morning, Andy came down for breakfast, however he didn't say a word about the Prom. When his mom threw in a few carefully worded questions about what he did, he would answer them generally, telling them he had fun, that he had chatted with a lot of his buddies, but that the food wasn't that good. His father forgot for a moment that Samantha was trying to gain insight into what had happened, when he mentioned how it sounded like the Prom he had been to. Sam ignored him and got to the point, asking Andy why he had come home so early. Andy danced around the question, saying the dance was boring and he had a headache, so he came home. He made no mention of Milly. That was all he would tell them. Being alert to his mood, Samantha wisely decided to leave it at that. Mark was going to question him a bit more, until he saw the look Samantha gave him and wisely decided to follow her lead, turning his attention to the local news on their television.

Two days after the Prom, both families noticed that Andy and Milly had started talking again, but what they didn't see was the context. Their conversations were curt and not as open as they had been. Their families figured they had some sort of fight during the Prom and had worked it out, but that wasn't the case. Twice during the week, Matthew Grimes had called and wanted to talk to Milly, once while Andy was there. Milly declined to take the call and Andy didn't say anything, but she knew he was angry even though he had no right to be, their long romance had finally fallen upon rocky shores.

She chose that analogy because of Andy's insistence finding excuses to life's challenges such as choosing a career or applying to school, often slipping away quietly to sail with Finn on his boat. He even asked her if she would join him a few times, but Milly was more interested in her education. She was doing well in school and had decided to concentrate on a degree in design.

Before the Prom, he had taken Finn up on his invitation, to sail out onto the Atlantic, get a little taste of the 'Salt Sea'. When Andy finally reached the Atlantic, he was hooked, even in the face of high seas and small squalls, he never lost his taste for sailing. Milly declined often to attend as their senior year was winding down as did Andy's mother, which caused Finn to lament about how these trips would be better if she had come along. Then a few days before graduation while Milly was looking at colleges with her family, Andy's parents had a huge argument and enraged, Samantha stormed out. Mark refused to say what happened but did ask Andy to find out where she had gone and to report back without letting his mother know. Mark saying it would seem like he didn't trust her, which made Andy wonder what his father wasn't saying.

This argument had upset the family and just added to Andy's own loss. His parents were having problems just like his relationship with Milly. This was on his mind as he searched the town, looking in his mother's usual haunts, not locating her in these places. In the past, when she was angry, she would often retreat to an antique store near the Pamlico River. When he didn't find her there, he was about to head home when his mother called his cell, asking what was going on at home. Following his father's instructions, he just told her that things were okay, though everyone wanted to know where she was. There was a bit of muffled conversation, obviously his mother had placed something over the phone so he would not hear, then she came back on to say she was fine and would be home later, after she had calmed down.

Andy tried to ask what their argument was about, but Sam simply repeated she was fine and just needed to get some fresh air. She would call back on her way home. In the background, Andy heard a familiar voice, it was the only word just before the call ended, but instantly recognized it as Finn and knew where he had to go. He wasn't far away and raced there, narrowly avoiding a speed trap when a car passed him going even faster and was suddenly pulled over when a police car put on its lights.

Parking in the same spot he often used, he walked quickly to the dock where the Munck was usually berthed to find it gone. He looked out on the water and saw what he thought was the Munck sailing away. Thinking quickly, he walked to the Marina office and borrowed a small boat powered by an outboard motor. He'd been there often enough that he had no problem convincing the Marina owner that Finn had forgotten some medicine for his mom, and he wanted to drop it off. In no time, he was on the water and following the ship's course as it was no longer in sight.

Opening the throttle, Andy loved the fact that his boat was cruising at a good rate and soon caught sight of the Munck, the distinctive battery charger atop the sail, allowing him to pick the boat out and close the distance. Getting close enough to see onto the boat, he cut his motor and grabbing the emergency binoculars that were stored on board, scanned the boat quickly spotting his mother and Finn sitting in the stern. Seeing nothing unusual, he started the engine again, keeping it at a lower speed to reduce the noise as he began to close the distance.

He didn't need the binoculars now as he was close enough to see them clearly. They were talking and Andy wondered if it was just his mom's way to calm down, when he suddenly saw his mother kiss Finn on the lips, which reminded him of the first time he and Milly had kissed on the Ferris Wheel. He slowed at that point deciding he'd seen enough. Turning his craft around, he opened the throttle forgetting, in his haste, that it would cause more noise. Throwing a last look over his shoulder, he could see Finn stand up and look right at him.

Getting back to the Marina, Andy returned the craft and thanked the owner for the use of the small boat. When asked if he had found them, Andy lied and said he hadn't and that he would call his mother and let her know he had her medicine, explaining it wasn't serious, only some sea sickness pills that she probably didn't need. With that, he headed home to tell his father he hadn't found her, but also that she had called and given him the message.

His father nodded and Andy felt compelled to try once more to find out what had happened, as his parents were usually happy with each other, but obviously, there was something wrong here, and her racing to Finn meant once again, the pain of hurting another. As he thought about it, he remembered that first time when he saw them sitting together, well he wasn't about to add to any sorrow and kept the secret of what he had seen to himself. Once again, he wished Nathan was around so they could chat, being his confidant and with his own relationship probably over, he knew he would never find the answer to the questions that were boiling in his brain.

There wasn't much time to brew on this question as he had to get ready to graduate and he threw himself into preparing for it. Contacting Milly, they agreed to act nicely to each other, it being, after all, a great achievement in their lives. Walking to the school that night, they talked about the colleges Milly had visited. She found the college she liked in northern Florida and chose to attend it. Andy looked at her then, shocked. He had wondered if they couldn't fix their relationship but that depended on her attending a college closer to home. He had never been to Florida, except for one trip to Disney World the summer before Milly arrived in Aurora.

Milly tried to put a positive spin on it, saying it was only a five-hour drive away and he could easily visit. Secretly though, she wanted the chance to be on her own for a bit and make her own decisions. To her, their relationship was over but she also thought that maybe her absence might rekindle his interest in her and let him realize how important she was to him. She told him how her chosen college would allow her to major in interior design, with a minor in mechanical engineering, two areas she enjoyed immensely, and if they decided they were right for each other while she was away, well who knew what would happen? Then, she added their years away would allow him to explore the world.

This didn't sit well with Andy. He saw right through what she said and told her, it was her life to live, and she could do what she wanted. The remainder of the walk to the school was one of silence, both of them lost in their thoughts.

The graduation ceremony came and went in the flash of an eye. Milly was a half dozen students ahead of Andy, and when she crossed the stage, she was handed a bouquet of flowers, the card not signed. When Andy crossed the stage, he saw Milly holding the flowers and looked around the room, centering his gaze on Matthew, who smiled at him and nodded, then pointed at Milly, letting him know he had given her the flowers. Andy settled back in his seat without a word.

When the ceremony was over, Matthew walked up and had his photo taken with Milly, who was grateful for the flowers, and she graciously smiled and held onto him. Andy saw this and would have charged in, had the other graduates not blocked his way. He did manage to get close to her later and told her that it was obvious Matt might be good for her, believing that Matt had been accepted to the same college and trying to be gracious. Milly became so upset over what she felt was a nasty comment, that she left the school without saying anything more to him. It was only later that Andy had learned about this and realized why Milly was so angry.

As he waited for his family to join him, Andy suddenly saw Finn coming up to him. "Hey there, Andy, I had trouble getting up to you," he said, not smiling.

Andy just nodded, not sure how to respond.

"I just wanted to say congratulations," he said seriously.

"Thanks. You come to the party at my house?"

"No. Think it's better if I don't. Your dad doesn't like me around. Best if I make myself scarce."

Andy nodded. "Maybe you're right. Can I ask you something personal?"

Finn shuffled his feet. "Go ahead."

"What's going on between you and my mom?" Andy asked, his smile now gone.

Finn took a second to answer. "You're a man now, so I'll give it to you straight," he said, seeing Andy's family moving toward them from among the crowd.

"Honestly, I have always loved your mom. When she was younger, we used to date, secretly. If your grandfather had found out, well, it probably would have caused trouble for us, well, me. Then your father came into the picture, and I decided it was best to leave for a bit, let her get her life together. I didn't know they stayed in Aurora, but when I saw her in the hospital, it just brought back all the memories of our time together. Before that, I thought we were over each other, your mom being married, and she had you kids, but all the old feelings came back the minute I saw her."

"I know it hurt you, seeing us together, so I decided to leave again, maybe head up to New England for a spell. I won't try to see her again. Oh, and I never told your mom you were in that boat, didn't want to worry her and all."

By now, his family had managed to maneuver through the crowd and Finn gave Andy an envelope, while his father looked on. He looked at Samantha. "Just wanted to wish Andy well and tell him I'm leaving for a bit."

Mark looked pleased and Samantha surprised. "When are you come back?" She asked.

"Don't know if I will," he said as Mark smiled slightly. He shook Andy's hand, whispered something in his ear, and after hugging Samantha, walked out of the auditorium.

His parents looked at Andy. "What did he give you?"

Andy held up the envelope. "Not sure. It doesn't look like money," he replied. "I'll open it later."

The family headed home where there was a joint party for him and Milly. They were both cordial with each other, knowing it would hurt their families if they argued, so they smiled with everyone and took photos, as people came up to the graduates and asked what their plans were. Milly looked at Andy for a second, then saying where she was going to college. Andy didn't know what to say when they asked him. The best he could come up with was, "I'm going to explore a bit before I determine what I want to do."

The rest of the evening both families hung out and when it got late, several of Andy's friends showed up and asked him to join them as they visited other parties. Andy looked at Milly, asked if she wanted to come along, but she declined, saying she was tired and was hoping he would stay with her.

Andy thought it over, but his friends wanted him as well and he told her he had to go. She nodded, kissed his cheek, and told him to have a good time, then she turned and headed back to her parents.

Andy knew their relationship was over, even if others didn't. He told his parents he would be careful and not drink any alcohol. Mark nodded, especially since one of his friends was driving. Samantha also said was fine, though she seemed distracted as Andy said he'd be back later. In a flash, he was gone.

Milly watched him go, saw him looking at her as the car sped off, then told her parents she was going home for a bit to hang up her robe. When she got there, she cried for over an hour, even as her family arrived. When her siblings and her father were in bed, she sat with her mother, confiding in her that their relationship was over.

Mary put her arm around her daughter. "I've known that things were difficult. But Milly, no one can see the future. In time, you might find that maybe things aren't over. That's my wish for you. Now, congratulations. I'm so proud of you. Tomorrow your future awaits."

Chapter Nine
Surprises

I like the dreams of the future better than the history of the past—Thomas Jefferson

The day after graduation, Andy awoke feeling alone and lost, even the thought of taking a trip out to sea with Finn did nothing to spark his mood. He lay on his bed, noticing that Robert was already out of the room and giving him time to ponder what had happened. Putting on a pair of shorts and sneakers, he walked quietly outside where he stretched his muscles before heading out for a short run. In the past, he would often run by Milly's house, stretching a bit more to allow her time to dress and join him. It was something he enjoyed and was like an infusion of strength when she did. She always joined him with a smile and her positive attitude working in ways that always seemed to bring him up when he was down. Not today. He stopped running by her house, the way he usually did, looking up at her window for a sight of her, but today, she didn't appear. That happened sometimes, but he had hoped it might be a chance to overcome their problems. He accepted that she wouldn't join him and feeling sad, he just started running again, not so happy this time.

He didn't know that Milly was standing at her window, hiding in the shadows as he stretched outside her house. She debated with herself about what she should do, but this time, it was different for her, difficult. Part of her was torn; he was after all her first love, but deep down she knew that he would never change, and she remained rooted to the shadows. The love she had expressed for him was over and she felt she had to be strong for herself, though she cried a bit when she watched him start running again without her.

The next few days were similar, he would run by her home, and she would not come out, and by the third day, he knew she was avoiding him. It bothered him at first, but as the days passed, he accepted their relationship was over, which set him free to concentrate on his goals. Instead of running their usual course, he changed his mind and took a different route, getting back home just as his father was starting to wash the family cars.

As promised, Mark and Sam purchased a car for Andy and gave it to him after graduation. It was an older car, a dark maroon, but it needed work. Andy and his father had spent time working hard to refurbish it. Even after hours on the car, it still needed work, but it was his and he loved it. Now his father was cleaning it, attempting to erase some of their handprints and the grime it had received when Andy took it out for a spin.

"That was a fast run," his father said, looking at his watch as his mother came outside carrying some rags. She was followed almost immediately by his brother Robert who was now fifteen and teasing their little sister, who was almost six years old. She was a bit of a surprise for them all, which was similar to Milly's mom who had given birth to another sister, Monic, almost exactly a year later.

Robert was carrying some books and a broken picture. "I'm sorry, Andy. Sarah and I were just clowning around, and we broke the glass. They fell over your graduation envelopes. Can I get rid of them, or what?"

"Hey, wait," their father stepped into the conversation. "Andy, did you open all your graduation envelopes? If there were presents in there, you need to respond with a thank you to everyone."

"Dad, I did. I opened them all," Andy responded, a bit peeved that they were checking up on him.

"You never told me what Finn gave you," his mom said.

Andy suddenly had a startled look in his eyes, of something he hadn't done. "Oh, crap. Okay, go ahead and yell at me. I opened everything people gave me at the party, but what the heck did I do with Finn's envelope?" He moved quickly into the house and emerged about ten minutes later carrying it. "I forgot, I had stuck it in my cap when we were leaving graduation and just found it now," he said, showing them the crinkled envelope.

As Andy tore the envelope open, his father stopped spraying the car he was working on and looked at him, while his mother came over and leaned on his father, her forearm resting on his shoulder. As he opened the envelope, his father asked, "What's in there?"

"Wait, Dad, I'll let you know. Okay, it's a letter, wait a paper." He unfolded it and as he read, his mother looked at it as well, curious what Finn would write to her son and not tell her. As he opened the thick paper, he looked it over. "I don't know what this is," he said.

"Let me see it," his father said, walking over to look.

"It says 'Title'," Andy responded, looking at his father, who grabbed his hand and held it stead while he too looked at the paper Andy held.

"Oh, my God," Samantha said, putting her hand to her mouth. "He gave you the title to the Munck? Why would he do that?"

"I don't know, Mom, I really don't," he stated, then looked up at his father. "Dad, you remember he whispered something to me. I thought he was talking about mom, but it didn't make sense."

"What did he whisper?" His mother demanded of him.

Andy was a little taken aback by the forcefulness of her question. "He said, 'take care of her', that was it. Take care of her. He wasn't talking about you, Mom, he was talking about the Munck."

"Oh, my Lord," Samantha said. "Mark, I have to check on him." Mark lowered his head then nodded, and when he looked up, his wife was already heading for the car, the same one that was partially covered with bubbles. She didn't seem to care, just grabbed the keys off the picnic table where Mark had put them and headed out of their driveway.

"Dad, mom looks upset," Andy said quietly, hoping to not upset his sister or brother. "Should I follow her? I know where she's going."

Mark looked at him. "Yeah maybe, take your brother, make sure she comes home," he responded.

"I understand, Dad. I kind of figured things out. I'll make sure she gets home."

Grabbing his own keys, Andy tore out of the driveway, his brother in the passenger seat. As they raced by Milly's home, she looked up and waved. Neither of them waved back, but there was something in the eyes of Robert as he looked at her, something bad, she could sense it. She hurried over to Andy's house, seeing his sister on the small swing set they had built for her, and Andy's dad sitting nearby, his head in his hands.

"Mr. Thompson," Milly said quietly. "Is everything okay?"

He looked up and she saw the tears in his eyes. "Oh, I'm sorry. Hi, Milly," he replied, as he tried to wipe the evidence of his tears from his face. "Sorry, Andy just left with his brother. You'll have to come back another time."

"I know, I saw them drive by. I want to know if you're okay."

He looked at her and offered a kind of strained smile at her. "I'll know soon enough," he responded. "Keep your fingers crossed."

Milly had no idea what he was talking about. She knew this might be a way back to Andy, but she paused. She didn't want to get him back this way if there was some tragedy at work. She wanted Andy to come back to her on his own terms, not because something was bothering him. "Well, I'll keep my fingers crossed and say a prayer for you," she responded as she began to walk away.

"Thanks, Milly, I could use it," he had trouble keeping himself composed, but Milly was on her way out of the yard.

"Bye, Sarah," she said, not looking back at Mr. Thompson.

As they pulled into the Marina a few minutes later, Robert spotted their mother's car. "There it is," he said. Andy parked right behind her, blocking the car in, just in case. The two were out of the car and moving down the dock quickly to the Munck, right where it had been for years. The two boys slowed to a walk until they saw their mom sitting on the dock crying.

"What now?" Andy said quietly to himself, as he and Robert reached her and pulled her to her feet.

"Mom, what happened?" Robert asked her.

She looked at her youngest son, wiping away tears, "He's gone," she said. "He didn't even say goodbye. He just left. Why?"

Andy looked at her, but decided it was best to just leave things as they were. If she knew why, she might despise him, or maybe she would want to try and find Finn. *Would she really do that,* he wondered, *leave her husband, her family behind?* Another reason it was good to break things off with Milly, he believed. It hurt, breaking up with her, but it was for the best.

While Robert stayed with their mom, Andy went to the boat. He looked around. It appeared to be deserted, as he had suspected. It looked exactly like it had the last time he had been aboard, but there was more. He wasn't sure what it was exactly, just that it was like Finn was still with him. He looked about but nothing appeared out of place, just that feeling stayed with him. Shaking the feeling away, he couldn't find anything, a note or any articles that indicated he would be back. Finn was gone.

Chapter Ten
Assault

Life is inherently risky. There is only one big risk you should avoid at all costs, and that is the risk of doing nothing—Denis Waitley

Andy followed his mother as she drove into the driveway, Robert sitting in the passenger seat next to her. Robert got out of the car first and walked up to his father. "Finn is gone, but he left his boat."

As Samantha got out, she gave a strained smile to her husband, then rushed into his arms. He looked at Andy, who nodded as Robert, and he collected their sister and announced that they were going to head over to the ice-cream parlor and would be back later. Mark had to admit, whatever had happened between his son and Milly, it had changed him a little. He was more aware of the needs of others, and Mark needed to be alone with his wife. He started to reach into his pocket to pull out his wallet, but Andy held up his hand, signaling he didn't want money.

Robert and Andy walked while holding their sister's hands, allowing her to jump up as they swung her in the air, as they talked in code about what they had witnessed. When Robert made it clear that he thought there was something going on between their mother and Finn, Andy just waved the thought away. "She's good. Dad will take care of it," he responded.

"Hey," Robert stated, "we should check out the boat later, see what shape it's in. Maybe you can take us out on the water."

"I want to go out on the boat," Sarah stated. "I've never been on the Munck before."

Andy laughed at this. "I was kind of thinking the same thing, but before we take it out, we need to check it over carefully. Last time I was on it, I noticed some wet areas near the galley," he replied.

"Wet areas?" Robert asked.

"Yeah, might be nothing, but if we want to take this little munch…" He stopped short, realizing he was just about to call his little sister what Finn called his mother. "This little punk," he corrected. "Sarah, I promise, we'll take you out one of these days, we just have to make sure that it's safe. Okay?"

"Yeah, but can we just go on it later?"

"Yes. Maybe mom and dad will want to come and see how it is. I don't think dad has even seen it," he said, as he thought about that.

When they returned home, their parents were gone, Robert found a note on the fridge, which both read quickly. The note simply said their parents would be out till late and to make some supper for Sarah. At the end of the note, the boys saw the little circle with a crossed checkmark inside it, which they knew was how their mother always ended her notes to them. It was a code that only the boys knew, meaning, things were okay, and not to worry.

Samantha had come up with that symbol after some of the arguments between her and their dad when they were younger, something she never told Mark. The circle meant that she was okay, and the little crossed checkmark meant so was their dad. Just something she felt the boys needed when the arguments, though few, sometimes led to shouting and the boys would get upset.

Robert saw the symbol and let out a sigh of relief. "Don't know what happened between mom and Finn, but I think they've both calmed down. Bet, dad is taking her out to dinner."

"Well, at least their relationship is still solid. Wish I could say the same thing," Andy responded.

"What the heck happened between you and Milly, anyway?" Robert asked.

"We broke up at the Prom," Andy responded, then started to fill his brother in on what had transpired that evening.

"That son of a bitch, Grimes. Man, I hate that guy."

"So do I," Andy replied, "so do I."

The rest of the evening, the boys kept Sarah occupied. As it grew dark, she asked if they could play a game before she had to go to bed. Eager to keep her happy, they agreed, but Andy almost spit up his cola when Sarah returned with the board game, Life.

"Oh, man," he started. "There is a God and she's a woman."

Robert almost spit out his cola as well. "What the heck did you just say?"

"Nothing, it was Milly's favorite game and here we are playing it again."

"Oh, man, God is a woman!"

This started off a laughing spurt, Sarah joined in, though she didn't know exactly what they were laughing about, she just wanted to be a part of the fun.

When their parents arrived around midnight, Andy was awake and saw they were holding hands; the crisis, whatever it was, had been averted. He stood from the couch and looked at them. "You two have fun?"

His mother giggled a little, okay, alcohol was involved, Andy knew. When his mom drank, she always got a bit silly. "We're fine," his father answered. "Is Sarah asleep?"

"Yeah, she passed out in the middle of a game of Life. Too bad, she was winning. Robert fell asleep a little while ago."

"I'm awake," his voice came from the recliner. "It's amazing how much energy Sarah has. Hey, Dad?"

"Yes," he answered, grabbing his wife and squeezing her a little, to which Samantha just laughed more.

"We were thinking of heading down to the boat. You want to come along? Andy thinks it might need some work and with your knowledge of construction, we thought you might give us some ideas."

"Maybe, I need some sleep right now, check with me in the morning. I think I'd like to see it."

As their parents walked out, Andy sat back on the couch. It was such a relief, something he hadn't experienced much lately. He blinked a couple of times, and suddenly opened his eyes, wide. He thought he saw someone looking in his window. He looked over at Robert, but he was sound asleep. The clock on the wall showed it was almost 2 a.m., so he must have fallen asleep as well. Andy heard a noise outside then. Someone outside their home at 2 a.m., making noise was no joke and he was determined to find out who it was. Quietly, he rose from the couch, picked up the family emergency light, it was a copy of a police light, encased in light steel and shone a bright beam which could be expanded if you pulled back on the bulb housing.

He threw a shoe at his brother, who didn't even stir, so he knew he was on his own. The town of Aurora wasn't a place known for trouble, it had its share of cops, but generally there was seldom any need for their response, especially in their neighborhood. Moving to the rear door, Andy opened it quietly and stepped outside. The night was warm, as was usually the case in the summer, and he moved toward the side of the house where he thought he saw the face looking in the window. There was movement outside, near his car and Andy moved to the side of the house before turning on his light.

The beam blasted out and the first thing he saw was the hose his father had been using, laying partially across their picnic table. He raised the light and quickly noticed someone by his car, the door was open, and the person was bending over the seat. Andy advanced quickly as the person in the car turned around using their hand to try and block the light. It was a male, Andy was sure of that, but he was wearing a mask over his face. Andy didn't waste a moment; someone was trying to steal his car. The man tried to run away as Andy took off after him, when the man bumped into the picnic table in the dark and fell back. In seconds, Andy had closed the distance and swung down with his light, hitting the guy's arm.

He was rewarded with a Yelp, then his knowledge of Karate kicked in. Andy dropped the light and hit the man on the side of his head, knocking him back toward the lawn. Andy advanced quickly, but as he was about to kick out at him, something hit him over his back and now it was his turn to cry out. The blow really knocked him for a loop, and he fell to his knees for a second, only to have the first guy come up and kick him in the stomach. Andy went down hard and tried to block successive blows as now two men were attacking, and then something hard hit him on his arm. In the dim beam of the fallen flashlight, Andy saw it was a crowbar, and the pain on his arm probably meant it was broken.

With one last kick, the assailants turned and fled from the yard, or rather they tried to flee. Suffering from the beating, Andy could only watch, sparse light from the streetlamp down the street gave him a sort of shadowy view of someone now fighting with his attackers. In a lot of pain, Andy used his good arm to try and rise. He managed to get upright mostly, when someone grabbed him around the waist. "Easy, lad, you've taken a good beating," the voice said.

Andy looked up. "Finn?"

"Yeah, it's me. Come on, let's check out that arm, matey."

Too confused to argue, Andy allowed Finn to lead him to the picnic table. "What are you doing here? I thought you left?"

"So did I, but I forgot my gun. I went back to the Muck to get it and then your mom showed up, so I hid in the boat, little storage shelf in the galley. Saw you come on board and then leave. I was hoping you wouldn't see me, would have made a mess of things, even more, if I had been spotted. So, I stayed hidden till you and your family left. Good thing you did, that tight space was playing hell with my legs, cramped them up something bad."

"Did you know those guys were going to break into my car?" He asked, as he looked at the two men, who were now getting up and staggering away.

Finn looked at them as the two made their getaway. "Vile scum. They'll be sore tomorrow, that's for sure. And no, I just happened to look in your window, wanted to leave you with something."

"Should we call the police, try to catch them?"

"You might also want to call an ambulance first. I think they broke your arm. The police can come later, they'll catch those bastards. Look, let me help you get inside, then I'm gone. Don't tell anyone I was here. Take this."

Andy was hurting too badly to argue, he just took the proffered envelope. "You already gave me the Munck. I can't take anything else from you," he responded.

"Horse shit. The Munck needs a lot of repairs. I thought of scrapping it, but then figured you might want it. You love the sea as much as I do, this envelope is just something to help get it back to shape, and I think your mom will appreciate it if it stays in your family. I owe your grandfather a lot, and this is just something to help me repay that debt," he said, as he gingerly helped Andy to his feet.

On their way to the house, Finn said, "Your mom told me about the trouble with your girl. From what she said that girl is a keeper. You need to get a grip. Live your life, sew any wild oats you have, but when you're ready, find that girl and marry her. That was a mistake I made, and I regret it deeply."

"You mean my mom," Andy said, as he struggled up the few steps to the back door.

"No. Your mom means so much, but she was too young for me. I mean the girl I let get away before I met your grandfather. Sam is great, reminded me of her, and now that I'm old, it's too late."

"How old are you, anyway?"

"I'm only seven years older than your mom. Met your granddad in the Navy; he was the officer on my ship and he kind of liked me, kept me out a Philippine prison, bad place. Afterwards, he kind of kept an eye on me and I repaid my debt to him on time; we were in a bad spot. I followed him here after we both got out of the Navy. That's when I met your mom."

"I was wondering," Andy said, the pain now really starting to hurt as Finn helped him to a chair then grabbed the phone.

"Tell the dispatcher what happened, but don't tell anyone I was here. It'll only cause problems. I saw how badly she cried when she thought I was gone, but now, she's over me. She has your dad, he's a better man than I ever was."

He made sure Andy was sitting in a chair, grabbed the phone and handed it to him, then stuffed the envelope in Andy's pocket, before he headed out the door.

"Thanks for your help," Andy said quietly, as the 911 dispatcher came on the line.

Chapter Eleven
History

Life is what happens while you are busy making other plans—John Lennon

The sound of sirens outside woke the family. Sarah ran to her parents' bedroom in tears, and they came down the stairs to the sight emergency lights flashing through their windows and spied Robert standing to the side while two EMT's worked on Andy as he lay on the floor in the kitchen. "What the hell happened?" Mark screamed at Robert, who stood there with his mouth open.

Samantha passed Sarah to Mark and raced to Andy. He was a mess, sporting a gash along his left eye and while one of the EMT's worked to staunch the bleeding, the other was wrapping Andy's arm in an air cast. "Andy, are you alright? What happened?"

Andy looked up. "I saw a couple of guys trying to break into my car. I thought there was only one and was doing a good job on him, when someone else hit me with a crowbar," Andy replied through clenched teeth.

A police officer came through the back door and taking in the view, asked one EMT what he knew, then he spoke to Mark, while Samantha cried over her son. "We received a 911 call from your son saying he was attacked. It appears he suffered a beating and may have a broken arm. The men breaking into his car got away, but not after they were beaten by someone else," he said flatly, like it was an everyday occurrence.

"What? Who was the other guy?" Samantha asked as she fought to hold back her tears.

"I don't know. I was busy getting kicked. Some guy just came out of nowhere and beat the hell out of them after I was on the ground. Next thing I knew, he was helping me inside and then he just left. I'm not sure who he was," Andy replied.

"You don't know who he was?" Samantha again asked, sensing that he wasn't saying everything.

"Ma'am. We need to get your son to the hospital for x-rays and treatment. You'll have to wait and question him later."

"Robert, why don't you help your brother or at least come and get us?" Mark demanded.

Robert just stood there his mouth open, not sure what he should say.

"Wasn't his fault, Dad," Andy said for him. "He was asleep on the couch and when I heard a sound outside, I went to investigate, thought it was our neighbors."

With that, the EMT's had him lie on a gurney as they covered him with a blanket and rolled it to the door, then to the ambulance which was parked in their driveway. By now, the whole neighborhood was alerted, and people were gathering outside, blocking the lights from the ambulance and arriving police vehicles with their hands.

Andy was starting to feel the effects of the pain medication and his head moved from side to side, his vision blurry. Even as this was going on, he kept remembering what Finn had said. He was back in Andy's life. The image of Finn standing by the table looking down at him, and how the hell did Finn take those two guys out? Sure, he could have taken them himself, if he had been more alert and had seen the second guy before he was attacked from behind, but Finn, he was older than his parents. He smiled at this. The old man was still tough enough to take down two armed criminals and he didn't get a scratch, at least not that he could see in the darkness and through his pain.

And then there was what he said. Andy was hurting then, but his words made sense even as he endured the beating he took. Milly was important to him, that much he was sure of. He still wasn't ready to just settle down and forget all he wanted to do, but if he could just talk to her, maybe they might come to an agreement.

As they were removing Andy, Mark, still holding Sarah, spotted an envelope on the floor with a bit of blood on it. Handing Sarah to Robert, he reached down and opened it, finding it was full of cash with no note. He took the envelope and put it in his robe pocket, having grabbed it when he was awoken. He looked at Robert and asked him what this money was about. Since Robert had no idea, thoughts crept into Mark's mind, and he decided not to mention it to anyone.

By this time, Andy had been loaded into the ambulance and just as the doors closed, for a split second, he looked out and looked into familiar eyes. He tried to get the attendant to hold up a moment, but it was too late, the ambulance doors were closed, and it was already starting to move. Andy looked through the door window, clearly seeing Milly standing in the street, wearing a robe as she moved toward his family.

Milly had been awakened, like everyone else, by the sirens and the flashing lights. Her parents were up as well and staring out the windows. "What's going on?" She asked them.

"We don't know, but it looks like something happened in our neighborhood," her mother answered. "They're just a few houses down our street. Oh, my God."

"What?" Milly asked, even though she already suspected the answer.

Her mother looked at her. "I think they're at the Thompson's house."

Milly moved to the window and looked out. Her mother was right. She remembered the fear she had seen in Mark's eyes, the hurt she had seen earlier. Quickly, she grabbed her robe and started out the door. Her mother was about to stop her but thought better of it and let her go, explaining to her husband, Ned, that it was alright.

Milly walked quickly down her street, passing the other houses. Yes, it was Andy's house. She moved to the sidewalk, standing by several neighbors when she saw the gurney come out. She was too far away to see who it was, but even if she'd been closer, she would have had problems seeing, since the person on the gurney was covered with bandages and a blanket. She managed to get close to the ambulance as the door closed and was looking in the back and she knew. She saw Andy looking right back at her. The EMT closed the ambulance doors and soon it departed, its siren blaring and lights flashing.

Looking around, she saw the Thompson's as they were making their way to their cars. She could see they were terribly upset; Samantha was even shaking. Milly walked quickly over to them. "Hey, what happened? Is Andy alright?"

Mark looked at her like he hadn't seen her in years. "He'll be fine. He stopped some men from stealing our cars, or something and he got a little banged up. Excuse us please, we have to go."

Milly stepped back, moving toward Robert and Sarah, who were standing by the cars as their parents took off and left for the hospital. She saw that

Andy's car had the doors open and wires were on the seat. Being that Andy was very fastidious when it came to not leaving a mess, she knew that he had interrupted the people here.

Robert had his sister by the hand. She was crying and obviously upset and when she saw Milly, she pulled free of Robert and raced to her. Milly scooped her up as she spoke to Robert, learning of the events from him. When he was done relating what Andy had said, she asked a question. "So, who was the man who helped him out?"

"He said he didn't know the man, that he showed up during the fight and after he helped Andy get inside, he just left," Robert replied.

"Huh. I wonder who it was, must have been a neighbor," Milly replied.

"Seriously? Do you know our neighbors, I mean besides your family of course. I have an idea of who it was, but I'm not sure."

"Who?"

He waited till she had put Sarah down and was heading inside, then as she started up the steps, he whispered his idea to her. "Finn."

"The guy who owns the boat you guys go out on?" Milly said, not knowing what had transpired. "If it was him, why wouldn't he have stayed around? He's friends with your family, right?"

"Yes and no," was all Robert replied. "You want to come in and wait for Andy to come back. I mean, if he isn't too badly banged up and they don't keep him overnight," Robert asked.

"Not tonight. I got a job today working at a restaurant on Middle Street. I have to start early, so please just text me with how he's doing when you hear."

Robert nodded and thanked her for helping to calm Sarah down, but as she started to head home, he added one more thing, "I sure wish you and Andy would settle things. I miss seeing you."

Milly walked back, gave him a hug and whispered, "I miss you as well," she said as she headed out.

Robert got Sarah to calm down and before long, she was again asleep; this time sleeping on the couch. Robert sat there looking down at her, thinking about what he had told Milly.

<center>~~~</center>

79

In the hospital, Andy was wheeled to a room, the same one he had stayed in when he was a kid and where he had met Finn, these similar circumstances made him shake his head. Both times, Finn had played a part in his life, only this time, he wished Finn were here, at least he would have someone to talk to.

As if by magic, his parents entered the room. His mom stopped and looked at the other bed, now occupied by another older man. "Andy, isn't this…" She never got the chance to finish the question before Andy answered her with "Yes." It made her think that all of this was more than a coincidence.

It took his father a second to realize what they were talking about, and he began to wonder more about the man who supposedly helped his son. He didn't bring the question up since his relationship with his wife had improved with the disappearance of Finn, and he wasn't about to open that thought pattern in his wife if he didn't have to.

His parents talked to him until the cops showed up and started questioning him more. Andy was as truthful as he could be, except for the part involving Finn and after half an hour, they left, saying they would increase patrols in his neighborhood for the next couple of weeks. They were interested mostly in trying to identify the men, or why Andy hadn't called for help earlier, and where the men went. Other than one or two questions more about the man who helped, they left him to his parents' care.

A few minutes after they departed, two nurses came into the room and announced to Andy and his parents that the x-rays taken when he first arrived showed a broken arm and several bruised ribs. He also had to have the gash in his head stitched and they believed he had suffered a concussion. All things that Andy expected, and instead of being wheeled out of the room, the nurses brought in a medical tray and began working on him there. Occasionally, a doctor would stop in, review what they were doing, then leaving after asking Andy how he felt.

The nurses had given him some sort of shot for the pain in his arm and began placing a cast on it. What he disliked most were the shots placed directly into his head, a local, one of the nurses stated. His head felt a little better, but when the nurses started to stitch him up, he wished he had another shot, the pain being as bad as when the one guy hit him with the crowbar.

Two hours after being admitted, he was discharged and sat in the rear of the vehicle as his parents drove him home. Both declined his offer to drive. It was only a joke, but he realized they were too shook-up to realize he was kidding. When they arrived home, they found Robert asleep on the couch with his sister, the TV blaring.

Andy suggested leaving them be instead of waking them to go back to bed, and his parents were so exhausted, they agreed, though his father suggested he sleep on the recliner, just in case the two men came back. Andy said he thought the recliner would suit him better than laying in his bed and he said he would call 911 immediately if those men came back. Though he really wanted to crawl into bed and get some sleep, he realized his parents needed the comfort of being together again.

As they departed the room and Andy took his seat, Robert awoke and saw his brother sitting on the recliner. "Hey, you're back. What did they say?"

Andy pulled the blanket away and showed him. "It's broken."

"I figured, but your face. You look like you had a fight with a bear, and lost," Robert said, smiling.

"Ha ha. You're not funny," Andy replied. "I feel like shit, so I'm staying here. You can go back to bed, I'll be up."

"Are you kidding? No way. If those assholes show up again, what are you going to do, spit at them? No, I'll stay here and help keep an eye on things. What time is it anyway?"

Andy looked at his watch. Usually, he kept it on his left arm, but he had their mother put it on his right since the cast prevented his wearing it there. "It's after five. Well, if you're going to sit up, make sure you have the phone in your lap and I'll catch some zzz's," he said with a yawn.

"Anything happen after I left?"

"No. Oh, wait. Milly stopped by to see what happened," Robert replied casually.

"What? I did see her," Andy said quickly.

"In the hospital?" Robert asked.

"No, as they were closing the ambulance door. I wasn't sure it was her, but it must have been. How long did she stay?"

"Not long. Just helped calm Sarah down and said she had to get home to get some sleep. She's starting a new job at the restaurant on Middle Street."

"Joe's Crab Barn?"

"Yeah, I guess so, that's the only restaurant on that street. Must be there."

Suddenly, Andy wasn't as tired. Milly had showed up and Finn's words kept echoing in his mind, 'find that girl and marry her'. "I may have to stop by and see how she's doing one of these days."

"Yeah, whatever," Robert replied. He put his head back against the couch and quickly back to sleep as Andy looked at him.

"He can sleep anywhere," Andy replied, as he started watching some horror movie on TV. Even though his mind was racing for a bit, thinking about Milly, the adrenaline was wearing off as the pain medicine the nurse had given him began to kick in. He was asleep on the recliner less than ten minutes after his brother closed his eyes.

Chapter Twelve
Navy

There is nothing more enticing, disenchanting, and enslaving than the life at sea—Joseph Conrad

It took Andy almost a month of rest before he was feeling good enough to see Milly. With a broken arm and a battered body, he was unable to drive; so, one late afternoon, he walked down to her home having learned from friends that she got off work about this time and he felt it would be better if he waited for her at her home so they could talk without interruption. He walked into her yard and saw that there was no car, so he knew they were gone, and he simply sat in one of the lawn chairs which he pulled back a bit to get out of the sun. He replayed their Prom night together, realizing he hadn't been ready to commit and had acted like an ass. It was time to set things straight.

He was just thinking about what he would say, relishing the idea of seeing her face as she noticed him sitting there on the chair, when a cherry red Mazda pulled into the yard. He saw the passenger door open and out stepped Milly, looking like she had experienced a rough day. Seeing her brought a smile to her face which quickly disappeared when the driver's door opened, and out stepped Matthew Grimes. Neither of them noticed Andy sitting in the shadows and he watched as Matt walked around the car and stood close to Milly, speaking quietly.

He couldn't hear what was being said, but noticed she laughed and pushed him playfully. Then Matt walked back to his car, got in and pulled out, tearing away on the street. It was only then that he coughed lightly to announce his presence.

Milly jumped at the sound and to his surprise, she didn't seem to calm down when she realized it was him. "So, you're spying on me now?"

"What? No," Andy answered defensively. "I just came over earlier to see you, to talk. When I saw Matt, I didn't know what to say."

"Right, and you just sat there quietly to try and see what I would do," Milly replied angrily.

"That's not what I was doing. I didn't want to interrupt, but I didn't want to just sit here without talking to you," he replied, his head down.

"Talk about what?"

"You, me and us, I'm ready to talk now," he replied, this time raising his head to look her in the eye. He felt this would show he was serious. He was wrong.

"You've been sitting around your house and didn't attempt to call me, or contact me somehow," she said, still angry.

"What did Matt say?"

"None of your business. Wait. I'll tell you. He asked me out, again."

"That bastard caused this rift between us and now he's giving you rides home?"

"He didn't cause this, you did! I wanted to be with you, spend my life with you, but you were selfish, immature. I can't take it, I really can't," she said, tears forming at her eyes. "You hurt me then, and to set the record straight, other guys have asked me out as well, some of your friends even," she blurted out, realizing instantly that this was a mistake. She saw the hurt in him when she said this.

"Which friends?"

"It doesn't matter. I don't want to have this conversation now. You need to leave," she almost shouted, tears now flowing freely.

Andy slowly got to his feet, anger making his face red. "Fine, I'll leave," he replied as he began to walk out of her yard, but he stopped before he reached the street. "I'm sorry, I hurt you. Really," and with that, he walked out of her yard. He didn't look back or he would have seen her sit in the swing seat, her tears flowing heavily now.

For the next few weeks, Andy walked around in a fog. He had been ready to commit to Milly, but circumstances had intervened to disrupt that attempt. To help get over his anger, he spent a lot of time working on the Munck, especially when his father paid to have the Marina pull the boat out of the water and store it on hard ground. Only then did Andy see the number of repairs the little boat required. Planks were warped and a large portion of the hull on the port side, where he had seen the damp wood in the galley, needed to be replaced at a hefty price, unless he did the work himself. However, with his arm only recently healed, he knew it would be a challenge. There was even one spot where someone, probably Finn, had simply stuffed rags into a small hole which allowed the wood there to soften.

After a day of looking at all the damage, he muttered to himself, "No wonder why Finn thought about scrapping it."

Andy naturally turned to his father for help in getting the boat seaworthy, having forgotten about the money Finn left him until Mark pulled him aside and handed him the envelope. "You want to tell me where this envelope came from? I found it on the floor in the kitchen."

"Oh, shit, I forgot about that," he replied, closing his eyes for a second as he raised his head.

"Are you involved in something? Is that why those men came to our house? It has blood on it."

Andy chuckled a bit at that, then lost his smile immediately when he saw the look his father gave him. Explaining this wouldn't be easy and he had to be careful. "That money came from Finn."

"The night you were attacked?" Mark asked, his eyes wide with worry.

Andy decided to modify the answer, knowing if he told the truth, it would cause problems. "No. That was money I earned working with Finn over the summer. I just don't remember how much is in here."

"Why does it have blood on it?" Mark asked, wondering if his son was telling the truth.

"I never counted it, just stuck it in that envelope, thinking I would give it back to Finn. Then he left, so I was stuck with it. The blood is mine. I remembered the money that night and was going to count it when I heard something outside. I put it in my pocket before I went outside and I guess it fell out when that guy brought me inside," he said, doing his best to appear truthful.

"Finn gave you that money? Why didn't you say something before?"

Andy was ready for this question now. "I told you; I was going to give it back. How much is in there anyway?"

"Five hundred and eighty dollars. You're sure that money has nothing to do with those men?"

Andy nodded, being truthful now was much easier than spinning a lie and he relaxed. "Yes."

Mark smiled, and Andy could see the relief in his face. His father had been worried about the origins of the money and he understood why he had been curt with him in the recent past. "Well, now you have a little bit to get started with repairs."

Andy thought it would be a good start, but quickly realized why his father said it would be a start as the money disappeared quickly when he got to work on his boat. Occasionally, Robert would join him at the Marina and the two learned many lessons about dealing with boats and their upkeep. Sometimes, other boat owners would lend a hand, showing the boys shortcuts for repairs, or how to carefully waterproof the hull, keeping them so busy, they would not return home from the Marina until the sun had gone down. Still their progress was slow.

While all this was going on, Andy kept hoping that Milly would show up one day to talk, but she didn't: sometimes making him angry, mostly at himself. With the summer ending, he still had no idea how she was doing or if she even missed him. He didn't know that she was busy making plans to leave for her college in Florida. Her mother came in one day and asked if she minded inviting Andy's family to her going-away party.

Milly looked at her, knowing that besides her current situation with Andy, the families were still friends, and her parents would sometimes join his for dinner, so she told her mother it would be fine. When the night arrived, she was surprised when Andy didn't join his family at the gathering. Mark explained that he was working on his boat and was having a difficulty which prevented him from attending. Milly just nodded, a part of her disappointed, but she had expected it after the way she had spoken to him the last time they were together.

She excused herself during the dinner for a moment and slipped away while the families were in the backyard, heading down to Andy's house, but like his father had said, he wasn't there, and she returned dejectedly, thinking that it was her last chance to try and mend fences before she left. A part of her still cared deeply for him and she would have liked to say goodbye, so she returned quietly to the party and never let on that she had gone to see him.

The next day, one of her friends who was also attending the University of Central Florida, arrived to pick her up and all her thoughts were on her new future, a life as a college student. Still, as the car pulled out and they drove by Andy's home, she looked out and waved at them, though Andy wasn't around.

When Andy arrived home later that evening and heard that Milly had waved as she headed to school, the news upset him with the thought that his life wasn't turning out the way he had hoped. He had no job, no girl and no money. That night he lay in bed, his conversation with Finn prevalent in his mind. He had spent his life at sea, meeting people, making good friends and meeting girls. *That must have been a good time*, the thought bringing a smile to him. Finn had said those days of his life were the best, a life at sea, serving his country.

Andy suddenly sat up in his bed, the idea he had like a bolt of adrenaline to his body. The Navy, he could enlist in the Navy like Finn had done. Then he thought about the Munck. His pay would enable him to make the repairs, but if he were sailing in foreign waters, he wouldn't have the time to finish them. What he needed was a part-time job, enough to purchase the material he needed, but a job that would allow him to make the repairs himself. That's when he decided on the Naval Reserve.

The next morning, a bright July Monday, Andy told his parents of his decision. His father liked the idea since he could learn a trade and possibly go to college and the experience would help him mature and possibly prepare him for his future. His mother though wasn't happy with this choice. Yes, her father had also served in the Naval Reserve, but she remembered the difficulties that came with that job, things she had never discussed with her own family. She didn't know if she would like her son to follow a life like that of Finn and it gave her mixed feelings.

The next day, Andy drove to the closest recruiting office and spoke with the sailor in charge. He learned that he had to take the entrance exam, then pass the physical, which the recruiter told him would be no problem. His broken arm had healed properly, and he was in good physical shape, so the sailor said it should be a routine experience. Andy's greatest concern then was what sort of job to choose, which became even more difficult when he did well on the entrance exam.

Sitting with his family that night, his father helped him decide, suggesting he take a job that would train him how to make repairs on the Munck. Andy liked that idea and when he went to his recruiter the next time, chose the job of Machinery Repairman Technician. It was a long title, but it would offer good training and an excellent opportunity to learn more about boats and how to repair them.

Another stroke of luck was that the recruiter told him there was an opening to leave for basic training at the Great Lakes Naval Training Center north of Chicago, in only a couple days. He eagerly accepted the assignment. When he got home, his mother wasn't as eager to have him leave so quickly, but he explained that even though he would be unable to finish the training before Christmas, he would be able to return home for the holidays, at least that's what his recruiter had said. His father thought it was a good idea, not much time to dwell on training and to get on with his life. Best of all, his father said he would continue to pay the storage costs and his brother said he would do what he could with the Munck. That was good enough for him.

Three days later, Andy arrived for basic training on a Friday morning, and he shuddered in the cold air. He had departed North Carolina on a sweltering July morning, and now the cold air felt more like a December evening; however, he endured the training, which his recruiter said was one of the hardest, and had to work out like never before. It was especially difficult because of his lack of exercise while he was injured, but he endured and concentrated on his studies. While at the Great Lakes Center, he made a lot of friends and excelled in his class. To him, it was one of acceptance, do what he was told, follow the rules, and push himself to complete the challenges presented, made it a little easier to finish basic training near the top of his class and at graduation, he eagerly awaited the chance to attend his advanced training class, which was held at the same location where he had undergone basic.

On the first day of class, Andy dove into the training material, which taught him the important facts of how to maintain a vessel. While accomplishing this, he also learned how to use the wind to propel a craft and the needs for maintenance and emergency repairs, especially in rough seas, something he knew would be vitally important when he took his boat to sea.

The Christmas holidays arrived, but Andy was stuck at his base, unable to go home due to a holiday blizzard closing the airport for two days. He did skype with his family nearly every day and was able to watch his siblings open their presents, which allowed him to share their joy, some. Then the holidays ended, and it was back to school, where he received an intensive course on how all ships worked and more about the importance of working as a team.

One of the most fascinating things he learned, though he did not believe he would use on the Munck, was how to repair weapon systems and how to board suspicious vessels or move about on land, should the need occur.

This part of the training was fascinating as it was taught by a sailor of an active SEAL team and he was thrilled by the professionalism these men displayed when they walked about in a confident manner, never boasted or threatened and they were always ready for a challenge, no matter how hard, or how dangerous. Their demeanor was one that he tried to emulate and took great pride during an exercise when a SEAL member praised his job performance and dedication. He even went so far as to inform his Chief Petty Officer that he would be a great candidate for their teams.

The Chief Petty Officer nodded when he was told how Andy was singled out for his performance but pointed out that Andy was only a reservist and was therefore ineligible for acceptance into the teams, how the Navy described the SEALs. To Andy, this was a huge blow, and he left the men feeling dejected, only to be told by the SEAL he had befriended that he could apply to the teams, he would just have to switch form Reserves to Active status.

To Andy, this was a major decision and one that he struggled with over the next few days. He even went so far as to call his parents and discuss the benefits and difficulties of switching. To his surprise, his father informed him that he and Robert would continue to do work on the Munck, but it would be Andy's responsibility to pay for storage and materials, since it was his boat. These would take a big chunk out of his paycheck being that he was only an E 2, Seaman Apprentice, but it was something he wanted to do, and he felt strongly that he could complete the difficult training.

Hearing this news helped Andy make up his mind and the next day, he asked to switch his enlistment from Reserves to Active. The sailor in that office said his losing command wouldn't like that, but he was sure Andy could do this and it would allow him the chance to apply for the SEAL teams when his technical school was complete. With his concerns about the Munck now assuaged, Andy was free to concentrate on something he found he wanted to do. He knew his acceptance into the teams would mean he would be away for a long period of time, months if not years, but with him no longer attached to Milly, there was nothing now to hold him back. He was going to become a SEAL.

Andy had to wait at the Great Lakes Training Center until he was finally shipped off to California where he awaited the start date of the next class, which happened to start March 1. Now part of SEAL training, what was referred to as Basic Underwater Demolition/SEALS, or BUDS for short.

Chapter Thirteen
Seals

When you take risks, you learn that there will be times when you succeed and there will be times when you fail, and both are equally important—Ellen DeGeneres

"Gentlemen!" The short instructor yelled in a deep voice. "Welcome to BUDS training. That training begins now! Into the surf," the instructor announced. Andy raced into the Pacific Ocean surf, feeling the water pound into him and almost knocking him off his feet with the force of each wave. This was his first day of what was termed Hell Week, and he was as ready as he felt he could be.

After graduating from his technical school, Andy applied and was accepted into SEAL training almost two weeks after applying. Instead of being home during the harsh winter, he found himself at BUDS training. Basic training, though difficult, was nothing compared to this new course, which was designed to encourage discipline and whittle down those who could not endure the harsh challenges.

When they were wet, the instructor ordered them to roll in the sand which covered their bodies and rubbed their skin. Andy accepted this, knowing from the preparatory school that this would happen. From there, it was on their backs, and they did flutter kicks, his stomach pounding after only a few minutes, but he refused to give up. The whole day was like this, running in the sand, swimming in the cold ocean waters and then exercises on the sand again, they didn't even stop for lunch, just kept going when the instructor told them they weren't hungry yet. Already, the class of 250 candidates had been whittled down by three men who couldn't stand the torturous exercises.

By evening, Andy could no longer feel his legs and he relished the chance to rest, even it meant sitting in the stinging swell in long lines, as close as possible to the man in front of him, the man behind him doing the same. They shared body heat that way and kept some of the freezing cold from their bodies. During this time, Andy took this moment to close his eyes a bit, not believing there were still six more days of this crap. Still, he felt he had to endure.

Around midnight, the class had been whittled down by almost twenty more students when the little instructor called a halt for the night. The men were double timed through the sand to the barracks area where they were told to get some sleep. Some men simply fell on their racks while wet and fell asleep, but Andy felt it would be better to strip his wet clothing and remove some of the sand he had collected. This only took a couple more minutes, some of the others following his move, and he was so tired, he fell asleep on his rack without drying off.

Unbelievably, the lights flicked on in the dorm and the men were told to stand at attention at the front of their racks, where a new instructor, a huge hulking muscular man walked up and down the aisles. Those who slept in their clothes were dropped for a hundred pushups, then ordered to strip and get into new uniforms. Luckily, Andy and those who had stripped before sleeping were spared, though they were all ordered to dress in clean utilities before being rushed to breakfast before the sun had even risen over the horizon.

Breakfast, that was a joke. The men barely had time to grab toast and maybe a handful of eggs before they were ordered to store their food, which meant throw it away and stack their trays, then they were rushed out to a new madness, the boats.

Andy had seen these large black boats that were lined up on the shore, and they were told these would be the same types of boats, Rigids, they were called, that real SEALS used when conducting operations, or missions. Having seen a few movies about this sort of stuff, he knew they weren't about to climb in them and motor around the ocean. Instead, the candidates were instructed to lift the Rigids above their heads and to extend their arms. Andy knew about this, but he didn't know about the weight, these Rigids were heavy, and they had to run around the sand with the boats above their heads.

Several times, the candidates slipped and fell, which put more strain on the rest of the team. In Andy's case, two candidates fell, and he was forced to hold up a larger percentage of the Rigid which really strained his arms. One of the men quickly returned to his place, but the other simply crawled up the beach to the Drop Bell. This bell was the way out for those who did not want to continue the class and it didn't help things when the instructors, there were five of them now, kept yelling and encouraging them to ring the bell and drop out.

The entire day was spent doing this and then dropping for more of the flutter kicks, and then more running. There were times when they rushed into the ocean, it was just as cold as the day before, to endure more waves knocking the remaining candidates around so they had to scramble back to their spots, but they weren't allowed to get up and run to do this, instead those knocked out of line had to scuttle their way on their arms and legs just above the water, and God help the man who took too long to return to the line. When this happened, everyone in that line was forced to do pushups in the water, making it hard to catch a breath.

Andy endured this all till the end of the day, when they were lined up and told that almost seventy of their fellow candidates had opted to Ring Out. Each candidate was encouraged by the instructors to ring the bell and just quit, but Andy remained where he was. Once again, the candidates were double timed through the training base, but instead of heading to their bunks like they had the day before, this time they had to run for two miles. More men stopped and headed for the bell.

All week long, this continued, the candidates taking abuse and injuries. By the last day, the class was down to only thirty-one men. One instructor wasn't happy about this, telling the remaining candidates that the number was too large, and he wanted it paired down by at least five more. He kept running the candidates until one more man chose to ring out, and the instructor smiled. That was when Andy saw something that surprised him, women in bikinis came onto the beach in the darkening sky and began to drink beer, encouraging anyone who wanted a beer to join them as the instructors moved away. Some of the group took the offer, walking up to the women, but turned away when they were told they had to 'ring out' first. Andy was tempted, but then images of Milly kept coming to his mind and he quietly compared her to the women on the beach.

Only this kept him from moving until the instructors returned and walked to the bell. As one of the instructors reached down and rang the bell thirty times, the lead instructor, Master Chief Ronondo called out the candidates. He yelled one of the best things Andy had heard in a long time, "Secure from Hell Week!"

He had done it, and this time, instead of being doubled timed to the dorms, the BUDS graduates were marched to the dorm and told to sack out. Those sailors who had held out, were no longer considered candidates, but were BUDS graduates. They were told to get some sack time and that they would continue their training in the morning. Of the original 250, only 28 men, including Andy, remained.

As the graduates stood before the dorms, afraid to move, the instructors dismissed them and walked off, letting the graduates cheer and pat each other on the backs. Andy was excited, but he needed sleep and he made his way to his rack, stripping down and dropping on it. He wasn't the only one, as the rest of the team soon was in their racks as well.

Then the challenge. They had only been asleep a short while, when every instructor came charging into the dorm, banging cans and setting off fireworks. The exhausted graduates staggered from their racks, trying desperately to collect themselves, when the instructors pulled in a wagon full of beer and proceeded to toast the graduates. All of them were exhausted, but Andy realized this was an important part of the graduation ceremony, the bonding. Carefully, he pulled on his utility pants and joined his comrades in toasting the end of the week. Even graduates who were not legally of age to drink, which of course included Andy, were encouraged to join in, as one instructor explained, they were old enough to fight and die for their country, so they should be entitled to bend the rules this one time. However, the instructors knew their graduates were at the point of exhaustion and the ceremony was rather short. Andy enjoyed it, just like the others, but he was even more grateful when he was able to hit his rack again.

The next morning, the graduates, now referred to simply as BUD grads, which signified they had completed only the first portion of their training, were awakened at 05:00, military terminology for 5 a.m., and ordered to clean their utility uniforms, or turn in those that were damaged during Hell Week. A lot of the trainees ended up doing this since the rough training had worn holes into their pants, or shirts were ripped when they fell into obstacles.

After he graduated from BUDS, he spent the next two months in the SEAL Preparatory School, which meant more physical training and learning some of the basics that all SEAL candidates must be trained in. After two days of recuperating, during which they still had to participate in physical training, the grads moved on to weapons training, learning how to use weapons from other countries, or how to use explosives. When these were done, they were transported to the next major obstacle in their training, SERE, or Survival Evasion, Resistance, Escape. This training used what they already knew and placed them in a position to avoid capture and if they were, how to resist and hopefully escape.

Andy was dropped off with five others, a standard SEAL unit. Armed with blanks and the usual equipment SEAL teams carried, the grads had boarded a helicopter and were flown to another spot on their island just off the coast. Instead of landing, they were kicked out the door about twenty feet above the sand. One of the men, Seaman Benjamin Yoates, injured his ankle slightly when they hit the ground but felt he could keep up with his team. Andy and the others split up his load while one of their number helped the injured comrade move. They couldn't leave him, the SEAL Motto, 'Leave no man behind', had been drilled into them constantly over the three weeks they had been training and this being their first exercise, they followed their mantra. The team took off immediately but was delayed by Yoates, who had trouble keeping up even with the assistance of his teammate.

Their established objective on this mission was to scout a staging area, locate three Americans being detained by the Opposition Forces called OPFOR, who were actually SEALS who had complete similar training, in a bamboo hut. Then they had to devise a plan to help the detainees escape and return to the extraction point where they would contact a helicopter and fly out. Their advisors, other SEALS, had warned them repeatedly of the challenges and what they could expect if they were captured. The treatment by their cadre would be brutal and not to expect them to be lenient. This exercise was designed to be as real as possible and extremely challenging. A last warning from their advisor was that it was serious, and some trainees had died through mistakes. He didn't elaborate, just pushed them out the helicopter door and then they were alone in a simulated hostile environment as the chopper departed.

Being only a Seaman Apprentice, Andy was ordered to follow the orders of their Petty Officer Second Class Thompson, a man with the same last name, but not related to Andy. To avoid mistakes, Andy was referred to as 'Junior', his namesake became 'Senior'. The other team members also had a nickname, and though the six had never trained together as a team, they seemed to mesh and carry out their orders. Andy was told to scout ahead of the team and search for any traps or problems even though they had only a vague idea of where the bamboo huts were located. He moved through the foliage as quickly and quietly as he could, doing his best to keep from becoming entangled. The area was aswarm with insects, both mosquitoes and stinging red ants which would climb on his boots and clothing every time he stopped, which was often as he surveyed the surrounding foliage.

About ten minutes into the trek, he walked onto a small trail and came to a stop once more, even as the ants started to attack. Ignoring them and avoiding pushing them off, he checked out the trail. It was heading in the direction he needed to advance, which would make getting to their objective easier. Then he noticed a thin string, almost fishing line to the side of a large rock. It was a booby trap he realized and as he looked more carefully, he saw more strings along the trail and decided to return to the wild, where he waited for the others, making sure to mark the trap so the others wouldn't trip it.

When they joined him, he pointed out the traps and Senior told him to shadow the trail by cutting through the jungle foliage. This made the trek harder since he had to make his way through the jungle growth as he searched for other traps, just in case the OPFOR had set them up there as well. They had, as Andy discovered some distance further on. Another trap set up at a small stream and Andy quickly sprayed the line to make it more visible before moving on.

An hour later, another of his team, who had taken over the lead, located the target area and they all realized how difficult freeing the hostages would be. The target hut was located on the side of a small hill, surrounded by a wire fence with three towers surrounding the wire and the OPFOR troops moving through the dense growth. These men were alert and appeared to be searching for them which meant there could well be more OPFOR troops in the area they passed through.

When their scout came back and reported this to the team, it was up to Senior to develop a plan on how to assault the target and achieve their goal, to rescue the hostages and return to the extraction point. SEALs work strictly under orders but were encouraged to suggest options which the team leader would add to his mission before devising and assault plan. One of the other grads suggested going in hot, using their weapons to target and eliminate the defending forces. Even though their weapons were armed with blanks, laser designators were attached and would register a hit on their opponents, the tags would count each hit as a kill or a wound. Senior decided to assault the target from the front and see if they could penetrate the gate defenses and remove the hostages from there instead of cutting through the wire.

Andy listened passively before offering a slight change. He said, with Seaman Yoates not able to move quickly, why not send him to the extraction point now while the rest of the team attempted to assault and free the hostages. Yoates could walk, though not as quickly as the others and if he left now, he could get to the extraction point, secure the perimeter, and contact their ride early, allowing the rest of the team to hopefully arrive and board their helicopter before the enemy located them.

Senior nodded at this, but said they needed to determine a way to assault the target. One of the other grads suggested heading back to the trail and setting off a booby trap there to draw the enemy away. Senior thought this over and liked the plan, thinking the enemy forces would probably not expect them to attack in daylight but under the cover of darkness. If they set off the traps now, the OPFOR would obviously investigate, allowing the rest of the team to move up and assault the remaining guards while they were off balance, hopefully resulting in them freeing the prisoners and making their way back in the daylight to safety, instead of trying to navigate in the darkness.

Senior liked this idea and chose Andy to move back along their path and to set off one or more of the traps since he knew where they were, then move to the evacuation point and provide additional security until the rest of the team arrived and they would all depart together. Andy felt it was kind of simple, but Senior said a simple plan was best, less chance for something to go wrong. Everyone agreed and the team immediately started moving into position. Yoates hobbled off as quickly as he could, but in his haste, set off the steam booby trap, announcing their presence before their team was ready.

This happened at the worst possible time, just after the SEAL candidates had split into two teams without being near their target or the extraction point. Andy, only a few yards behind Yoates, dropped to the ground when he heard the explosion, then immediately heard a second explosion. Not sure what had happened, he realized that his team was now in danger, Andy moved toward the stream, hoping to distract the enemy when they appeared, which might still allow his teammates to successfully locate and rescue the survivors. He didn't have to wait long.

Just minutes later, he heard gunfire ahead and took cover. He managed to surprise several of the OPFOR, his laser scoring three 'kills' of the six. Realizing his location was now known, he tried to move away from there and in his haste, accidentally set off another trap, one he hadn't seen, a flash bang grenade which was designed to disorient anyone nearby. Andy stumbled about, disoriented, until something hit him across his back, and he dropped to his stomach and seconds later, two OPFOR were on him, while one stripped him of his rifle and placed a rope around his neck, the other tied his arms and they pulled a sack over his head. Andy struggled to free himself, but a kick to his stomach knocked the wind out of him and he was dragged along, the rope choking him as the scratchy nylon squeezed his neck and made breathing difficult.

Not long afterwards, he was pushed to the ground where he could only wait, and soon afterwards, he heard scuffles and another person hit the ground next to him. In the distance, the two could hear more shooting and were certain their team members were either defending themselves or were assaulting the compound. With the bag over his head, all he could do was kneel where he was dropped and wonder what was happening.

The sound of shooting became closer, and Andy took this opportunity to whisper to the man next to him, only then learning it was Yoates. He had tripped the booby trap and was attempting to move faster when he walked into another, set by a patrol from the enemy force. He too was disoriented by this new blast and as he tried to clear his head, several OPFOR were on him and tied him up treating him as roughly as those who captured Andy.

Andy listened quietly, when there was suddenly another loud bang and the two prisoners hit the ground and laid there thinking it was some trap, set up by the enemy team to get them to try and escape. Two more flash bangs hit, and Andy's ears rang so badly he couldn't hear anything except other shotting. Then, someone pulled him to his feet and the bag was ripped off his head. Andy turned ready to head butt his attacker when he realized it was Senior. Both he and Yoates were freed, and the team made off, Andy helping his SEAL brother along since he had no longer had a weapon.

There was no time to question what Senior was up to, just do what he could to help Yoates keep up. The man was big, and his rough handling hadn't helped his leg, so Andy hiked Yoates onto his back and kept moving through the undergrowth, made even more difficult by the tremendous girth of his friend.

Then it was simply the challenge of trying to navigate the rough terrain, especially the razor-sharp bamboo grass that Andy hadn't noticed before. He figured Senior was simply trying to get them all safely to the extraction point and realized the mission had been a bust as the prisoners they had been sent to rescue were not with them.

Finally, the team broke into an open area and Senior was already on the radio, calling in their ride. Andy took this moment to rest, trying hard to catch his breath, sucking down water from a borrowed canteen, since his had been taken by the enemy force. He took cover when more firing occurred close by, counting the seconds on his watch as they waited in what cover there was. Finally, in the distance, he could hear the evacuation helicopter, which landed just seconds after he first heard it. The team struggled aboard, all of them pulling Yoates on and seconds later, they were safely away.

When they arrived at their staging area, still on the island, the team was rushed off the helicopter and hustled inside to face muster and mission debrief. As the six BUD/S graduates stood at attention, Senior stepped up to and stood before their SEAL team leader, Lieutenant Buerl, who looked at each man for several minutes before instructing Senior to explain why they had failed their first task as SEAL candidates. The description of them as 'candidates' wasn't lost on the men; it was like they had been reduced in status with the use of a different term.

Thompson explained to his superior why they had failed. He covered everything very carefully, from the injury to Yoates to Andy's discovery of the booby traps and the location of the objective then their aborted attack. Buerl just listened quietly as they spoke while other SEALS remained in the background, some writing down what was said, others watching the faces of the other team members while Senior spoke.

When he was finished, Senior ended with a crisp, "That is all, sir!"

Buerl stood there like he was mulling over what Thompson had said, finally he nodded and looked the men. "Did you learn anything from this assignment?"

Senior mentioned how they had done all they could, explaining that their lack of intelligence of the target and the unexpected booby traps, had caused the mission to fail.

Buerl nodded at this. "True, which is why SEALs practice a mission like this constantly. However, as you know, sometimes, a mission goes bust. The important part when that happens is to protect the team and get out with everyone while you can. Thompson, you realized that your attack would not succeed and made the right choice. When a mission fails, others will determine what went wrong and will try again. The fact that you led your team well, managed to recover your men and then got them all to the extraction point was a good move," he said, showing no emotion on his face. Then he spoke one word, "Junior! Step forward!"

Andy's nickname. "Aye, sir!" Andy answered after stepping forward one step.

"You carried that Sasquatch looking ass out of the interior even though he's almost twice your size?"

Andy smiled only briefly; his friend Yoates had just earned his team name. "Yes, sir."

"You worked your ass off to help ensure your injured teammate was able to evacuate. Because of your caring for a fellow SEAL, you are here by promoted to the rank of Seaman. Good job," Buerl said.

Following tradition, Andy saluted, shouted, "Aye, Aye, sir!" Then stepped back into line.

"Senior, have your men clean up, collect new gear and prepare for your next mission," he stated, which meant the team would go back out as soon as they were combat ready probably to complete the mission, or maybe a new one. That was the way of the SEALS, the mission was critical, and the needs of the team members would be noted and attended to, if they could be. If they couldn't, the mission still needed to be conducted.

Sasquatch Yoates was excused from this mission, only because his injured leg would have to be tended to. He would wait for the next BUD/S graduate team to continue with his training, being that it was learned his ankle wasn't sprained, it was broken.

Twenty minutes later, the BUD'S graduates were back in the air, heading to their same assignment, to rescue the three detainees at the compound.

Chapter Fourteen
Losses

Act with a determination not to be turned aside by thoughts of the past and fears of the future—Robert E Lee

Andy finished the SERE portion of his SEAL training, but not without difficulty. During his return to the island that night, now better prepared for what to expect, he was out the door before he could be pushed. He hit the ground and immediately took up a defensive posture until Senior tapped him on the back and they trotted into the jungle. Since it was now dark, the team had arranged to use only signals to communicate with each other. The original members of their team, except for Yoates, were present and included a new member, 'Pistol' who was integrated into their team after recovering from surgery for a serious back injury. Pistol had earned his team name earlier for his ability to hit targets with great accuracy.

Moving into the jungle once more was even more dangerous. Andy had difficulty seeing much even with his night vision goggles on his head, and they had been deposited in a different area this time with a new mission, to reconnoiter a simulated ammunition dump and place explosives, something their instructors told them was a common occurrence for teams.

Once more, Andy, now referred to only by Junior, his team name, took the lead once more as he led the team through the jungle growth at an even slower pace. This time he didn't see any booby traps as he moved carefully through the foliage. Not seeing them didn't lighten his mood any, since he was sure there had to be something and he checked every place ahead before moving his foot. Unsatisfied with the slow progress, Senior relieved him from this duty and let Pistol take over.

To Junior's surprise, Pistol took off his night vision goggles using hand signals to relay that he could see the ground better without them. Junior just shrugged but their pace did increase until they reached a position close to their objective. As the morning sun threatened to clear the horizon, Senior had them select sleeping positions. *Sleep, yeah*, Junior thought, *just like breakfast during Hell Week*. He simply pulled himself into a spot near Petty Officer Third Class Chello, whose team name was Comp, short for composer because his name was pronounced like Cello was sporting a sling.

Junior tried to get rest, but every time he did, he was assaulted by those same red ants or mosquitoes which seemed to find ways to bite him even through his protective netting. Finally, he did fall asleep for a bit until he was slapped by Comp to take over the watch after only a couple hours of sleep. Though tired, he knew this was all part of his indoctrination into the elite unit. Then the sun began to set, and the team began to move toward their objective.

As expected, they noticed some OPFOR units moving through the jungle as well and they had to detour often on their way to their target. Thankfully, they managed to reach the ammunition storage area and going through the wire which surrounded the structure, the team was able place their explosive charges, also simulated along the building by digging small holes and hiding the charges in these holes which were covered so they would not be discovered.

The entire operation had taken longer than expected and by the time they were ready to leave, the sky had started to turn from black to deep purple. They still had to leave the area and place clips on the wire removing evidence of their penetration spot and by the time they were done, they no longer needed night vision to move. Senior ordered them to move out as quickly and quietly as possible and they had almost reached the jungle's denseness when they were spotted.

An alert went up at once, alarms blaring and OPFOR moving to cut them off before they could get away. Now part of rear security, Junior kept checking their six, military slang for the area behind them as Comp led the team through the jungle growth. In their haste to exfiltrate the area, Comp tripped a booby trap, this time a large net which grabbed him and another team member pulling them into the trees where they were surrounded by the OPFOR troops and captured.

Still referring to each other by their team names, Junior was the last captured and like the others, spent the next four days undergoing captivity and some use of torture and interrogation, things designed to harden him for life in the field. The treatment was brutal, all of them fed small portions of rice in bowls until the day when Andy, now alone in a cement cell with no roof, heard his name called softly from above. He looked up and saw Pistol above him and with his help, was pulled up. There, he moved about the prison area and helped pull the rest of his team out of their cells.

When the entire team was collected, they all crawled to the edge of their cell block, then dropped onto a lone guard, disarming him and taking his weapon. Since it was dark, the team then made their way to edge of the facility and using their bare hands to pull the barbed wire open enough to allow them to escape, the team slipped away into the jungle. With only one night vision goggle taken from the guard they overpowered, and armed with a single automatic weapon, the six team members made their way toward the evacuation area, encountering another group of friendly SEALs, actually another team sent to extract them, and the combined team continued to the evacuation area where a rescue copter soon arrived.

Once on the copter, the team had their injuries treated and Andy, now called by his actual name, was never so thrilled to be free once more and able to relax a little. In a short time, the copter arrived at their base where they were escorted into the debriefing area to meet once more with Lieutenant Buerl. As usual, Buerl had a scowl on his face as the newly liberated team stood at attention.

He expressed his concern that they had been captured but then the scowl left his face and he actually smiled at them. This was a first that all of them realized, and he told them how their mission had been a success and said, "Well done," as he continued to explain that the action to take more time to hide their charges under the ground had been missed by the OPFOR at the target area and their mission had been considered a success.

"Good job, Senior," he stated. Then he gave the command, "At ease," which meant the team was able to able to stop standing straight up and to place their arms behind them and step apart, which was an easier command for the men as they were able to relax as they discussed their actions on the mission, once again covering what they had done right and what they could do better on future missions.

When they were finished with this, Buerl promoted Senior to First Class and told the team they had graduated from this part of their training and to stand down for a couple days to recuperate and prepare for their next assignment, the Underwater Demolition Training which would be conducted in San Diego.

There were a lot of cheers for their successful mission and the group was treated to a steak meal and beer which they had seen being prepared as they arrived. Sitting in a chair where he was no longer bound by ropes was unusual for Andy. The other SEALs stating the same thing but digging into a fire cook steak and drinking a cold beer, made them all appreciate what they had accomplished. As they ate, other SEALs around them discussed their mission, giving advice on how to relax and overcome some of their experiences.

Andy took this in quietly, until they all heard a familiar voice behind them. Turning as one, they saw Yoates standing on crutches as he asked if he could join them. The team, including Pistol, told him what they had done and how challenging it was, but they were sure, once he was fit again, that he would join them before they finished UDT.

Three days later, they arrived at Underwater Demolition Training, also called Combat Diving. To Andy, this part of the training was more enjoyable. It was also the closest he came to home during his training, operating out of the Naval Base in Virginia. There were no red ants eating at his skin, or mosquitoes to swat at, just the cold waters of the Atlantic. While some SEAL candidates became seasick with their first experience on the ocean; for Andy, it was almost easy since he had already learned about how to overcome seasickness when he sailed with Finn, and he finished this portion of his training and received another promotion. From the cold depths of the ocean, he moved on to Basic Parachute and High-Altitude Parachute Training, or simply Jump School.

This first part of training was conducted at an Air Force Base in California, where the team was taught how to jump from aircraft along with Special Operators from the other services. All of them learned how to leave an aircraft, specifically an aircraft with propellers, called a C-130. On his first jump, Andy watched as the tail ramp lowered and they were ordered to stand up, then told to move forward after checking their chutes and equipment for the umpteenth time. When it came his turn to leap from the aircraft, Andy just closed his eyes and simply leaped into the open.

As soon as he jumped, he opened his eyes and assumed the drop position, which meant facing the ground and bending his arms while he kept his legs open as he dropped. This move, which some had said could be challenging, came to him easily and he quickly located those who had jumped ahead of them. Since this was his first jump, he waited until his altimeter beeped and pulled the chain on his chute, holding his breath until he felt the jerk, meaning his chute had opened cleanly and his speed dropped. Feeling like he was suspended in midair, he floated to the ground, but came in a little fast and he fell back, his buttocks hitting the ground. It hurt, but he was young, and he shook it off as his friends laughed at him.

His next four jumps were easier, and with them he received his jump wings, showing he was a qualified parachutist. The rest of the training was a bit more difficult, having to learn how to jump from high altitudes where he had to use oxygen since they were so high up. This proved more difficult, but it was easy compared to learning how to operate fixed winged suits and ultralight air kites, something the Navy began to incorporate into their training. Still, he finished this training when others failed and were removed from the program and was close to becoming a full team member. It was now July and he was expecting to finish up this portion of his training before moving on to Land Combat and Sniper training.

Chapter Fifteen
Accident

Never let hard times break you. Be strengthened by the adverse circumstances you are going through and allow yourself to gain from these experiences—Anurag Prakash Ray

It was the last day of training in the Parachute Course and Andy was in good spirits as he and the rest of his training team loaded into a pickup truck moving toward the site of their drop off point for a briefing. It was now late September, and the California air was soft and warm on his aching body. He just let the air wash over him realizing that he mostly wanted the briefing to end so he could get a hot shower and wash off the encrusted grime that made his skin itch and maybe something to eat. He looked around him, his brother SEALs all chatting and relaxed, when he spotted another Navy pickup out of the corner of his eye heading right at them. He tried to yell a warning but couldn't get out the words when the other truck plowed into them. Most of the occupants were thrown from the truck along with their equipment as the truck flipped several times.

Sitting at the point of impact, Andy's leg became trapped in the collision and as the truck flipped, he was attached to it as his body was tossed about and he was knocked unconscious. As his truck finally came to a stop on its side, Andy's leg had been almost severed just below the knee and his other leg was pinned under the truck. Even though everyone on the truck had been injured to a degree, they immediately began to administer first aid, one team member applying a tourniquet to Andy's leg, saving his life, before continuing to apply more first aid.

When Andy awoke, he was in the base hospital, aware that the pain in his leg was the concern of the many people leaning over him. From his visits to the hospital to gain some medial knowledge which he would use in his SEAL position, he recognized one of the base surgeons and knew he was hurt more than he had first realized. He could remember the accident, the car hitting and his attempting to get away at the last second and then being trapped, but nothing else until he woke up here.

"Seaman Thompson," the doctor spoke to him, as a couple of the medical staff around pulled back suddenly. He didn't know why, possibly they were his friends or people he knew. "You've suffered a serious injury. We are going to prep you for an operation to try and stop the bleeding. You need to follow the directions of our medical staff and not fight them. Understood?" He did not mention that Andy's leg had been almost cut from his body.

Andy didn't know why the doctor was taking the time to talk to him, though it didn't matter since he couldn't stay awake. While under, the doctor, having seen similar wounds at many battle sites like Afghanistan, Iraq, or Syria, worked feverishly on the leg, finally announcing after six long hours that the limb had been reattached and seemed to be responding to treatment properly, though it would require extensive rehabilitation before his patient would be able to gain full use of the leg. His greatest fear was that of gangrene appearing and he ordered round the clock observation of his patient.

When Andy finally came around, he was in a cloud of mist, there was intense pain, but his most immediate concern was the mist, which he couldn't shake away. In desperation, he tried to use his arms to clear it but someone was holding his arms down, telling him to stop moving and take a few deep breaths. Andy followed the instructions, opening his eyes slowly and looking up at a nurse who had a smile that matched Milly's.

"Milly, you came," Andy said, the words barely audible, but the woman heard him.

"Seaman Thompson, I'm not Milly. I'm Angela. How are you feeling?"

Andy concentrated his gaze on the young woman, seeing the silver bar of a Lieutenant Junior Grade. "I'm sorry, ma'am. Your smile reminded me of someone I knew," Andy said quietly.

"Is she your girlfriend?" She asked.

"Used to be, maybe again someday, once I finish my Navy training," he stopped there noticing the unmistakable pause by the nurse, and Andy had a sudden fear. "Am I being kicked out?"

The nurse refused to answer the question, but the Naval Corpsman did. "Well, they might let you stay, but I for one think you're too clumsy to keep in the Navy. Jesus, Andy, next time a truck comes at you, jump!"

The nurse looked at the Corpsman and smiled. Patting Andy on the arm, she said, "I'll let you two catch up a bit. Don't tire him out much, Corpsman," she said before leaving.

"So, you joined the Navy," the Corpsman said with a slight smile. "Just like me. You know, I blame Finn," he continued as he checked the medical drip of Andy's intravenous.

"You know Finn? I don't recognize you," Andy said, looking at the man in confusion. There was something about him, something familiar in his actions or voice maybe.

"Haven't figured it out yet, huh? Okay, let's try some key words. Oil rig. Monkey bars, Milly," he said with a smile, watching as Andy finally put it together. "Figured it out yet?"

"Nathan?" Andy asked, the idea completely impossible.

"Good job, you got it on the first try. Well, you were always better at figuring things out. What are the odds we would both end up in the Navy and at the same location of all things? Damn, I'm so glad to see you again, though I wish it were under better circumstances," Nathan said. "They arrested the Seaman who hit you, driving like an ass; said, he was trying to get somewhere fast when he lost control."

"Did they amputate my leg?" Andy asked suddenly, afraid to look down at his body.

"The truck just about did that, but the surgeon, Captain Leonard, saved it. He worked on you for a couple of hours, though he did mention your SEAL buddies did a great job keeping you alive and getting you here in record time," Nathan replied.

Andy thought back, remembering glimpses of things he saw. His teammates, some of them injured as well, working to keep him relaxed and then commanded a Humvee. He kept passing out, not remembering the ride to the hospital, but at peace because he knew his teammates wouldn't quit, no matter what it took. It was one of the reasons why he wanted to be a SEAL, their dedication and resolve never to give up.

Andy laid there looking at his friend. "I figured when I saw the lieutenant's face. How bad is it? I'm not paralyzed, am I?"

"No, you're injured but you can move. The biggest danger now is gangrene. That appears, it's a whole different matter. If we don't see it, you'll recover, how much your leg will function, we don't know yet."

"How long have you been in the Navy?" Andy asked him.

"Not long. In fact, this is my first posting and when I saw you come in on the gurney, I couldn't believe it. Now, you better do your part to pull through and when you're doing better, if you want, I'll make sure your parents know you're okay. And I'll tell Milly as well."

Andy couldn't believe it. "That will be great, but Milly and I broke up," he said, growing tired. "My fault," was all he said before the medicine pulled him to sleep.

Over the next couple of days, Andy grew stronger and was able to find time to chat with Nathan, his best friend from a lifetime ago, learning how he and his mother had moved to Texas and he had to start over at school making friends, but it wasn't like his time with Andy. His mom did find a new guy, but he was an ass so right after graduation, he enlisted in the Navy as a Corpsman, his top choice. After tech school in Fort Sam Houston, which was close to home, he was assigned to gain some practical experience before being assigned to this area. That was how he ended up here.

Andy told him about his life after Nathan left and how he had gotten so close to Milly and how they drifted apart. He left out many of the details about the Prom and how stupidly he had acted, then mentioned Finn and about his relationship with his mother and then how Finn had given him the Munck, as a graduation gift. Nathan's eyes lit up.

"You have a boat of your own?" He asked, completely missing the rest of what Andy had told him about his life, though Andy was a little skimpy on details, in case he ever returned to Aurora.

"Yeah, I do. I only joined the Navy Reserve to learn about ship repair, but then I met the SEALS and transferred to active status. Now, I don't know what the Navy will decide about my future," he said, falling back on his pillow as he thought.

At that moment, half a dozen SEALs came walking into his room, Lieutenant Buerl in the lead, followed by Yoates and several other members. Petty Officer Third Class Chello, had been on the truck with Andy and even with a broken arm, was the man who managed to lift the truck up enough so the others could remove him and get him to the hospital.

Lieutenant Buerl looked at him. "Seaman Thompson. We've come to check on you," he said. "Not only your team, but other SEAL brothers as well. How are you holding up, Junior?"

Andy smiled. "They managed to save my leg, but I don't believe I'll be able to finish my training, sir," Andy replied. "What does that mean?"

The lieutenant said he would find out and walked out of the room, while the rest of his SEALs sat around kidding him. Andy introduced Nathan and all of them talked about what had happened and how tough Andy had been. There was a lot of ribbing when Lieutenant Buerl returned.

"You men, can you give me a few minutes with Junior?" He asked.

When the others cleared out, the lieutenant gave Andy the bad news. His leg was in a bad way and there were signs of infection. Because of this, he would not be able to finish his training, possibly for a long time, if at all. At this point, he was told if the infection didn't clear, he might still lose his leg, in which case, being that he didn't finish training, he would not be able to remain in the SEALS. If it did heal, he would have to wait until he was cleared medically to be allowed to rejoin the teams, only it would be a tremendous challenge. He would have to redo the Underwater Demolition Training from the beginning and then the rest of his training sometime in the future.

When the lieutenant was finished, he looked Andy in the eye. "I'm sorry to give you this news, son. It's definitely a gut punch, but the choice will remain unknown. Most importantly is your leg. The other stuff will come after that." Andy took the news stoically, but it did hurt. He had thought the worst was behind him; now, he knew that wasn't true. He told the lieutenant that he would check with the doctor and keep in contact and let him know.

Buerl looked at him as he stood. "Andy, I've got to say, I've known a lot of SEALs in my day, but you rank up there with the best of them. The doctor says your leg doesn't look good and it might still have to come off. He'll know later today, and he'll keep me informed. I need to get these guys out and finish training, but before I go, let me tell you, you're one of us. Come hell or high water, you're one of us."

Andy thanked him, then said his goodbyes to the rest when they came in behind the lieutenant. They had all been briefed on his condition and it was a sad meeting. Sasquatch looked at him as they were starting to depart. "You keep fighting the good fight, Junior. If you need me in the future, call. I'll do my best to be there to help you," he said, tears starting to form in his eyes. He shook Andy's hand and followed his friends out.

When they were gone, Nathan returned. "I guess they gave you the news?"

Andy nodded. "Yeah, when will we know for sure?"

"Soon," was all Nathan said.

The news came later that day. His leg was not healing properly and showed signs of gangrene. It would have to be removed.

Three days after Andy's leg was removed, he was recuperating in the hospital when an orderly came in carrying a bundle of letters. Andy's mail had finally caught up to him and he was given the letters that had come in while he was training and here. As he was going through the letters that had been held, he found one from Milly. It was a 'get well' card, in which she wrote a simple phrase, 'thinking of you and hope you get well soon'. He read this short statement over multiple times, even showing it to Nathan, who patted him on the back and told him he was lucky. The two talked for a bit about this, when suddenly he heard a commotion in the hallway of the hospital. He looked up to see his father poke his head into the room and look around spotting him as he stood in the hallway.

"You know, Andy, this infatuation with hospitals is getting a bit ridiculous," Mark said, before being pushed into the room from behind by his mother. She pushed past Mark and rushed to her son. Andy was thrilled to see them. It was now September and he had been away from home for over a year. Instantly, his mother was in tears seeing her oldest in this condition, then his brother and sister also came in to see him. There were a lot of hugs and tears. A few minutes later, Andy looked at his family and smiled telling them he had not been hanging out alone here.

When his mother asked him what he meant by that, Andy pointed to the Corpsman standing off to the side, a big smile on his face. Nathan looked at Andy's parents and said, "Hi. Remember me?"

It was his father who first recognized Nathan and rushed to give him a huge hug, followed by his mother. Robert didn't remember him well, since he had been small when he left, and Sarah hadn't been born yet. The family could only stay a few days, but they were some of the best in a long time. They all talked over what he and Nathan had discussed, and then it was time for his family to return to North Carolina, Andy making sure his parents would pass on his thanks to Milly for the card.

The day after his family departed, Andy was transported to the medical treatment wing, his condition being upgraded to 'recovering'. This was where his most difficult training began, that of learning how to operate on his one remaining leg and a prosthetic. The fitting was easy, however trying to learn to balance himself and then walk was so much of a challenge for him. He had to deal with new pains and cramping, but gradually learned to walk and then to run. Granted leave over the holidays, Andy was able to return home for Christmas and enjoyed some much needed 'down-time'.

Being the rest of his body was in great shape, Andy took the training like a SEAL, holding in the pain and the fear and doing what he could to understand and accept the damage his body had taken and after two months of intensive physical therapy, Andy was given his honorable discharge and a one hundred percent disability rating, meaning he would retain his pay and receive gradual increases, called COLA or Cost of Living Allowance. His team wasn't there to see him off, but Buerl was, and he reminded Andy that if needed help in any way, to contact them and they would be there for him.

It was a touching moment for Andy as he left the Coronado Training Center, for the last time, his dream of being a SEAL was over. Now, it was time to head back home and try to rebuild his life.

Chapter Sixteen
Civilian

A man travels the world over in search of what he needs and returns home to find it—George Moore

To Andy, SEAL training had been the toughest he had ever experienced, but the next two months in physical therapy strained him in ways he didn't know he could endure. The first thing he faced was getting used to a prosthetic and right after, he had to learn to walk again, which was so much harder than he could imagine. When he finally could walk once more without support and without falling, he was forced to attend tough weeks of physical training to help him rebuild his endurance and physique. This training was almost as bad as the days he had suffered in the mock prison, or Hell Week, and the only way he was able to endure was through the support of Nathan. The two of them would sit in his hospital room and relive their past, Andy even admitting how badly he messed up with Milly as Nathan sat there, unable to give him advice. When he received calls from home, his family checking on his progress and offering their thoughts of support and prayers, he would always ask about Milly, how she was doing and anything new in her life, but the answer was always the same, they didn't know or that her family said she was fine.

That was Andy's life for many weeks until some shocking news arrived, Nathan received orders to transfer from the hospital in California to a cruiser in the 7th Fleet, now sailing in the Pacific. Nathan was happy with the assignment but was worried about how Andy would react, but he accepted the news stoically. Usually, an assignment took several weeks or months before it happened; however, this transfer had a fast turnaround time, as Nathan was needed to replace a Corpsman who had become injured in some way and Nathan was told to pack and ship out in only two days. He and Andy spent as much as they could chatting about life aboard ship until it was time to leave, and Andy was alone once more.

Finally, the day arrived when Andy was told he had improved enough to be released from training and was presented with his honorable discharge as an E-3 Seaman and released from active duty. He didn't tell anyone how nervous he was at this, not knowing what he would now do. These thoughts were in his mind as he called his parents and told them he was being released and would be heading home. The Navy assisted with this as well, providing him with an airline ticket and arranging to transport his personal effects home with him. Still, the day he had to turn in his active military ID card and then receive his inactive card was, he felt, one of the hardest things he had to do.

Andy returned to North Carolina almost sixteen months after leaving to join the Navy. It was now December and he returned to a small snowstorm which brought back memories, especially after having bumped into Nathan in the hospital. His parents picked him up at the airport in Raleigh, worried about his walking in the snow with a prosthetic, but he managed to negotiate the short trip to their car, and they were soon on their way home. While sitting in the back, his mother turned and asked how he was feeling. Andy just smiled and told his parents that he was fine and looking forward to some rest. Of course, his next question was about the Munck, and instead of answering him, his parents just smiled.

His father looked at him in the mirror. "Let's take a short side trip before we go home, okay?"

Andy could see by the way they were smiling, that it probably had to do with the Munck, so he nodded and looked at the landscape passing by, his mind lost in thought. After an hour, they were entering Aurora and his parents took the road to the Marina. However, the sight of the Munck sitting out of the water took his breath away. His father had said the family would continue working on his boat, but the craft now on land was like a new ship.

As they parked, Andy got out of the car and walked up to the boat. There were so many improvements; it was like a totally new boat, with a dazzling white paint job and the name proudly listed on the side. To his surprise, both his brother and sister were waiting for him on deck, wearing heavy coats because of the cold, but they waved when he came up, his mother having called them from the car when he landed.

Andy walked along the boat seeing new planks where the warped old ones had been and ran his hand along the bottom, feeling the repairs that were made. These were nothing. When he climbed the entrance ladder, he found himself on the deck, now sporting a new awning to keep the snow out and noticed the gas powered outboard where the small electric engine had been and the tiller was gone, replaced by a steering wheel attached to a pedestal about three feet forward of the rail.

"You both did this? It must have been expensive. How did you afford it?" Andy asked in shock, looking at his parents after they both climbed aboard and were standing there.

"We did the work, but you paid for it. Don't you remember?" His mother asked. "You gave us what was left of the cash and then your military pay." Andy had arranged some of his pay back for when he returned to make the repairs, but his parents had used that money to surprise him.

"This is your Christmas present," his mother said.

"But I didn't send that much home," Andy protested.

"Well, we added a little," his father replied smiling. "Actually, we worked for three days straight when we were certain you were coming home. It was hard but we managed to get it done in time. But that isn't all."

"There's more?"

"Go in the galley," his mother said.

Andy moved the cabin door aside and stepped down into a new kitchen and walked down the few steps which were nicely varnished with a dark wood stain. As he got to the bottom, he saw the new equipment and more importantly, Milly's parents sitting in the cabin enjoying a cup of coffee. That explained how his brother and sister had gotten there since Robert was still too young to drive. Andy looked around quickly, but Milly wasn't there. His parents saw him looking, and Milly's mom saw the disappointment. She had always liked Andy and wanted desperately to find some way she could help get them back together.

With Milly refusing to come, she decided to cover for her daughter. "Milly couldn't make it," she said thinking quickly about how she would answer his next question. Her husband also threw her a look.

Andy knew it was a lie and decided not to add to her mom's discomfort. "Well, tell her, I would have loved to see her again," and left it at that. He did notice the sigh of relief from her mom though.

Then Robert smiled at him. "'Bout time you showed up, we've been waiting here for over an hour."

"Sorry about that. Dad drove slowly in the snow. You and dad did a magnificent job. Finn wouldn't recognize it," he said, then threw a quick look at his mother, but she just smiled and shook her head. *Phew, close*, he thought, as he started looking around the galley.

Robert and Mark were eager to show him around, even though it was so cold. "Tell you what," his father said after a few minutes. "Your mom and Milly's parents are freezing now. Why don't we head home and make plans to come back here and show you everything when it's a little warmer?"

His mother agreed with that idea, so everyone gathered their things and locked up the boat as they headed for the ladder. Mark made a big thing about passing the keys to Andy, telling him how the boat was now his. However, he did add one thing, that because of all their combined work, Andy needed to take his family out sailing and added Milly's parents when Ned mentioned briefly how he had lent a hand from time to time. Andy thanked him and Mary for their help and Ned took this opportunity to talk about how he worked on a few boats when they lived in Italy, and he had added a few special touches. He stopped to point out how the deck area was larger in size and how the steering had been attached to a pedestal. Andy looked at where he was pointing, until they were interrupted by Mary, who told them they needed to wrap this up quickly, and Ned nodded.

"Won't be good if I piss the old girl off now," he said smiling.

"I heard that, Ned," Mary said loud enough for everyone to hear. Ned just made a face like *oops.*

When they were in the car again, Andy asked about the boat, but they were home before they were able to talk more about it, and as they entered their home, once more, Samantha asked the question that he was expecting.

"I guess you were hoping to see Milly."

"Yeah, but it's okay. I know she's probably home right now, watching her brother and sisters," he said quietly, seeing his mother nod off to the side. "I messed up during my senior year, saying things that I couldn't take back."

"Is that why you broke up?" Mark asked.

"Yeah, seeing Matt with her at the Prom just pissed me off and I kind of made a fool of myself and really hurt her when I saw him kiss Milly during the dance," Andy admitted.

"You should have punched him in the face," Mark said, quieting when he saw the angry look from his wife.

"I almost did," Andy admitted, "but I made it worse when she wanted to know if we were going to get married someday," he answered, remembering the Prom like it had happened last week, not a year ago.

"Kind of trying to rush things a bit," Ned said, thinking. "What did you say, if it doesn't hurt too much to talk about it," he added, not wanting to put a damper on the family get-together and ruin the mood.

"It's okay. It happened over a year ago, I've come to grips with it." Andy replied. "I told her, at the time that I didn't see us living the same dream. I wanted to see the world first and she was talking about marriage and our future together. When I told her this, she was so hurt, so embarrassed. I felt so bad after this and tried to make amends, but she was to upset and I felt like I had ruined things, for both of us."

"That's why you joined the Navy," Samantha said.

"Yes, and I wanted to get some experience with boats," he said, then carefully added, "And Finn had a bit in that. He told me about his time in the Navy, how he met gramps and how they became friends. He also told me a bit about you, Mom," he stopped there when he saw the look on her face, one that said, "don't go further with this discussion," and he complied by nodding. "It was mostly what he did in the Navy, what he saw and how it helped him grow up."

His mother breathed in; glad he had switched the topic back to something less dangerous.

"Now, that I've seen a little, and what I experience when I was a SEAL," he paused here, the hurt of his being denied the chance to finish his training, evident to his parents, "I guess I felt I was ready to tell Milly how I feel about her now. But it'll have to wait."

"Why?" His mother asked. "You should tell her this."

Andy shook his head as he smiled. "Not yet. She's not ready. And she may have changed her mind," he said, not bothering to mention the card he had received in the hospital. He had time to think that card over a lot, and decided it was simply a courtesy. There was nothing else, no hidden message he had been able to decipher from the card. She wasn't ready. Then they were home.

Mark jumped into the conversation, trying to change the subject when it became bogged down a bit. "Hey, we've got a great dinner planned for you. Robert, Sarah, can you set the table please?"

This took Andy by surprise a bit, seeing how his father had insight into what he was thinking, and he had forgotten his siblings were in the room, their being so quiet, which wasn't how he remembered them. They had matured a lot as well. "Yeah, let's see what you've prepared," Andy said to them, as he helped his siblings get the dishes.

Chapter Seventeen
Searching

Our finest moments are most likely to occur when we are feeling deeply uncomfortable, unhappy, or unfulfilled. For it is only in such moments, propelled by our discomfort, that we are likely to step out of our ruts and start searching for different ways or truer answers—M Scott Peck

Christmas morning, the weather cleared, and Andy was finally able to go see his boat. It was still a little cool, but Andy, his family and Ned all drove to the Marina and went to the boat. As Andy climbed aboard again, Ned pointed out how the deck was enlarged somewhat with the gunwale pushed out. Ned explained that when they redid the deck, the gunwales were removed then reattached to the deck over the sides of the boat and from there to the hull. It only added about a foot to each side but allowed for a small bench to be attached, so guests would now have a place to sit and where he could steer the boat from the wheel. They also added an awning which could be set up or removed in storms, providing some relief from the sun while on the water.

Andy was impressed, but that was nothing compared to the bow. Here, his family had raised the deck and installed four solar panels between several newly installed windows in the middle empty space, which allowed a person on the deck below to walk around the space without bending over. Further, the bow pulpit where he and Nathan had ridden on the river was extended and the front had a small removable windmill attached. Between the windmill and solar panels, the boat now had the capability to power all the electrical items, like the radio, interior lights and some galley equipment that had been installed instead of turning some off as others were used.

Andy was amazed and ventured with them through the interior, starting with the galley, which he viewed the other day, was now clean with new kitchen equipment installed, including a small fridge and a propane stove which was placed aft, the propane tank stored under the deck above in a previously unused storage area. The biggest surprise here was that the interior wall had been extended forward, offering guests a place to sit and relax, or where they could sit at a small dining room table. He also saw the small privy had been pushed aft, a door now installed and instead of a bucket, there was a chemical toilet.

"Dad, this is amazing," Andy said, taking in everything.

"Now, a lady guest has a little more privacy," his mother stated.

"We didn't have enough room to install a shower, so we installed a hose for showers on the deck above, and with a removable curtain for female guests," Ned said, but looking at Samantha as he said this. "Won't be much fun in colder weather, but your father told me, you were thinking of sailing in the Caribbean."

Andy looked at his father. "You remembered what I said. Wow, I know you put a lot into this, but I think I need to find a job now. I'll still have my military pay, but that won't be enough to keep up maintenance on the Munck. I'll have to figure things out," he said.

"What about using the Munck to make money?" Ned suggested. "I'd love to take an excursion out on the ocean, and with that new engine, you could get there quickly."

Andy thought about it for a moment. Yeah, Finn had mentioned something about that in the past, how he used to take people fishing, or just sightseeing; only this wasn't the place. If he wanted to make real money, he'd have to go where the money was and that was the Caribbean. There was no better time to go than now during the winter season. He made his mind up right then to go.

January 2 arrived, and Andy was there when a crane lifted the Munck off the stands and lowered it into South Creek and it brought back such happy memories. Saying goodbye to his family once more and Milly's parents as well, Andy took command of his boat. *His* boat. It was a thrill for him that was more important now after learning the traditions and importance of that position in the Navy. As a parting gift, his mother had purchased a captain's cap at the Marina gift shop, and he was sporting it along with an all-weather jacket, it was still winter after all.

Once on the water, Andy felt he was once again in command of his future. Over the holidays, he had arranged a place to dock and compared prices and locations where he could establish a business. His parents had helped him stock up, his mother being afraid he would starve on his own. He just laughed to himself as she made sure his pantry was filled. As she was storing this food, Andy saw her reach down and touch a portion of the galley wall, like she was rubbing something. When she paused and stared at the spot, Andy crouched down and looked at the spot as well.

She noticed him and suddenly tried to stand, but Andy's position behind her prevented this because the small kitchen table had been extended. He saw her look up at him, embarrassed, and turned to his side seeing the mark his mother had dropped her hand away from and he had just enough light in the cabin to see the initials. 'SB & PG' in a carved heart.

"You and Finn?" Andy asked.

His mother nodded. "I forgot it was there until I started putting these groceries in this cubby. It's hard to see with the table here now," she said quietly. "Don't tell your father."

"I won't, Mom, don't worry," Andy answered.

"Maybe you should sand it off, just get rid of it," she added suddenly.

"It's my boat, Mom, and it's a part of you I will always have here. So, it stays."

"But you don't know why we put it there…" She started to explain but was cut off by Andy.

"I know more than you realize. Let's just leave it at that. The initials stay and I'll cherish them," he replied as his mother started to tear. "Get rid of those tears. If dad sees them, he'll be concerned."

Samantha smiled and hugged him then. "You be safe out there. Take care of the Munck and it'll take care of you."

Andy remembered that exchange as he left South Creek and entered the Pamlico River. It was strange this time; he was now piloting the boat where Finn had always been the one to do this and Andy took orders on how to safely navigate the river. Suddenly, the gravity of negotiating the waterway safely hit him. He had piloted boats before; however, they were small Rigid SEAL craft which were easy to maneuver on the open ocean. Here, he had to pay attention to other craft on the river and remember the rules when approaching other craft, especially the larger trawlers or cargo ships which shared this waterway with all craft to move to port, or the left side when passing other boats.

Thankfully, Andy was able to reach Pamlico Sound and more open water. Waves here were not as big as they would be on the open ocean, but they were still dangerous. He remembered his first trip into the Sound, how Finn had instructed him to keep a sharp lookout, their boat not equipped with any sort of radar. That, however, had been rectified by his family, or Ned, or both, he didn't know who exactly, just that his boat now had a small radar set located near the tiller allowing him to identify any craft near his position.

It was still cold, and Andy was glad he was wearing the all-weather jacket as the spray was fierce. He had carefully watched the weather; a small front had moved through the area yesterday, the aftereffects still evident. In the distance, he could just see the storm clouds pulling away. The air was very cold on this section of the water, but he felt now was the time to make his way south and head for those areas like south Florida where he could locate people who would want to charter his boat and allow him to earn a living. It sounded so easy when he thought about it, but now that it was about to happen, he wasn't as sure about it.

He crossed the Sound and then tragedy almost struck. Just as he was about to pass by Portsmouth Island, the last piece of land separating the Sound from the Atlantic, a larger boat pulled through at speed and the Munck almost floundered. Andy was tossed to the side as his boat was hit by the large wave and tipped dangerously on her side. Thankfully, his father had installed a safety harness near the rudder, only this allowed Andy to stay on the deck. Still, it was an eye-opener for him. The fate of a smaller craft didn't seem to matter much to larger ocean vessels. He would have to keep a more careful eye on them in the future. That's when the words of Finn came to mind, to be vigilant and careful. Andy intended to take those words to heart.

Once he had the rudder firmly in his hands, Andy steered his boat through the opening and out onto the Atlantic. The waves here did not seem as big as those he had faced in California, but they were still large. Watching his radar and seeing no other vessels nearby, Andy locked the rudder in place and inspected his boat, moving first to the bow to ensure his power generating equipment had survived the passage, then moved to the galley and looked about. Some smaller items had been thrown around, but most importantly, his coffee pot was still attached to the coffee maker.

If there was one thing he had learned to appreciate as he got older, it was the joy of a good cup of coffee. Like most sailors, he opted to drink it black, enjoying the warmth of the brew and savoring the taste. His small maker quickly made him a hot cup of coffee, which he took with him onto the deck.

Taking a check of his compass, he quickly chartered the course he would follow to his future, first Florida and finally, the Caribbean.

Chapter Eighteen
Caribbean

Andy took another sip from his beer as he charted the Munck through some 'rollers', just larger waves. Rollers wasn't really a nautical term but was how he liked to describe the waves they encountered to his clients, since they would roll the boat from side to side as they passed. His clients on this excursion were busy fishing for swordfish, or other large sport fish. So far, the trip had been a bust, having hooked a smaller shark, which Andy cut away as it neared the boat and a few small fish.

He looked at the gathering clouds moving in from the southwest, *thunder boomers*, he thought. Not good for a boat on the open sea. He announced they would have to head in, to the boos and catcalls from his guests. Andy ignored it, knowing if he stayed, the severe waves would make them all sick, or worse, one of these drunken businessmen might even fall overboard, something which had happened the year before on one of his outings. If it hadn't been for the help of another boat, the man might have been lost to the sea. Thankfully, the man had presence of mind to hold onto a float and the bright orange design allowed the other boat to spot and pull the guy from the sea.

Andy quickly started up the motor after making sure everyone was carefully seated and strapped in, telling them for half price, they could try again tomorrow. Secretly, he hoped they would decline the offer, but he had adopted a policy of making his clients happy and it had resulted in his business increasing, which wasn't easy with all the other boats and charters he had to compete with.

Thankfully, the drunken businessmen announced they had a flight to catch and would have to be up early for it the next morning, so Andy did what he could, giving them coupons to a local bar, which had provided him with the coupons if he would send additional clients to their establishment. For Andy, it was arrangement, they provided beer at cost and suggested his services to people looking for an adventure, and he encouraged patrons to visit the island bar where they could get cut rate drinks allowing this bar to increase their business.

It was a good call on Andy's part, for as soon as they docked and exited his boat, the skies erupted with a torrent, the rain quickly becoming a deluge. Thankfully, he was docked close to the bar and his patrons had to move quickly. Andy made sure they were well on their way before settling in and prepping his gear for the next day's charter, whatever it happened to be. That was one of the joys of having his own business, he could take a few days off and his military pay, sent electronically, allowed him to pay any dock fees. It wasn't a bad life, but it also wasn't what he had expected life in the Caribbean to be. Sure, he took days off to prep the boat or just to meet people and network new clients and businesses, but there was often little time to travel and explore other islands.

"Hey, Barb, you all set down there?" Andy called to his waitress who was now working to finish cleaning the galley, which meant storing what food had not been consumed and putting the empties in plastic bags for disposal. That was one thing that bothered him in the Caribbean, few places recycled plastic or glass and he was forced to place the refuse in bags to be collected in the morning by workers, each bag removed coming at a hefty price.

Barbara called up and said that she was almost done. Thankfully, there weren't many things to clean up, the fishermen concentrated mostly on the beer and wine coolers Barbara had served them in her duties as a waitress. It was a compromise the two had worked out. Barbara could remain on the boat and would help with clients and in return, she could keep her tips and not have to pay for a place to live.

They both shared the Munck, showering on the deck utilizing the removable screen Ned had installed, and sleeping in the small berthing area by the galley, or on the small couch in the galley itself. It was close quarters, but it allowed them to save money and they got along, mostly. As for food, well they usually ate what was left over after a charter, or if they managed to catch something from the sea.

Andy had met Barbara more than two years before after a long night of partying at a local bar. He was there to celebrate the upcoming wedding of a friend he had made and, feeling tired, had settled in a booth seat across from Barbara, who was working as a server. She wasn't feeling well and had sat to help her stress headache, but to Andy, she seemed depressed. Taking a swig from his drink, he started talking to her and that was up when she confessed, she was losing her apartment and didn't have enough money to return to Georgia. Feeling badly for her, he suggested she spend the night on his boat. She was getting a bit desperate and since Andy was cute, she took him up on his offer, showing only a little surprise when Andy removed his plastic leg.

The coolest thing about his leg, Andy had said to friends earlier, was that it was plastic and was the same color as his skin, so when he wore shoes and shorts, few people would even know he was sporting a prosthetic limb. Barbara didn't freak and simply listened to how his injury had happened, but to learn he was a SEAL, that was something that made him more attractive to her, and the fact that he didn't boast about it beforehand, meant he was a better than average male. Something she hadn't seen lately.

In the morning, Andy awoke to a sparklingly clean galley. Barbara had risen earlier and cleaned the place well, even his coffee pot, which he had to admit he hadn't cleaned in so long, he couldn't remember the last time he had. She was grabbing her stuff and preparing to leave, when the next charter showed early and graciously, she helped get them situated on the boat and joined him on the trip, a cruise around the island. She did such a good job that Andy asked her if she would be interested in joining him on future trips, the two working out a plan of what her responsibilities would be and after a time they had merged into a team, one that clicked and helped each other shine to their customers. They had been working together ever since.

Andy wasn't thinking about this when he came down onto the dock and headed toward the local hotel, where his mail was collected and saved, for a price of course. No one did anything for free here in the Bahamas. On his way, he stopped by the bar where the waitress on duty introduced him to a future client. Andy shook hands and talked to the man, who said he was bored with the Bahamas, and wanted a little excitement in his life. He asked if he could charter his boat to Martinique where there were casinos. Andy looked at the man, thinking it was about time he had departed this berg and continued with his goal of exploring, not knowing this trip would change his life.

Andy agreed and went back to the boat to tell Barbara, who wasn't that fond of the idea as she had been dropping hints that she wasn't happy here and was thinking of a change, possibly heading back to her home in Georgia. Andy thought this would be perfect for her, but she told him she missed family and friends, and she wanted to go home. She did, however, agree to accompany him to Martinique if he agreed to help pay for a plane ticket to Florida, where she could rent a car and fly home.

He looked at her, his companion for the last year and now he would be alone again. He managed a slight smile, though he was pained as he agreed to her request. They made quick plans to collect the supplies necessary for the journey, Andy collected extra fuel for the engine and Barbara gathered food and drinks for the voyage that he estimated would take a full day to reach, longer if their new client didn't hustle back to their boat.

Looking at his watch, Andy asked Barbara to head to the hotel to collect their mail, and maybe put in a forwarding address since he didn't get there earlier and wasn't planning on returning anytime soon while he went to the bar to let them know he would be taking an extended trip and he collected the small amount of money he was owed.

As he waited on the boat for Barbara to return and then his clients, he looked over his finances. He had been tracking what he made over the past two months and was a little surprised to see that he had made a fair amount, even after he gave Barbara her share. He could afford to add a few things to the Munck. Then Barbara returned and looked at what he was doing while he went through the mail she had brought back.

"You know, you might want to think about selling this boat," she said to him.

Andy looked at her. "Are you kidding? This thing was a present, I couldn't sell it," he replied.

Barbara pulled up his finances. "Well, if you paid attention to your finances more, you'd see that you have a nice little nest egg. If you sold this boat, I think you'd get enough money to buy something larger, which means more people on tours or charters. You could clean up."

Andy let out a deep breath of air before answering. "I know you're right, but this boat, it was named after my mom. And the owner is a family friend, well, friends with my mom anyway. I would have to think of a new name for another boat," he said, lost in thought.

Barbara looked at him and smiled. "Why not Munck Two?" She spoke. "You know, but the two would be the number spelling, not the word spelling."

Andy looked at her then grabbed her around her back and pulled her to him for a deep hug and a gentle kiss. "You're a genius. I wouldn't be giving up the Munck, I would just make it larger. I could do that," he said, a smile coming to his face.

He had to leave that thought when they heard their clients on the dock. "Time to make the bacon," he said to Barbara, who pushed the wrinkles out of her blouse and skirt as she joined him on deck.

A half hour later, Andy raised the sails once in the Atlantic. He could have used the motor, but that was for emergencies, and sailing allowed him to save the fuel, plus he loved traveling by sail, letting the boat crest over waves, the spray invigorating and cooling in the hot sun. His clients, Dave, who had made a small fortune on some internet system and his girlfriend, Clarice, seemed to enjoy the ride as well, spending a lot of time in the pulpit at the bow, copying scenes from movies like 'Titanic' or running back and forth on the deck.

They were goofing around, so Andy made his way forward to caution them about running on deck especially with the wind increasing and with the ocean waves increasing they should put on their life vests as a precaution. Clarice seemed to understand, but Dave chose to ignore his advice, saying he was a good swimmer and paying for this trip. Of course, trouble occurred short afterwards when the front of the Munck dipped in a wave trough and both of clients were thrown about the deck. Clarice grabbed hold of a support line, but Dave hit the deck and then rolled over the edge and into the water, the Munck now moving at a fast clip away and Andy knew they had to act quickly.

As Barbara took the wheel, Andy grabbed a life ring and threw it off the back of his boat knowing how quickly they could lose sight of David in the choppy seas. The ring landed close to Dave, who either didn't see the ring or was panicking so badly he was in danger of drowning. There was only thing to do, and as Barbara lowered the sail, Andy jumped off the rear and swam to the man. The water was cold and choppy, Andy suddenly remembered his first day in SEAL training as he started swimming toward him as he floundered in the waves for some reason ignoring the life ring just a few feet away. Fifty yards or so didn't seem like much unless you were fighting time and danger, and Andy used all he had learned in training as a SEAL and how he could overcome any challenge placed before him.

He reached Dave and pulled at him even as the man was in total panic and swung at him in the water hitting Andy in the face. Without thinking, Andy blocked another blow aimed at him and punched the man hard in his face, calming him down enough for Andy to put his arm around him to keep him safe. He looked around and saw the Munck now turning back toward them, the sail down and Barbara manning the engine. He also saw Clarice standing on the bow filming the adventure.

Andy felt better until he saw the shark fin knifing through the water some distance off and suddenly remembered when he and Nathan had gone swimming, and something hit their legs. The fear of being attacked in the water returned and he began a rapid backstroke pulling David along. The fin wasn't moving in their direction yet, but Andy knew the shark would sense their motion and would no doubt come to investigate. He looked back at the Munck, it was still about a hundred yards or so away and moving toward them rapidly, but he also knew Barbara would slow down as she came closer, the increased size of the waves making it difficult for her to keep track of them, so he pulled off his bright colored shirt and began waving it in the air, relaxing a bit when Clarice pointed at them and started yelling at Barbara. Now, it was just a matter of time.

The fin turned and to Andy's horror started heading in their direction. When Dave saw what Andy was looking at, he began to panic again and pushed away from Andy, who let him go and concentrated on the menace quickly approaching. His training kicked in; SEALS were trained to live in the sea, work with the sea, and deal with the sea. He remembered this exact scenario, put something between him and the approaching shark, and he spotted the safety ring floating not far away. However, he knew when he moved toward it, the shark still concentrated on Dave.

He decided to splash the water, causing what commotion he could as he swam to the ring and reaching it, pulled it between him and the imminent threat. The shark kept coming, centering on him and its mouth clamped down on the ring, its rows of teeth grabbing the ring and dragging it beneath the water. Andy got a good look at it, a Tiger, probably six or seven feet long, a killer. It wasn't as deadly as a Great White, or a Bull shark, but any shark was unpredictable in the open ocean and now he had lost his only barrier.

Then the Munck pulled nearby, and he saw Dave grab the ladder and begin to climb aboard, Andy swam as quickly as he could toward safety. He reached out and his hand grasped a portion of the ladder as well. He started to climb when he saw the Tiger coming at him again. Pulling as fast as he could, he knew he wouldn't make it, then got an idea. Pulling the top part of his body out of the water, Andy pushed his prosthetic at the shark, hitting the shark on its snout.

The shark lashed out, thrashing the water as Andy kept trying to get up the ladder. The teeth of the shark clenched onto his leg, pulling him down a bit, then his prosthetic pulled free from his leg and Andy was able to pull himself out of the sea and up onto the deck. As he fell over the bulwark onto the deck, Clarice screamed, thinking the shark had bitten his leg off below the knee since there was blood.

Barbara was there in a second but realized the bleeding came only from a small gash on his leg, probably caused by the straps that held his prosthetic on, as Andy yelled that he was alright. A few seconds later, his prosthetic bobbed to the surface and Barbara was able to use their fishing net to snag his leg and haul it on board. Clarice continued to scream as she grabbed her boyfriend and clung to him.

By now, Dave had recovered and helped Clarice to calm as well before approaching Andy as Barbara attended to the cut on his leg. Andy was looking out on the ocean, watching the shark which had attacked earlier, now swimming in loose circles around the boat. It was a mesmerizing sight for all of them for a few minutes, until Dave stepped down on the ladder they had used to climb out of the water.

Clarice yelled at him, as Barbara thought he was in shock, but Dave simply reached down and pulled in the small rope attached to the float Andy had thrown to him earlier. He pulled the damaged float into the boat and then handed it to Andy. "Now, this is a trophy, you should keep," he said.

Andy took the float, noticing the large tear on the ring where the shark had closed its teeth on the float and tore it. There wasn't much left of this portion. That shark had done its best to rip the ring apart but released it when there was no taste. "Can you imagine what it would have done to us if we didn't have this ring?" Andy said.

"Well, to you." Dave said back. "I was already hauling my ass out of the water. Sorry for leaving you behind, I guess I panicked, and I owe you so much for saving my life," he continued. "When I saw you exit the water without part of your leg, shit dude, I almost threw up. How'd that happen?"

"When I was a SEAL," Andy answered, not really wanting to get into how.

"You were the Navy's elite," Dave said, surprising Andy, who thought he was too young and selfish to know what the SEALs were.

"Yeah, was. My leg meant a medical discharge. Now, here I am."

Dave reached down and shook his hand, "Always wanted to meet a hero."

Andy shook his hand, "I wasn't a hero, just tried to calm you down and get you out. When I saw that shark, well, I just wanted you out faster."

Dave started to laugh. "I wanted out too, but I know you splashed the water to make sure the shark came after you, so I could get out. Damn, man, you are a hero. Admit it or not."

"Well, my leg still works, and we've got a schedule to keep," he said, as he refastened his prosthetic to his leg. He stood and tested it. Like the safety ring, it had some bite marks now and was slightly dented on one side, but he told everyone they were battle scars and he would keep both his leg and the ring as a remembrance, not of how he almost died, but how he survived. That was his way, the glass always half full.

The rest of the journey to Martinique was more relaxed. The ocean seemed to calm somewhat like in salute for Andy's surviving. He didn't know why, the meteorological service he listened to had said the ocean would have huge swells and there would be periods of rain. That didn't happen and they pulled into Fort-de-France Bay later in the evening.

As Dave was preparing to leave, he handed Barbara an envelope and told her to give it to Andy once he and Clarice were off the boat, slipping her fifty dollars to ensure this request was met. Both of them hugged and before departing and invited them to the casino tonight for some dinner and gambling fun.

Andy looked at Barbara, who nodded slightly, so he said they would, and after they moved out of sight, Barbara handed him the envelope along with his mail that they hadn't gotten to because of the excitement earlier.

Andy opened the envelope from Dave and was shocked to see two checks made out to him and Barbara for fifty thousand dollars each. Andy sat there in shock for a few minutes before handing Barbara her check. She looked at it and began to cry, explaining to him that she had vowed to return with money when she left, and had been worried about confessing to her parents she was broke. Now, she could show them she was a capable adult and had made enough money to prove it.

When she said this, Andy lowered his head and looked at her with knowing eyes. "Ah, I see. You made quite a bit helping with that rescue," he said with a huge smile.

Barbara swatted him on his arm. "Hey, you said we were a team, so just, shut up!" Then she stormed down the steps into the galley. Andy could hear her tossing things around and decided he wasn't going down there for a bit, at least until she stopped throwing things.

That night they enjoyed their dinner with Dave and Clarice and when they were done, Andy confessed that he wanted her to go home with a good meal, and about how he would pay for the plane ticket, so Barbara could show the check to her parents and use it to start a new life. This brought Barbara to tears again, worried how he would be able to continue without her.

Andy held up his hand. "You know, I was thinking of finding a place to store the Munck and maybe I'll head home as well—"

He was cut off by Barbara. "Why? I mean, I thought you wanted to explore Martinique, so I thought you would want to stay for a while, check out the local population," she responded as a very attractive woman in a bikini walked by their table and smiled at Andy. She looked at Barbara and turned her head away.

"Bitch," Barbara said quietly, but loudly enough for Andy to hear and start laughing.

Then he held up a letter. "I didn't get the chance to tell you about this," he said, holding it up for her to peruse which she did.

When she was done, she looked up at him. "A neighborhood block party. What's so special about—" She paused as she said it. "Oh, your friend Milly might be there."

Andy smiled. "Maybe, but I would also like to see my family again, and if she happens to show, then yes, it might allow me a chance to catch up. However, the party is in three days, so instead of storing the Munck here and flying back, why not sail home. If we leave tomorrow, we could be there in two days, and I could leave the boat in my hometown. We can rent a car there to drive to Raleigh and get you a plane ticket home. You wouldn't have to worry about customs, and I could head to my town and join the party in plenty of time."

Barbara smiled, but it was a sincere smile. "You're a great guy. You know my number, so just keep me in the loop, let me know what happens. Maybe I can offer some advice on what to think?"

"I would really like that. So, what do you think about my idea?"

She picked up her glass of wine that a waiter had just filled and held it up to him. "Hard to say no to the boss."

"I also thought I could pick your brain a bit first. You have a good head for business, so with that said, what do you think about an idea I have, to invest this new money in some business ventures here? I have a former SEAL buddy, who lives in the Virgin Islands and when I called him today, he said he had some good ideas on what to invest in."

"Is it safe? You don't have much experience in this area that I know of," she said earnestly.

"If my buddy says it's a good deal, then it is. SEALs look after their own. Always have," he responded. After dinner, they set about preparing for their journey the next day.

Chapter Nineteen
Reminiscing

Do one thing every day that scares you—Eleanor Roosevelt

Milly stood off to one side holding Drew's hand as her parents walked ahead of her to the party. She had arrived home with Drew just an hour before, hoping to have time to introduce him to them, but the traffic had been a nightmare and their normal four-hour drive took almost six to complete. She and Drew had finally arrived tired, and a bit off their game. On top of this, her family had little time to talk with them as they were helping to get the party started, her mother telling her they could talk after the food was served.

This wasn't what Milly wanted or hoped for. She wanted her parents to meet Drew, who, to her, was a brilliant and funny guy, once you got past his arrogant brashness. She had to admit, she hadn't liked him much at first either, but over time, she began to tolerate and then to like him, her field of mechanical design hadn't allowed her to meet many males. The field was dominated by women and though she made many friends, available males were few and far between. She did date a few other guys she met in college, but she kept comparing them to Andy and nothing serious developed.

When she graduated from the University of Central Florida and returned to Aurora, she concentrated on seeking employment, but the job market was tight and it was only when she bumped into Matthew Grimes, of all people, that an opportunity presented itself. She learned he had left college after his second year and started working in a hotel chain that needed help. Matthew worked out of Raleigh and was home for the weekend and he suggested she visit him there and meet his supervisor. Skeptical of his intentions, she nonetheless agreed and while there, he introduced her to the manager, who was meeting with the chain's owner, Angelica Lawton. Milly impressed Ms. Lawton with her knowledge and education and before she knew it, was offered a job offer working with the company. She accepted, thinking the job would be in Myrtle Beach, South Carolina, but at the last minute, she discovered it was in Charleston, headquarters of the hotel chain.

Myrtle Beach was only about three hours away by car, Charleston an hour further away and farther than she wanted to travel, but her father said it best, 'go where the jobs are', and she did. The family came with her to help find an apartment and she was nervous about her first day at work, especially when her new team warned her about their supervisor, Drew Lawton, Angelica's son. He had learned from his mother about Milly, and he was prepared to put her through the ringer on her first day, but when he met her, he thought twice about that, being captivated by her beauty and knowledge.

Though she had dated a bit in college, she found Drew to be more distinctive than her college dates. He was handsome and charming, but he was also serious about making a mark in this world and insisted on perfection when it came to his staff, utilizing their successes to prove to his mother that he had the right stuff to run the company, something she thought he lacked, but Milly saw his determination as a positive trait and before long, he asked her out, taking her to an exclusive restaurant. He spoke French fluently, which was similar to her native Italian, another plus, and the two hit it off. Milly didn't notice his disdain for the servers, but his demeanor was impressive and before long, they were an item in their hotel community.

Afraid of what others might say about her, Milly tried carefully to maintain a professional image around her co-workers. She insisted that Drew respect her wishes, but as their dates continued, he pestered her to become more involved. It was hard for Milly, but she saw a chance to impress his mother and finally agreed, albeit he didn't match up to Andy in other areas. Drew did have his own flair and he was also better in some ways, though sometimes, he could be equally odd at times, like his embarrassing way of talking down to those beneath him, or demanding more of his workers, something Andy never did. Drew though was better when it came to intimacy and took pains to ensure Milly was satisfied, though she did have to admit, Andy had started on that journey without experience, he had been clumsy in bed, something Drew was not, and she did enjoy making love with him, but it sometimes made her feel guilty as well.

Sometimes, after making love with Drew, Milly would walk into another room and wonder what life would have been like with Andy. At times, she felt angry at the life not lived, then she would bring her thoughts to the present and review her life. She knew she wasn't over Andy and would sometimes curse him for his immaturity, a defensive trait, which allowed her to think of her life now with a fulfilling job and a bright future. Still, there was something missing and she would often cry with sadness.

Then, during the summer, she received a phone call from her mother about the upcoming block party and she felt it would be a good opportunity to introduce Drew to everyone and get their opinions about him. She did wonder if Andy would be there, but her parents told her Andy was off chasing his dream in the Caribbean and though he too had been invited, no one knew for sure if he would attend, or if he had even received his invitation. It was over four years since she had last seen him, and wondered if he would attend and what he was like now.

Now at the party, Milly felt completely out of place until she noticed some of her friends, especially Maria. She told Drew she would be right back and left him standing there, totally out of his element and he was a little pissed. He had been concerned about visiting Milly's family and now she was off chatting with her friends and enjoying herself, ignoring him. He had used his stature at work to build a relationship with her, but this could wreck everything. He was no longer in control and felt he had to make sure he got her away from here as soon as he could. Only they had just arrived, and he couldn't think of some way to draw her away, especially if she was talking with her friends. Still, he decided, she was hanging with other females. There were other men her age around, but so far none of them had attempted to chat with her, and he wanted to keep it that way.

Milly stood there chatting with Maria and several of her friends from school, explaining what she was doing now and then pointed out Drew, who was standing by himself with his arms crossed, looking like he wasn't having a good time. "He seems like a bit of a dork," Maria said. "Seriously, Milly, what do you see in that guy?"

Milly looked at him, obviously noticing he wasn't happy. "He is a nice guy," she responded, but then began to remember some of the things that she had noticed when they first met. "I guess he just takes some time getting used to it. Come on, let me introduce you."

The small group of women started to follow Milly, when they noticed a commotion occurring off to one side. They all stopped and looked and to everyone's surprise, they saw Andy hugging his mother and father. "Oh, this is going to be interesting," Maria said to the girls as Milly started walking toward Andy. The girls all nodded, some sporting smiles.

"Damn, Andy's back," Angela, another of her classmates stated. "Sparks are about to fly." The other girls huddled together, talking about this turn of events.

Drew saw the commotion as well and then watched as Milly seemed to be walking toward it. His instincts were to get in front of her, stop this unexpected event. He didn't know who the man was, but obviously Milly did, and he needed to intercede. He was about to head toward her, when Milly's father stepped in front of him. "Hey, I've got some food cooking that I think you might like," Ned mentioned.

"Who is that man?" Drew said, completely ignoring Ned's statement as he pointed toward Andy.

Ned turned and looked. "Well, I'll be damned. Andy showed. You should meet him."

Drew looked at Ned and shook the question off. "Who is he?"

"Oh, that's Andy. He's Mark and Samantha's son. We didn't know if he would show up or not. He's been sailing his boat in the Caribbean, and we haven't had much contact with him," he said with a smile, knowing exactly why Drew was upset, which suited him fine. He had already decided he didn't like this guy. He wasn't a good fit for his daughter. "Don't worry, they used to date years ago, but that's over. I think," he stated, knowing he was getting to Drew, which he enjoyed for some reason.

Drew didn't hear him but was relieved when he saw Milly return to her girlfriends and begin talking with them. To him, the crisis had passed, and he wanted to make sure it stayed that way. In the meantime, he decided to take Ned up on his offer and walked with him toward the grill.

Milly had stopped walking when she realized her friends were not around her and walked back to them, wanting to know why they weren't coming with her to meet Andy. One of them explained that they didn't want to get in the way if she wanted to talk to Andy alone.

Andy was warmly greeted by his family, first his mother and then his father gave him a hug, and both had the same question, 'why hadn't he told them he was coming?'

Andy just explained that it took a long time for mail to reach him, and he had only gotten the letter a few days before, then he had to scramble to get back home, where he then bought a ticket for his friend to fly home before driving in heavy traffic to get here in time.

Of course, his mother wanted to know about the Munck, and how it was doing, which led to a short description of how well the boat was performing and what he had been doing with it. He told her she could see it again, since it was docked at the Marina, and she was very happy to hear this. At that point, they were interrupted when Robert came up and gave him a hug as well. Andy was surprised to see his not so little sister, who was now ten, with her next birthday just two months away in October.

Mark explained to his son how they had decided on the block party to ring in the end of summer and everyone in their neighborhood had decided to join the celebration. Both of Andy's parents had hoped he would come home for this, and Andy was glad that he had made the trip. Then he spied Milly. His parents noticed him become rigid for a moment and seeing where he was looking, his mother suggested he go say hello to her.

Meanwhile, Milly was chatting with her friends once more, throwing quick glances at Andy and her friends noticed it. "Why don't you go talk to him?" Maria said. "I'm sure he'd love to see you."

Milly was torn. She wanted to at least say hello, but she had Drew with her and worried about what he would think. Hell, she was worried about what she herself would think. This was the first time she had seen him in years, the last time was watching him being loaded on an ambulance, and now she didn't know how to react to his presence. She and Drew were dating and had been for a few months, so she didn't want to ignore him, especially since things between them were going well. She was about to talk to Drew, who was near her parents, when Andy intercepted her.

Andy excused himself from his family and walked quickly to where Milly was standing with her friends. He wasn't aware that she'd seen him, but the looks on her friend's faces, and one of them tapping Milly on the shoulder, made it clear that she probably had. He had waited for this moment for years, and now, he didn't know what he would say when he walked up to her.

"Hey," was all he could manage, kicking himself for the lack of a creative word. This was the first time he had seen her in years and all he could say was, 'Hey'. *Idiot,* he thought.

Milly turned to him and said, "Hey," back, which made Andy smile. *Idiots flock together*, he thought. "I'm glad to see you," she followed, then gave him a nice hug, while carefully looking over at Drew who seemed to be having a tough time with his food. She saw him drop his paper plate, but couldn't concentrate on what was happening, not without being rude to Andy. *Well, Drew will just have to deal with it*, she thought.

At the grill, Drew was making an ass out of himself. Used to finer foods, he hated being served on a paper plate like some pauper, and he didn't enjoy the food cooked on the grill. Hot dogs and burgers with some baked beans. On top of this, the paper plate bent and spilled his food on the grass. *Oh, will this damn party ever end*, he thought. On his way home, he planned to stop by the first restaurant they found to show Milly how a good meal was served on a ceramic plate, not some damned wimpy paper. He started to cuss a bit, until he saw Milly's father staring at him.

"Here, those paper plates are flimsy. Let's get you a double plate, that will help," Ned said, before turning and closing his eyes for a second. He returned a moment later and handed Drew a new double plate, this time with some sort of chicken and rice, but with a tomato sauce spread over them. "Let's see how you enjoy some good Italian food," Ned offered.

Drew knew others were looking at him, so he smiled and thanked Ned, before taking a plastic fork and trying the food. Surprisingly, he enjoyed it. "This is so much better," he said quickly, not realizing he was offending those who had supplied the other fare.

When Milly noticed that Drew was eating again and seemed happier, the respite allowed her to concentrate on what Andy was saying. It was mostly about his life now, and what he was doing, then he surprised her a bit, when he apologized. "Look, Milly. I just wanted to say how sorry I was for what happened during the Prom and then later at your house. I was so immature, and those comments I made. I wish I could take them back, take it all back. It was wrong of me. And again, I am truly sorry."

Milly looked at him, this time it was her lack of words to express how she felt. "I should have come to see you when you came home, after you lost your..." She didn't know if she should mention his leg, but it was too late now to think of something else.

"Oh, you mean this?" Andy said, pointing at his leg which was visible since he was wearing shorts and sneakers. "It was a shock, but I'm getting used to it, especially since it saved my life the other day."

"How?" Milly asked.

For a second, Andy debated whether to tell her what he meant, then he saw her looking at the bite marks the shark had caused.

"Andy, what happened to it? It looks like it's damaged it a little."

"Long story. Let's just say I learned how valuable it can be in certain situations," was all he said, since he knew if he told her, she would probably tell her parents, and by connection, his parents. He decided to change the topic. "I see you're still wearing that necklace from the carnival."

Milly smiled. "You mean this?" She pulled at her collar and held the necklace up, pressing the button. "You won this for me. I wear it all the time. It goes with everything, and it comes with such good memories," she stated, which started them laughing a bit as they remembered their ride on the Ferris Wheel.

"You know, I'd love to hear about your life. Would you care to join me for a cup of coffee later?" Just so we can catch up, "he added at the last second."

Suddenly, Drew showed up and placed his arm around Milly, giving her a quick kiss on the cheek. He had seen her talking to Andy and moved as quickly as he could to interfere with their conversation, having thrown his plate on a chair. The kiss was to let her old boyfriend know he was talking with a taken woman, his woman.

Andy knew exactly what it was and smiled a little when he saw how Milly reacted. She gave Drew a cold look, one that let Andy know she was upset, but the other guy hadn't learned to catch on. It was something Andy had learned over time, and he knew her new boyfriend hadn't learned to read her signals yet. Andy suddenly realized there was time for him to repair the damage, he would just have to take things slowly, carefully.

Milly saw the confrontation building between the two and her heart was torn. She still had feelings for Andy, deep feelings, but she was with Drew now and it wouldn't be fair to him if she displayed those feelings in front of him. Drew was a good guy, she thought, but he was not Andy and she had to decide, and quickly, before they started fighting, something she didn't want.

Thankfully, Andy settled her dilemma, by saying he didn't know she was involved now, and he quickly offered his hand in understanding. Drew grabbed it and shook. He squeezed it harder than he normally would have, just to let Andy know he had won. To his surprise, Andy's expression didn't change, in fact, he smiled gently, and Drew knew that this wasn't over for either of them. Not yet. Drew would have to do something big.

As Andy turned and walked away, he felt that same regret for not having done something sooner to land this woman. He knew how his heart ached when she turned him down though he would have been relieved if he had known that Milly felt the same thing and was kicking herself for not having told Andy sooner. She noticed how handsome he had become, how confident he was, and most importantly, how mature he appeared. To step back and allow Drew an out instead of fighting. That was great.

Andy returned to his family and friends for the remainder of the party, while Milly took Drew back toward hers. From time to time, Andy would see her boyfriend looking at him, a smug smile on his face, like he won a race or something. He decided not to let this guy bother him and concentrated on having a good time. As the party began to wane and people began to leave, Andy took his parents, and of course, Milly's parents with him to see the Munck. Milly wanted to go along, but Drew was complaining that they needed to get back on the road and she reluctantly bid her family, and Andy and his family goodbye even as Drew was sitting in the car, waiting impatiently.

On their way back to Charleston, Milly put on a smile and talked about the party, even though she would have loved to see the Munck, having only seen it before all the repairs. After she and Andy broke up, it just didn't seem right to visit the boat even with her father doing some of the work on it, and so she always came up with excuses why she couldn't go. After a while, her family just stopped asking and then Andy was gone. In her mind on that drive back to Charleston, when Drew had finally stopped talking, all she could do was think back to her younger days. Drew noticed her pensive mood and decided not to question her, knowing it might be about Andy and decided to dismiss getting a meal.

When they returned to the city, he dropped her at her apartment and suggested that he would like to join her tonight, but Milly said no. She was tired from the trip and the party and instead gave him a short kiss goodnight, before turning and heading to her apartment alone. Drew thought about parking and heading to her apartment to make sure the day ended on a high note, but as he was debating, a call came in needing his help to solve some problem or other and he looked up at Milly's apartment, seeing her shadow on the curtain, but he felt his workers would mess things up unless he took charge, and he left in a hurry.

Milly watched him leave and when he was gone, chose to sit and look through some old photos her family had stored on her computer, and she ended up calling her mom to find out how the trip to the Munck turned out. Not surprisingly, her mother mentioned how they were still on the Munck and how well Andy was keeping up the boat. She had taken many photos, which she would send to Milly once they got home. And that maybe Milly might one day visit the boat herself.

After she hung up, Drew called to say he was called in to work and asked if she wanted to join him since he would be there until late dealing with a logistical problem. Milly just laughed and said, "I thought you were tired and that's why we had to leave." She almost enjoyed his befuddled speech as he searched his mind for a valid excuse. She then laughed and told him it was okay and ended the call. After this, she walked onto her balcony and stared up at the stars, astronomy being one subject she wished she had taken in school. She saw Ursa Major first of course, known as the Big Dipper by most and followed it past the Little Dipper to Andromeda, her favorite group of stars.

Andy had interested her in the night sky, often mentioning how sailors of old had used them to navigate by using the telescope she had gotten him, and she remembered fondly those nights with both staring at the sky as they chatted on the phone. He explained how to find other systems, like Orion, or another favorite, Hercules. Tonight, she stood there alone, feeling like she was sharing the sky with someone else. She looked around but couldn't see anyone else on this warm autumn evening and wondered why she had this feeling.

In Aurora, Andy was standing on the Munck once more as his parents and Milly's were sitting on the deck beside him, enjoying some Mint Julips. Ned was especially happy to see his work was holding up well and commented on how clean the boat looked. As he sat there, he spied a safety ring, looking like it had been through a rough time. He pointed it out to Andy. "What happened to that?"

Andy looked at Ned and carefully whispered, "It had a little encounter with a shark."

Ned looked at him, and realizing Andy was talking quietly whispered, "Why haven't you gotten rid of it then?"

Andy smiled and pointed at it. "Just happened this week and I'm keeping it because it saved my life."

Ned stared at him. "You were in the water with that when a shark attacked?"

Andy looked around a bit. "Yeah, short story. A client fell off the boat earlier this week and I jumped in after him before I saw the shark. I used it to keep the shark at bay, while my crew mate turned the Munck around and came back to rescue us."

"What sort of shark was it?" Ned asked, getting a bit loud with his question so that the others now were listening.

Andy shrugged. No way to keep it a secret now. "A Tiger shark," he answered.

"What about a shark?" His mother asked quickly.

Andy took a deep breath. "Ned and I were just talking about a Tiger shark and how it tore into that safety ring there," he answered, pointing at the ring hanging on the inside bulwark.

Mark asked next, "Why keep it?"

"Because it's important to me," Andy answered, getting exasperated with this line of questioning, and then decided to come clean. He wasn't a kid anymore and he knew his mother would keep after him until he told the truth. Carefully, he explained what had happened and how his rescue had ended up with him thinking about home.

"I hope that idiot at least gave you a reward for saving his life," his mother said.

"He did," Andy replied. "A substantial reward which I'm going to put into some safe investments a fellow SEAL told me about. Hopefully, it will pay off nicely. With time."

"Well, for once, that artificial leg did you something good then," his father said.

"Yeah, I was thinking the same thing," Andy replied, kicking off his shoe and showing the bite marks along the side and bottom. "God was looking out for me," he replied, looking up at the stars in the sky.

As the parents talked among themselves, Andy stared at the night sky, seeing the familiar stars that he had shared with Milly, feeling almost like she was with him now.

Chapter Twenty
Friends

Land was created to provide a place for boats to visit—Brooks Atkinson

The day after the party, Andy again said goodbye and left Aurora, heading once more toward the Caribbean, wanting to meet with his former SEAL friend, Sasquatch, Benjamin Yoates. Andy had learned that Yoates had finished his training and then was wounded in the Middle East. Suffering the results of an Improvised Explosive Device (IED), a mine created from a large caliber shell which was detonated when Yoates and his team were riding through a remote section of the desert in an Infantry Mobility Vehicle (IMV), which was supposed to be mine resistant, but the mine was so powerful, it flipped the IMV and threw the SEALs around inside. Sasquatch suffered a massive head injury which resulted in his having to undergo multiple surgeries.

After the surgeries, Sasquatch had some trouble forming words and because of this condition, returned to the U.S. for medical support. He managed to regain a portion of his vocabulary, but when excited, word formulation was often difficult, and because of this, he was no longer considered fit for service and received a medical discharge. After this, he headed back to his home state of Florida, but as a former SEAL used to excitement, he found Florida boring and moved to the US Virgin Islands where he found contract work in the island casinos as a security specialist. This was more to his liking, and he gained valuable knowledge in video security. He contacted Andy and told him about the investments, especially in the casino on the island of Martinique, which is where he told Andy to invest his money. Andy jumped on this and invested his new wealth into the casino there.

Two days after leaving Aurora, Andy arrived in the Virgin Islands to meet Yoates on St. Thomas. As Andy tied off the Munck, he was suddenly gripped in a bear hug and lifted off his feet. Knowing it had to be his friend, Andy patted the huge arms holding him and asked him to calm down. When he was lowered to the dock, Andy turned and greeted his friend, Sasquatch. The man looked a little older, and the top of his head was misshapen, due to all the surgeries and the removal of some of his skull.

Yoates saw him looking at his head. "Kind of gross, ain't it?"

"Doesn't look much different," Andy responded to which Yoates punched him in the arm, hard. Andy didn't say anything, but that blow hurt like hell.

"So, Andy, what brings you to this part of heaven?" Yoates asked.

"I wanted to see more of the islands. Hell, ever since I was discharged, I've only been to a couple, so I thought it was time we visited that casino you mentioned," he replied. "And I just miss the excitement of exploring. You know, like we did on the island during SERE."

"Oh, don't remind me of that place. I hated SERE," Yoates responded. "That place was ten times harder than the desert."

"Well, you look good, and it looks like you're actually more muscular, though I don't know how," Andy replied.

"Helps when I have to deal with rogue types," Yoates said, picking up Andy's bag. "C'mon, I'll take you to my place. We can catch up there and get some real drinks not that watered down stuff they serve in tourist traps."

Andy followed his friend, walking through some busy streets people naturally gave way when the two moved in their direction, mostly for Yates who was holding Andy's seabag over his head like it weighed only two pounds, instead of the fifty pounds it did weigh.

Yoates led him to a nice single condo where Andy met an attractive young woman. "This is my girlfriend, Yolette. And this is my old SEAL buddy, Junior."

"Oh, that's nice, Y and Y, easy to remember. Tell me, does she know your SEAL name?"

Yoates turned red which told Andy she didn't.

"SEAL name. What's that?" Yolette asked, after meeting Andy and getting him a drink.

"It's the name all SEALs get in training. His is Sasquatch."

Yolette looked at her boyfriend and instantly burst into laughter which was contagious. "Your SEAL name is Junior?" Yolette said, bursting out laughing as Andy nodded.

After they settled down, Andy explained how he wanted to visit places he'd never been to and wanted to know more about those investments. Yoates explained about how the casinos wanted to upgrade their security and had created new ways of watching the crowds, as well as monitoring their cash flow. These cameras would relay information to various locations and the technology was linked to a facial recognition application, which had new technology implications for law enforcement and immigration offices, but they wanted someone with knowledge on how and where to install them.

"That's a good investment," Andy said. "I'd like to see it in operation. Think you can pull yourself away from this life of leisure and take a trip to Martinique in the next day or so?"

"Absolutely," Yoates and Yolette both responded.

~~~

THURSDAY, 9 SEPTEMBER

In Charleston, Milly had been working on small designs in a small cubicle, until she learned that she had been tagged to join a team for a major project after a couple of months. With the selection, she found that her location was also changed. Instead of a small cubicle working by herself, her new position was in a larger room with no cubicles, working with several other team members in an open floor plan among the staff. That took a little getting used to, but the place was well lit with large windows along two walls, letting in the sunlight and giving the place a pleasant feeling. There was even a potted plant on the floor near her desk, though on closer inspection, she found it was made of plastic. Still, it looked real enough and she felt it complimented her station.

Now, instead of working alone, she was a team member working with five other people. There were other teams as well, all working as teams around the room, to create or modify design changes for rooms within the hotel chain. The place was busy constantly, with messengers bringing in requests from the headquarters section, one floor above them, or small groups gathering to discuss a specific portion of rooms in other hotels.

The team Milly had been assigned to, which included most of the people on this floor, was to review existing blueprints of an extended-stay hotel the company had just acquired in Atlanta. When Milly arrived that first day, she was told she would be assigned to review and change the kitchen sections of
~~~

the hotel; her immediate supervisor having already been informed of her experience and production. To the team manager, a woman named Marci, it was a bit of a challenge, since the request to accept her in a place where the others had worked together for some time, had come from the top brass, which meant Mrs. Lawton herself. Marci had to wonder if Milly was possibly some sort of plant, a person who would watch what the team did and if they were really working, so most of the people seemed a bit nervous when Milly introduced herself.

Milly had no idea of this, but felt it was because she had worked hard on other subjects and the finished projects seemed to impress those around and above her. So, she accepted the assignment and was determined to give it her best effort, staying late some days to make sure her calculations were spot on and doing her best to be friendly with her new team. Her contribution to this team effort would only be small, but she knew she hadn't proven herself yet, and the hardest part was designing it in conjunction with the rest of the room, including the bathroom. Other members had those items and the team kept busy, constantly checking on the progress of one another and trying to formulate a working chart. The room dimensions had already been determined and now she had to adapt changes into existing designs. It required a lot of math and dimensions of the utilities, and though a daunting task, she felt up to it.

During a short break, Drew popped into the work room, stopping by Milly's station to see what she had going. As he was looking over her plans, he accidentally knocked over her coffee, which spilled onto her work. Milly tried desperately to wipe the coffee off, but it was a losing battle. "Damn, Drew. You've got to be careful," she said, as hours of her work were badly damaged, or even destroyed.

"Oh, it's okay. You'll be able to reconstruct it," he replied, still trying to push the coffee away with some tissues, which had partly disintegrated as he worked, making a further mess.

Milly pushed his hand away in disgust. "What do you want?"

"I was just coming down to see how it was going. Sorry," he said, hanging his head. "Next time, I'll be more careful. I promise. And don't worry, I'll explain it to your team leader."

Milly didn't want that. Him trying to explain what happened to her team leader would sound like she was incapable of taking care of her project and looking for excuses. "You don't understand. This is the first major project your mother has assigned to me. I need to do it well. Alone."

"I get it, I get it," Drew responded. "How long will it take you to do your assigned portion?"

"If I could work on it without interruption, I'll probably be done by the end of the week. Of course, then it goes for review and revisions, so that will take about a week and if there aren't too many changes, I should be finished with this project."

"Okay, just wanted to check. I just came down to tell you, my mother was interested in dinner with us tonight. Do you think you'll be able to tear yourself away from your work for one evening?" He asked her, crossing his arms as he looked at her. Milly sensed that he wanted a positive answer, and to get him out of her hair for the rest of the day, she said she would.

"Great! Dinner will be at seven, so I'll pick you up at your place, say, around six?"

"That should be fine. I'll see you then," she responded, then sat back down at her desk to try and repair what she could of her work. When Drew didn't leave immediately, she looked up at him realizing he expected a goodbye kiss. Milly looked around and several of her teammates were looking at her. Drew still wanted that kiss, but she didn't want anyone seeing her kissing him in the office; her being new was already a hindrance, and if they saw her kiss him, she didn't know what they would think.

"Drew, please. Can you just leave so I can continue here?"

He knew that he'd have to work extra hard to repair not only this damage, but what had occurred at the party over the weekend. "Fine," he responded, suddenly seeing the people all looking at them. "See you at six." With that, he walked out of the work area.

As he got to the doorway, he looked back. Everyone was again working on their own projects, and he knew he had to do something big. It was then that he spied the brochure for Martinique. He knew the company had purchased a building there about a week ago and they were talking about refurbishing it, their first international venture. "That's it," he said to himself, as he walked out the door.

Milly waited till he left their team, then saw one of her team, a woman named Eileen, coming over to her desk. "Oh shit," she said quietly.

"It's Milly, right?" Eileen asked as she stood in front of her desk.

"Yes, hi. "You're, Eileen," Milly said, happy that she remembered the woman's name.

"You've got it. So, can I ask you a question?"

"Sure, about the project?" Milly asked.

"No. It's just that, well," Eileen kept beating around the bush and Milly knew it was about Drew.

"You want to know about Drew, right?"

"To put it bluntly, yes. You see, a couple of us were wondering…" she trailed off, not sure how to put her question into words.

"We've been dating for a couple of months now," Milly answered.

"Oh, I see. I didn't mean to get involved in your personal affairs," Eileen said.

"It's okay. He had nothing to do with me getting this position if that's what people are wondering."

"Oh, no, of course not, we were just wondering what he thinks of the project."

"Other than messing up my work," she said, pointing at the spilled coffee, "he just wanted to see how I was doing."

"Well, if it matters, I think everyone enjoys working with you and it's just that," she stalled a bit, looking for a way to finish her sentence. Taking a deep breath, she continued. "Well, in the past, when he would stop by, he was a bit critical of the new people we've worked with. So, we, well, I, wanted to let you know your work is good."

Milly broke into a smile. "Thank you. I was worried about what people would think. I didn't get this job because of him, I interviewed with his mother, and she offered me this position before I even met Drew."

"Say, if you'd like to meet the rest of the team, we're planning on getting a bite to eat after work. Might be a good chance to exchange ideas with us, get to know everyone. Always helps to build a solid team and cement friendships," Eileen said with a genuine smile.

Milly knew she was supposed to meet Drew, but if she refused to bond with her teammates, it might put a barrier between her and them, just as they were getting started. She quickly made up her mind. She would call Drew a little later and let him know she couldn't make the dinner and would make it up to him later. "Yes, Eileen, I'd love to join you. Do we have to drive?"

Eileen waved her arm at the question. "Oh no. It's walking distance from here, just a burger joint down the road where they celebrate Happy Hour. You'll have a blast. Just meet me at my desk and I'll walk you to the place," Eileen said, as he waved and returned to her own desk.

When Drew got the news, about an hour later, he wasn't happy, but he didn't let Milly know. Then he thought it would give him time to formulate a plan on how to get her to accompany him; he just had to find a way to bring the trip up to his mother first. He started thinking about what he could say to both women. Besides, if she wanted to make friends with her teammates, it wouldn't do to tell her she couldn't and he wanted to give the impression that he was fine with that, and he started thinking about other things, like how to win over her heart, and he wanted to do it right. He started making plans right then.

Chapter Twenty-One
Work

Success in business requires training and discipline and hard work. But if you're not frightened by these things, the opportunities are just as great today as they ever were—David Rockefeller

FRIDAY, 10 SEPTEMBER

On the way to Martinique, Andy and his friends had a grand time talking about their training and Yoates let him know about the things he missed, like Sniper School and then medical training before being posted to SEAL Team Three, based on the East Coast of the United States. He told Andy of how his size made getting into and out of subs while underwater something of a challenge, but he got it done. And finally, being posted to the fighting in Africa, dealing mostly with Al Qaeda offshoots who mainly just terrorized the local populations in certain countries, mostly Niger and Mali. It was in Mali that his transport hit the IED, and he was forced out of the SEALs.

At the casino where they would invest his money, Andy got to meet the Casino Head Supervisor, who insisted on taking Andy's photo, which, since he was an investor, the casino required, and which would be displayed on the wall with other investors. Transparency, they called it. After this, they spent two days exploring or snorkeling in the warm and amazingly clear water. Andy loved it and took plenty of videos, sharing them with his family via the internet when he returned to the Munck. From there, they sailed back to the Virgin Islands to establish a new charter business.

After they returned to St. Thomas, Andy set up the business in a small office beside a tackle shop on one side and a clothing store on the other. He asked Yolette if she would be the receptionist, then asked Yoates if he was cool with this. Yoates simply waved it away, saying it was about time his girl started earning her keep, getting a hard swat from her which he didn't seem to notice.

"Sasquatch, you sure know how to handle a woman," Andy said after the swat.

Yoates just smiled. "Good thing I didn't teach her any combat tactics, or I might have ended up in the hospital again," he said smiling, then winking at Yolette, who just turned her head and walked off.

Within days, Andy's charter business was doing better than it had in the Bahamas. With the start of the fall, more tourists began to visit the island, he noticed an increase in clients, which had to be attributed to Yolette. Her natural beauty and charm attracted business and she handled the business end well. Then it was time for Andy to find someone to help crew his boat. Many people were looking for work, but Yoates wanted the job. He knew about boats and how to handle them, and suggested that they would make a good team, even accepting that Andy would be in charge.

Remembering the adage, 'never hire friends', Andy placed a call to Barbara at her home in Georgia. She answered right away and the two spent some time chatting before Andy asked her what she thought of taking his old buddy on as a crew mate. Ever the careful one, Barbara asked him what he thought of his friend and if he thought they would be able to work together. Andy thought about this and told her what Yoates told him. She responded that, though she didn't know his friend, he would be a good choice, since they had worked together in the past and had a special bond. Thanking her, Andy hung up and went to tell his buddy that he was hired, for now, after they held a trial run to see how things went. The next day, Yoates reported for duty aboard the Munck for a five-hour whale watching charter. The two stood there as their clients, three attractive women, all dressed in skimpy bikinis, climbed aboard. Andy looked at Yoates as both men smiled. "Too bad you have a girlfriend," then smiled himself as he watched the smile slowly disappear.

"Ah, c'mon, Andy. Yolette won't mind," he was getting mock angry.

Andy flipped him his phone. "Give her a call, see what she says."

Yoates almost threw the phone overboard, but instead passed it back to his employer. "Yes, sir," he said. "Can I at least flirt a little?"

Andy patted him on the back. "You can do whatever. SEALs keep secrets. Remember, brother?"

"Oh yeah, hot damn. You pick who you want first since you're the captain and I'll take what's left over," Yoates answered, eyeing the women like a child would eye candy.

"You're an idiot. Let's cast off," Andy told him, then asking the women to grab a seat. As he was about to back out of the dock, he caught sight of Yolette coming down to wish them luck. She didn't seem pleased when she saw her boyfriend smiling and handing one of the women, the one with a tiniest bikini, a beer. Andy looked at his friend, then just smiled and closed his mouth. *Why spoil the surprise now*, he thought, *best to wait till they got back, and he could tell Yolette about his day at sea.*

Carefully, he headed out the wharf area, moving slowly because of the number of boats docked on the pier but once in the designated channel, he opened it up a bit more, carefully monitoring the other boats as he made his way toward open water. For this part of the trip, he was using the outboard motor, it was faster and somewhat safer since it allowed him more control of his boat. Then he was slightly distracted when one of the women sauntered over and stood beside him.

Andy looked her over quickly. "Having fun?" He asked, to which she smiled and nodded. "Would you like to take the wheel for a bit?"

The woman seemed shocked for a second before replying. "I can do that?"

"Sure," Andy answered. "I'm going to help you until we get out of the harbor and onto the open water, but once there, you'll be steering the boat." He pointed up at the sails. "My crewman and I will need to get the sails up."

The job only required one person, but the two former SEALs had discussed letting their clients do some of the easier tasks as it would be a chance to allow them to experience a challenge that they would not usually do, helping to enhance their trip, and it worked. The woman at the wheel called her friends over and the three of them steered, they were thrilled when they ventured over a large swell and their screams of happiness made the two men smile.

After retaking the wheel, Andy called Yoates over. "I been sailing these waters for a few years now and the only time I experienced swells this close to land, a storm was brewing, only I don't see any clouds. What do you think?"

Yoates realized immediately that Andy wasn't kidding. He took a moment to look around at the waves. "Could be a storm out east here," he responded. "We should be okay for now, but it might mess up our chances of seeing any whales."

Andy agreed and he called the women over to explain to them why their whale-watching trip might be a bust. He suggested they try their hand at fishing, or he asked them if they would like to put into a different island, maybe hit the shops.

The women were disappointed at the news, though they did appreciate his honesty. "We didn't bring our passports on this trip," one of them said. "How could we shop?" The other two nodded at this.

"Hey, Yoates and I aren't novices, we're Navy SEALs, we've been trained to slip into enemy lands and scout positions, so if you want to hit some shops, we'll manage, or if you want more of a challenge, how about trying your luck going after some big fish?"

The three held a hurried conversation. They agreed that they could shop anytime, but deep-sea fishing, that was something none of them had done before and they chose that.

"Crewman," Andy called, "break out the gear. We're gonna try our hands at some deep-sea fishing."

~~~

THURSDAY, 16 SEPTEMBER

Drew called Milly and asked if he could visit her at her section, and since her project was now complete, she could only wait to learn what, if any, changes needed to be made, she told him that she was free and to come on down.

When she saw him approaching, she put her coffee cup off to one side even though there were no papers on her desk now and looking toward her team saw Eileen give her the thumbs up as he arrived at her desk. During her team dinner the other night, Milly had enjoyed cocktails with her co-workers before eating and since she spent a lot of her time at work, this was her chance to make some friends. The dinner did just that, and she found that her co-workers were pleasant and understanding people; they made her feel wanted and appreciated and she felt she made connections. Since that dinner, she had accepted invites to group lunches and some morning coffee with different people something she didn't tell Drew, but her most important connection had been with Eileen, whom she learned was widowed and had two grandkids, though they lived far away, and she missed seeing them often.
~~~

Because of this, Eileen became sort of an ad hoc mother for her and the two developed a strong friendship. Last night, in fact, Milly had invited Eileen over to see her apartment and the two of them sat on her balcony, which didn't offer the greatest view since it looked upon older houses on the next street, but the night was warm, and the alcohol led to some intense conversation.

That was when Milly admitted that she was starting to have some concerns about Drew, his treatment of others kept coming to mind and then what had happened at the block party, explaining how Drew had acted there and how she learned through a phone conversation with her mother a few days later, that her father didn't find him charming at all. That was something of a shock to her as he generally liked most people, and finally, the impression he had made on her friends. She kept mulling these things over in her mind, remembering a statement from Andy, when they were kids. How he said he just ignored rude comments from his friends about her first year in school and didn't hang with dumb people who had made fun of her.

Then Drew arrived at her desk, obviously excited about something. She put on a smile she didn't feel and looked at him, noticing Eileen in the background as she elbowed another of her team members and pointed in their direction. That didn't help matters as she tried to concentrate on Drew. He was talking about a hotel their company was going to establish on an island. Her mind instantly concentrated on the hotel, connecting his arrival at her desk and mentioning it, probably meant he was going to ask her to help design some of the rooms. This could be her chance to really show what she had been preparing for all those years in college and what she had been working toward after accepting a position with the company, accidentally drowning out what he was talking about.

She came back to the conversation when she heard his question. "So, what do you think?"

"Oh, that sounds good," she responded, not really knowing what he had asked but deciding to try and bluff her way through the question.

"Good. I think it's a great idea as well. Let's say, we pack and head out there next week. I can book a plane whenever we're ready to go."

"I'm sorry," she said. "My mind drifted for a second. What were you saying?"

"That's understandable," Drew said, a big smile on his face. "I'm sure you don't often get an invite to a tropical island."

Milly was startled, wondering what he was talking about. She hated lying and thought she could turn things around a bit, her mind quickly reviewing the best way to respond. Absently, she began playing with her necklace, which she did when she was trying to think. "Let's start things over. What about this island?"

Drew let out his breath, obviously annoyed at having to repeat what he already said, so he just cut to the chase. "Our company purchased a hotel in the Caribbean, and I wanted to take you there to look at it and get your opinion. Do you want to go with me, or not?"

Milly was startled at the question. "Yes, I suppose I can, but we've just started a new project and we'll be breaking into groups next week. How much time do you plan on spending there?"

"I just told you, and why do you keep fiddling with that glass necklace? I want you to come with me to the island to view the hotel, and don't worry about the project, you can start it and I'll just assign it to someone else next week. I know my mother will be okay with us going. So, do you think you'll be ready to go by next Friday?"

Milly looked at him for a second. "I suppose so. Do you mind if I bring the project with me so I can work on it there? How long do you think we'll be gone?"

Again, that annoyed look from him. "How will you be able to enjoy the island if you're working? Just leave it here and we'll be gone three or four days, maybe. Who knows, if we're having fun, maybe longer. Believe me, you'll enjoy this trip."

Milly looked over at Eileen who was shaking her head as if to say no, but she didn't have any valid reason to do this, plus she had never been to the Caribbean. "Okay, I guess I can ask one of my friends to do my job, at least until we get back. That okay?"

"Perfect, that will give me time to make all the arrangements. I'll plan everything, just make sure you take that cute little bikini you wore to the ocean last month. I liked that," Drew said, a mischievous smile on his face.

"I'll bring it. What's the forecast for the Caribbean?"

"Who cares, we'll have fun either way. I'm sure of that." And when he finished, he gave her a kiss in front of everyone, much to Milly's chagrin. She told him she didn't think it was appropriate in front of her co-workers, but he ignored her concerns, again.

As Drew left, she noticed he was singing to himself. Either this trip really excited him, or there was something he wasn't telling her. In a flash, Eileen was at her desk. "What was that all about?"

"He wants me to accompany him to the Caribbean to view some future hotel sights, and I guess he's really excited about it," Milly said, somewhat dejectedly.

"I thought you told me you were having second thoughts about staying with him?"

"I was, but it's the Caribbean. I've never been there, and it might be fun to see it once, especially if I'm not able to go again in the future."

"You go, girl. What island are you going to?"

"Wait, I don't know. You heard anything about any new hotels our company bought there?"

Eileen went to the desk of one of their team members, talked to the one guy who handed her some papers, which she promptly brought back to Milly. "Charlie said these are the new acquisitions," she said as she started to view the new properties. "Wait, here. This must be it. It's the only foreign purchase I can see. It's on the island of Martinique."

"Martinique. Wait, I've heard something about that. My mom was telling me the other night about my old boyfriend. He has something going on there. Wouldn't that be funny if I bumped into him again? Oh, Drew would be so pissed."

Chapter Twenty-Two
Plans

Through meteorology, we know essentially how hurricanes form, even though we can't say where the next storm will arise—Eric Maskin

SATURDAY, 18 SEPTEMBER

Andy was finishing his second beer with Yoates and Yolette at a small bar on Antigua, waiting for their guests to finish shopping before heading back to the Virgin Islands. They had taken a charter with two families, sailing from the Virgin Islands to Antigua for the day. Yolette commented after arriving that it must be nice to have money, to which Andy reminded her that it was people with money that kept them in business and the trip had been short and without drama. "Hey, just enjoy it. I for one am having a good time," he related.

The people they had encountered on the island were pleasant, though it seemed everyone thought that all Americans had money and they had to push past dozens of vendors who tried to hawk all sorts of items, from alcohol to CD players, things they were not interested in. They just found a nice bar and were enjoying the music and everyday commotion on the streets, watching with interest the number of tourists.

"You know, if we can find some place to advertise here, we might be able to book additional charters for any clients who want to visit, and instead of drinking, we can take others out for short cruises," Yolette said, looking at the two of them.

"We do okay," Andy said defensively.

"Yes, but you said yourself, you'd like to make more money. The Munck should have some updates in technology and maybe an overhaul. It's been like four years of constant use, right?"

"You're beginning to sound a lot like my old crewmate," he said to her.

"You mean, Barbara?" Yolette asked.

"How do you know Barbara?" Andy asked, totally shocked, she knew anything about her.

"She called this morning while you were piloting the boat and I answered your phone," she responded. "Who do you think gave me the idea?"

"I should have known," Andy answered.

"I'll head to the Munck now and talk to the dock manager, see what I can set up with him," Yolette said, gathering her things.

"You sure you can get his attention?" Yoates asked from his seat.

"Oh, don't worry about that. I have ways of getting a man's attention," she replied.

As she left, Andy looked over at Yoates. "You okay with her doing this?" Andy asked.

"Yeah, I trust her. That woman can handle herself," Yoates answered. "I met her about a year ago when I first came down here through a friend," he said, raising his eyebrows, though he didn't elaborate. "She was working as a cocktail waitress at a pub on the islands. She didn't care that my head was messed up, like so many others. She was just so honest and sincere, and I knew then that she was the woman I wanted to spend my life with," he related, acting a bit somber. "Besides, I think she's just trying to get back at me for the other day with those women on the boat."

Andy chucked at that. "Could be, but I knew you two had a connection. Just don't do anything to blow it, she's a keeper," Andy replied, echoing the words of Finn.

~~~

Over the Sahara Desert, the high heat of early fall had stirred up large windstorms which blew sand and dust all around, affecting the lives of people in Libya. Nomads were forced to take cover as the sand beat at humans and animals alike, the strong winds blowing against their tents and scattering those items which had been left around their camp. The winds continued heading west, causing small sandstorms to disrupt the lives of villagers around Zawilah, or Taraghin as well. The winds kept moving slowly west, collecting more energy in the heat as they moved toward the west where it would build even more strength within the next three days.
~~~

Chapter Twenty-Three
Martinique

Life is full of surprises—John Major

FRIDAY, 24 SEPTEMBER

The plane landed at the airport on Martinique and Milly was glad she had dressed casually, removing her sweater, and enjoying the heat as they departed. She followed Drew down the commercial aircraft steps and after collecting their luggage, they headed to the hotel their company had purchased. Once they were in their room, Drew had booked only one, after raising a fit when he was told the suite was not available; they checked into a spacious room on the second floor of the five-story building.

"The first thing I'm doing when this hotel is officially ours is firing that front desk person. Did you see how she treated us?" Drew stated in a fit of rage.

Milly shook her head. "She was nice. We didn't reserve the suite, but she found this room for us. Look around, it's beautiful," she said. "I can see some things we can do to make the place bigger, like getting more modern furniture, but the layout is very good."

Drew smiled at this. "You're still working, even in the middle of paradise. One of the reasons I really enjoy…being with you."

Milly noticed the pause in his comment, where he stumbled through the 'being with you' part. She was glad he didn't say 'love', that would have been so awkward for her, and the fact they would have to sleep together now didn't lift her spirits much. She decided to put it behind her, realizing why Andy was so enthralled in visiting these islands. *Damn, I'm doing it again, dreaming of Andy*, she thought. *This trip is going to be so hard.*

After checking out their room, the two headed down into the casino portion. "Drew, you never said this hotel had a casino," Milly said in surprise.

160

"Well, it does, but we won't have control over the casino, just the hotel portion," he responded. "Too bad, it would be fun to be able to risk a fortune and not have to worry about it if we lost."

"Where would the thrill be with that?" Milly stated. "The joy of gambling is the fear of losing. Without that, well, it just isn't as exciting."

Drew smiled, "Maybe you're right, but if this place brings in a lot of money, maybe I'll convince my mother to try and purchase it, or at least buy stock in it. Look at the amount of security cameras. No way anyone could rip this place off," he stopped talking, staring at something before turning away and focusing on Milly again. She noticed the forced smile but wasn't sure what it was that upset him.

After reviewing the hotel and the grounds, Milly asked if they could visit the center of Fort de-France Bay. She wanted to see how the people lived, to catch the flavor of this island. Drew agreed and soon the two of them were wandering the city, meeting the inhabitants, and generally having a good time.

Looking around, Drew could see the number of obvious tourists, which meant the hotel had been a good investment. He did notice other casinos, but their new acquisition, he was told, was an older building with a lot of history. It had been a jail for a short time and then an army barracks, and almost everyone he encountered knew something about the place. Milly was more interested in visiting a place she had never been to before. The room layout, at least in their room, seemed fine and any changes would have to involve doing extensive work on the walls and ceilings, which she felt would damage the flavor of the rooms and the hotel.

Wanting to see more of this land, they rented a car to take them around the island, stopping by small farm stands or small family-run restaurants, sampling the flavor of the country. When they stopped by a small farm, Milly played with some of the baby sheep. She picked one up, hugging it like a small child and Drew said she would make an excellent mom someday. He almost blew his secret when he mentioned her being a mom, but her look stopped him from his saying his wife. He wanted to keep the secret a bit longer, taking short videos and photos which, he thought, would be fun to show her and his mother after they had been married for a few years.

He thought of Victoria, his old girlfriend whom he had dated for almost a year in college, but just before graduation, she broke up with him, not knowing much of his background since he never talked about his mother or his life. She called him immature and shallow, worried more about money and prestige than in helping others. Drew was shattered by this and withdrew from others, wanting only to be successful so he could rub her nose in it. He kept track of Victoria a bit, following her on Facebook and Twitter and the more she did, the angrier he became.

Then he met Milly, her beauty captivating him. She was down to earth and he knew some would have told him she was out of his reach, but he made it his mission to win this woman over. She had, what his father would have called, Moxie, if he had survived, but he died in a car crash when Drew was only twelve and his mother took over. Not that she did much for him, she was always working, running the business she had inherited, increasing it, telling Drew all her hard work was for him, whenever she left him with nannies or babysitters.

Victoria had said he was too callous to find a nice woman and to him, Milly was just that person to prove Victoria wrong. She was attractive, hardworking and understanding. Even with the mistakes he made, she seemed to forgive him, though he wanted to ensure she took his ring before he would feel secure enough to let her do things on her own. That was why he worried so much at that, so-called party. More like a barn feeding frenzy, he thought it. Food undercooked, wimpy serving plates, the attitude that the people around him believed they were his equal. Please. Mostly, he didn't like Milly's father and he so wanted to see his face when Milly showed him the rock, he would give her. It was almost two full carats and had cost more money than this whole visit, but he felt it would be worth it. Milly was a great lover, caring, and she excited him more than any other woman. He had to, as his friends in college used to say, plant his victory flag on her, and that was what he was going to do.

This tour of the island allowed him a chance to determine how to ask her, finding out from the locals the best restaurants on the island and what was the most popular drink. As she moved from store to store, he watched carefully to see which items seemed to catch her interest most, a particular type of hat, or a nice pair of earrings. He joked with her a bit, knowing she was totally unaware, getting the impression that this was simply some sort of review of the hotel. Personally, he didn't care what they did with it, redo it, gut it and start from scratch, he was just excited, as was his mother, to finally be considered an international corporation. And if Milly wanted to be responsible for designing the rooms, or in the redecorating, he would make that happen. Her work was good, but she was going to be his wife and he was treading carefully, not wanting to scare her any, when she realized she would be a part of his family, entitled to more than she had been.

When Milly returned to their car after stopping at a local stand to purchase some fruit, he smiled at her, asked her if she was having fun, and of course she said she was. She just wanted to know when they would be getting back to the hotel so she could take some measurements. Drew just smiled, "Don't worry, we'll have plenty of time for that," he replied, as he put the car in gear.

~~~

Mark Thompson, Andy's dad, fancied himself as a junior meteorologist and he had equipped his den with some of the tools of the trade, barometers, thermometers, and a weather app that allowed him to keep track of weather around the world. He looked over his weather announcements, having been tracking a strong Low that had come off the African Coast a couple days ago. That Low had been building strength and was now a tropical depression. He knew the warm summer waters in that part of the Atlantic would probably help this depression grow into a nasty storm.

Grabbing his hurricane map, he marked off the location, listing the Low and its wind speeds. He had to admit this hurricane season was only getting started and it looked like it was going to start off with a bang. Local weather stations had been mentioning their worry that the Atlantic waters were so warm and how it might create stronger storms this year. It was only the latter half of September and hurricane season would continue into November. He wondered if Andy was aware.

~~~

SUNDAY, 26 SEPTEMBER

Andy was aware of the increased activity in the Atlantic, getting updates on his phone from the National Weather Service and since they were back on Martinique, updates from the Meto-France, the French Meteorological Service. Yolette had even recorded events on the way to this island again, knowing they had to keep alerted to anything that might interfere with their business, which was doing well, but Andy was a bit concerned with the growing tropical storm. The Low had intensified quickly, becoming a tropical depression in only a single day and now a tropical storm with the name, Genova. Forecasts had predicted it would soon become a level one hurricane as it was over very favorable water. The biggest concern for most was its future track. Less than a thousand miles away, some tracks had it moving through the northern part of the Caribbean which meant trouble for the Virgin Islands, but little by little, the track was beginning to look like it would hit the central Caribbean, which meant Martinique, possibly.

Andy and his friends were on Martinique because another charter Yolette had booked wanted to sail from Antigua to Martinique to check out the casinos and do some shopping. Andy looked at her and shrugged, as Yolette stuck her tongue out at him. "There will be no living with her now," Yoates said.

"I don't know how she did it, but she only talked to the dock manager last weekend, and we get a charter from Antigua to here. The woman scares me," Andy admitted.

Normally, Yolette would have remained behind to work in the office, but since she had set this charter up with the dock manager, Andy wanted her to come along to make sure there were no problems and to help with their clients, two doctors and their wives. If she could impress them, Andy thought, he might be able to get some good referrals for future trips.

To get an early start, the three had sailed from the Virgin Islands to Antigua the night before, sleeping on the boat with a quick ocean swim to freshen up before their guests arrived. When the two doctors and their wives arrived early, the Munck crew were ready, having hot coffee and Croissants, which Yolette baked in the tiny oven just before they arrived, on hand for their guests to enjoy. Then they took off and headed to Martinique where they arrived only a few hours later and docked.

After their guests departed, Yolette left to purchase some snacks for their return trip while Andy and Yoates headed to the casino. Walking in, the first thing he noticed was that it seemed less crowded than the last time he had been there. Yoates kidded with him, pointing to the photos of the investors which were displayed prominently near the entrance. He pointed out that Andy looked so distinguished in the borrowed jacket the casino had loaned him for the photo. Andy ignored him and walked to the security office, chatting with the people there and seeing how well the system he had invested in was working.

With that done, they went to Fort de-France to meet up with Yolette at a local watering hole they had discovered the first time they had been there and which they enjoyed, getting there only a few minutes later to find Yolette sitting at a table waiting for them.

"Did you two start gambling, or something?" She asked. When both said no, she replied something about them slowing down with their old age. That set Yoates off and for several hours, they discussed everything from the sea to the shore, a saying Andy had picked up from somewhere, as he sat watching a TV set up in the corner of the bar. The language was French, but it was about the approaching storm which was now eight hundred and fifty miles away and moving steadily in their direction.

Andy looked at his watch and then at his friends. "Guys, we need to think about heading back to the Munck."

Yoates looked at his watch as well. "Really, Andy? Our clients booked a six-hour shopping tour and we only left them about two and a half hours ago. They've still got three and a half hours left. What makes you think they might be ready to head back to Antigua now?"

"That," Andy replied, using his thumb to point over his shoulder at the TV.

Yoates was about to question him when he noticed many people paying attention to the storm. In fact, while he looked on, several more people entered the bar and were watching the news as well. Then he saw two tourists get up from their table, pay their bill quickly and hurry out.

Yolette grabbed Andy's arm. "You might be right, Andy," she said, looking at the number of people now moving a little faster down the city streets. "Let's finish our drinks and head back to the boat. If we're wrong, we can always enjoy a fresh cocktail on the Munck."

Andy paid the bill and the three headed toward the street behind him, almost crashing into Andy when he came to a sudden stop. "Now what?" Yoates asked.

"Thought I just saw someone I know," he said, as he quickly started heading up the street.

"Who?" Yoates asked.

"I told you about Milly, right? I thought I saw the guy she's dating. I know. Why would I see him here of all places?"

"Was Milly with him?" Yoates asked, looking around. He knew what Milly looked like from photos Andy had shown him earlier.

"No, just him as he got into a taxi. Hey, maybe he's following me," Andy said, jokingly, but he was almost certain it was Drew. At the party, Andy had looked him over carefully and was now certain it was him, but he didn't see Milly anywhere. If Drew was following him, Andy would take care of it, then he hurried along to catch up to his friends who were some distance ahead of him. Twenty minutes later, they reached the wharf and Andy's instincts were right on. Their guests were standing near the Munck, one of the wives looking over the bulwark and calling inside the boat.

"We're here. What's up, guys? We weren't expecting you back for three more hours," Yolette said. It was agreed that if their clients were there waiting for them, Yolette would be the one to interact, having a way of disarming people and making them feel more comfortable.

"Good thing we brought her along this time," Yoates said under his breath.

"We? I suggested it," Andy offered. "Her beauty is disarming."

Yoates looked at him. "You watchin' my woman?"

Andy smiled. "Not like that, big man."

Yoates tapped him on the arm, "Just messing with you, brother. I know you're honorable."

"You're a dick," Andy said, watching as Yolette was helping the people on board and gave the squiggly wave with her hand to let them know he was right.

The two walked up and climbed on board. "What's up?" Yoates asked.

There was one man who seemed to be the leader. He looked at Andy and asked him about the storm. "You haven't heard about that bad storm coming this way?"

Andy went to his cabin and pulled out the meteorological warning sheet he had checked as they arrived. "That big storm you're referring to just became a tropical storm this morning and it's almost a thousand miles away. Plenty of time to prepare for it."

The man handed Andy his phone. "When we booked this trip, I added that app to my phone, you know, to keep track of all storms and the like. Wife is scared to death of hurricanes. That says the storm isn't that far away and it's now a Cat One hurricane."

Andy looked at the phone, then showed it to Yolette and Yoates. Handing the phone back, he went to his small weather station and sure enough, unexpectedly, the storm had quickly been upgraded to hurricane status. Depending on the track, the hurricane could do severe damage to any island it traversed. Already, Andy noticed some boats pulling away, more than usual. Word was out and some of those with more-timid resolutions, were leaving now.

"Well, the clients want to leave, we leave," Andy said, as he pulled the anchor ropes from the dock and placed them on the deck. "Yoates, go forward to the pulpit. So much water traffic here, I want you to keep an eye out for boats near us. Yolette, please serve drinks to our guests and keep them comfortable until we're out of the harbor and can get under sail."

Once on the open sea, Andy noticed the number of boats which were sailing in every direction except east. With Yoates now on the wheel, Andy looked over the storm track with his guests. "Still kind of up in the air, but more computer models are suggesting a track through the central Caribbean. Hard to pinpoint exactly, but this hurricane, depending on how strong it would become, could do damage on a wide scale. You might want to wrap up your affairs on Antigua and prepare to evacuate if need be."

"If it hits Antigua, how bad would it be?" One of the wives asked.

"It depends on the strength of the hurricane," Andy responded. "A Cat One will have winds in excess of seventy-five miles per hour, and it would be more a nuisance than anything. Some downed power lines, some minor damage, things like that. Cat Two more damage and an increase in the storm surge, the amount of water it pushes forward. They can be bad. Anything over Cat Three, get out any way you can and as soon as you can. Those things are lethal to anything in their path."

"I've already looked into booking a flight out of the islands," the woman's husband said. "All the airlines are booked solid and you're saying we don't even know where this storm is heading yet. Why the rush to leave?"

"You remember Hurricane Anette two years ago, right? And the damage it did to Cuba and then Mexico. That was a Category Three storm. Genova is different. It formed just a couple of days ago and it's already at hurricane strength. Worse yet, look at the weather map here," Andy said, holding up the recent print out. "There is not much to interfere with the development of this storm, no sheering winds, just hot air and low pressure. That's a breeding ground for this storm. People remember the damage Anette did and they're not taking any chances."

"Well, our plane tickets aren't for another eight days. What do you recommend we do?" The husband, whose name was Roy, asked.

Andy thought about it for a moment, then asked the couple to wait a second while he talked with Yolette and Yoates. A moment later, he came back to them. "My crewmates have a home in the Virgin Islands, and they need to secure it first. But if you help us get their place ready for this storm, we'll sail you out of danger, no charge," Andy said.

"What about our stuff at the hotel in Antigua?" The other doctor, Sam, asked.

"I'm sorry, but it's too dangerous to clear out your stuff. Call the hotel, ask them to secure it and if this storm misses the island, you'll be able to come back later and collect it. If it does hit, it won't be there. We need to get to the Virgin Islands, and if you help my friends get their place ready, I'll sail you out. I mean, there is a chance this monster storm will change direction but if it doesn't, then I'll sail you all to Florida and you can catch a flight from there back home. What'd ya say?"

Accepting the advice, all four agreed to assist and Andy put on a little more sail, a way of double rigging to gain a bit more speed. It wasn't safe, but he felt speed was more important now. Every minute they saved would be an extra minute to get something done and there was always something more that had would need to be accomplished. While negotiating the sea, he put in a call to his parents using a satellite phone his parents had given him as a present when he was last in Aurora.

"I've been tracking that hurricane," his father told him after their greetings. "Gonna be a monster. Is it anywhere near you?"

"Yeah, Dad, it is. We're making plans to leave the area. I have some clients aboard. We just left Martinique and we're sailing to the Virgins to get their stuff and then they said they would help us get some of Yoates and Yolette's stuff in the islands second. After we're done with that, I'm sailing them to Florida. All the airlines are already booked, and I figured I'd bring them along, keepem safe."

"So, you'll ride out the storm in Florida then?" His father asked.

"Thought I might head up to see you and mom with a buddy of mine and his girl, stay a day or two while we're waiting for the storm to pass. If that's okay with you and her?"

"You're welcome anytime," Mark replied. "I'll let your mom know that you might be coming up."

"Good to hear, Dad. I'm at sea now, but if you hear more about the storm, contact me on this number, it's the satellite phone you gave me."

"I've got it, Andy. Take care," he said before hanging up. He looked at his wife, "Looks like that storm might drive your son home. He's in the track, so he might sail up here for a few days."

~~~

Hurricane Genova continued to strengthen though its course was a bit erratic, some meteorologists describing it as a drunken sailor. In a bar in Puerto Rico, an old sailor watched the news and listened to the meteorologists without emotion for a few minutes. A man sitting on the bar stool next to him leaned over. "What do you think, Finn? Is it gonna be bad?"

"Finn lifted his beer to his lips and took a swallow. The weathermen are wrong. Ol' Genova is just playing with them. She's doing a little dance. Once she gets her nerves up, she'll come right through the middle of the Caribbean, like some monster," Finn told him.

"Think we're safe here?" The other man asked, probably remembering Hurricane Maria years before.

"Hard to say, have to see which way she starts tracking first, that'll tell us a lot about her direction," Finn answered, taking another swig of beer. "I gotta make a call."

~~~

It took most of the day for the Munck to reach the Virgin Islands and immediately, the group worked to secure Yoates and Yelette's condo. Valuable papers were placed in a large safe on the bottom floor, which was big enough for everything, while their guests taped the windows to prevent their being smashed by flying debris. With this done and facing a time crunch, they headed back to the Munck.

As they hurried to the boat, Roy helped Yoates roll a large wooden chest on wheels down to the Munck. "Tell me, Yoates, what exactly is in this box? It's damn heavy."

Yoates looked at him and smiled. "Trust me, this container has stuff I couldn't part with. Important stuff," Yoates answered.

Roy looked at him. "I know it's probably got something I don't want to know about. Fine, another question. I heard someone say you're a Navy SEAL. Why aren't you serving still?"

Yoates stopped pushing and pointed at his head. "Little gift from Al Qaeda that I picked up in Africa. Kind of made me medically unfit for duty and left my head like this."

Roy walked up and looked at his scalp. "Did you know I'm a reconstructive surgeon? I've been able to repair worse damage. When this storm is over, you come see me. I can improve your appearance."

"Doc, I only get a small military allowance once a month and I work for another SEAL who lost his leg in an accident. I couldn't afford any sort of medical surgery for what I'd need."

"Didn't your fellow SEAL say, 'Quid pro quo?' Far as I'm concerned, you get my partner and our wives back to Florida safely, I'll make sure you get the necessary treatment. No charge. Of course, you'll have to fly to my office in Chicago for it. Ever been to the Windy City?"

Yoates almost picked the doctor up. "Doc, I went through basic in Chicago. Let's get this ship packed and you'll be seeing my ugly mug before spring."

"Great, I'll plan on it. So, back to my original question. What's in this trunk?"

It was late afternoon when they put to sea once more, Andy saying they would reach Florida sometime tomorrow night or early the next morning, depending on the ocean was in turmoil and the going difficult. Dozens of craft were on the water with them, all heading northwest, seeking to get away from the approaching hurricane. They had a couple of near collisions and only a quick reaction by Andy at the helm kept the craft apart. Thankfully, the other skippers knew the rules of the sea, turn hard to port and the boats were able to miss each other, barely.

Andy knew that panic was setting in and he remained on alert while keeping track of the updates. As he looked around, he had this strange feeling, he wasn't sure why, just that he suddenly felt like he needed to remain in this area. It was a feeling he couldn't explain or shake, so while piloting the Munck, he called several airports in Dominican Republic finding that there wasn't any turmoil there. He was able to make reservations for his guests at the Arroyo Barril International Airport located just off Samana Bay and told his crew they were headed in that direction. Now, to convince his guests that it would be best if they landed there and they flew back to the US, leaving himself in a better location for some reason he couldn't understand; just that it was important he remain.

Chapter Twenty-Four
Trapped

The most difficult thing is the decision to act, the rest is merely tenacity. The fears are paper tigers. You can do anything you decide to do. You can act to change and control your life; and the procedure, the process is its own reward—Amelia Earhart

SUNDAY 26 SEPTEMBER: EVENING

Drew was enjoying his third iced cocktail with Milly in the hotel bar, having spent most of the day swimming. The place was not as busy as he would have thought. "Hey, bartender," he called out. "This place was busy last night. I didn't think Sunday night would be such a downer."

The bartender, a young Polynesian looking woman looked at him. "Usually, it's busy, this is a vacation spot, but most people are out because of that hurricane," she said matter of fact like.

"What?" Milly asked. "Hurricane. What hurricane?"

"It's Geno or something like that," the girl answered. "Anyway, the French Agency of Weather is following it carefully," she responded in perfect English.

"Are you an American?" Drew asked, noticing how shapely she was.

"Yup, but I've always been fascinated with the islands. Came here one day last year and fell in love with the place. I don't know what all the commotion is about. It's just a lot of wind and rain," she said as she replaced the glass of Bourbon of an older man at the end of the bar.

"What do you think of this hotel?" Drew asked, trying to change the topic to calm Milly.

"I like it, kind of quaint. Heard it got sold though. Hope the new owners aren't jerks,"

Milly had to stifle a smile at that but began looking at her phone for updates on the weather, it was set for Charleston, so she was updating her location and listened as the bartender, her name was Odome, as she told them how she had been born in American Samoa, but her parents moved to California, and she loved seeing new places. Reminded Milly of Andy again, so she stopped that by asking Odome what she thought of the coming hurricane?

"I don't know. I've never been through one. Lot of people here say it isn't a big thing, just batten everything down and store some food and water and before you know it, the storm is over and it's back to life as usual," she said casually as she wiped down the bar with a nasty looking cloth rag.

"Isn't that a health code violation?" Drew asked, looking at her rag.

"Who are you, the cleaning police?" Odome asked as she slung the rag over the shoulder and went to fill some more drinks for the few customers there.

Milly debated calling her parents only because Drew was constantly telling her to make her own decisions and live her own life, not her parents. It bothered her at first, but going against her gut feeling, she decided to forgo the call, for the moment at least, but she started questioning herself when they walked down the hallway and passed several of the hotel's guests making their way to the front desk carrying their luggage.

"Are all these people checking out because of the storm?" Milly asked.

"Looks that way. The wimps," Drew responded. "Don't they realize the safest place to be in any hurricane is a solid building like this one? It was built over sixty years ago. It'll be safe here."

"I don't know, Drew," Milly said. "I just heard one couple discuss the tract of this storm. It looks like it'll be really strong and it's coming this way."

"Oh, Mill, trust me. We purchased this building, and we had engineers review it first. They said it was one of the best built they found on this island. I still think the storm will turn and we'll be able to enjoy this place with fewer people."

"That's good news, I guess. What did you learn that makes you think the storm will turn?"

"Just a hunch. Believe me, if I thought it would put us in danger, I'd be out of here in a heartbeat," he replied smiling.

"You mean, *we* would be out of here," Milly corrected.

"What? Oh yeah, sorry. *We* would be out of here," Drew said with a smile as they reached their room. "Look, it's time for supper. Let's go to the town and get something to eat. We can relax, enjoy a great meal, and see what develops."

Milly noticed the strange smile he had, like a child who had just done something good and was waiting for their parents to figure out what it was. She didn't know why, but it gave her the chills, so she decided to change the subject. "Where did you have in mind to eat dinner?"

"I took care of that already. It's all set. Wear something nice," he said as they entered their room and he walked to the closet.

Once there, he looked back at her, glad that she seemed oblivious to his plan. This night was going to be as special as he could make it. He had made reservations at one of the island's best restaurants earlier, doing it right after they had returned from their earlier jaunt, not letting on that he was rushing his plans a bit. He had hoped to stretch this stay out more before he brought up his proposal, but when he almost gave away the surprise a few minutes before and knew he had to accelerate his timetable, especially after he saw Andy as they were getting in the cab. Thank goodness, that ass hadn't called out as Drew rushed Milly into the cab before she spotted him. It would have ruined everything. It was like fate was challenging him.

As Milly went into the bathroom, Drew pulled out the small box and looked at the engagement ring he'd purchased the day before they left and hoped his rushed timing would still work. Then he thought, it wouldn't matter, Milly loved her job, loved him, though she hadn't used those words yet, and he had taken her to their newest location, a beautiful island in the middle of the Caribbean; who cared if a damned hurricane were to hit? What damage could it do? This evening would be theirs.

Milly entered the bathroom bringing her wardrobe with her. She pulled out a nice dress, then thought about it. No, the dress wasn't right. If Drew was going to offer her the chance to take charge of this location, she wanted to be wearing the right clothing, so she pulled out a smart pant suit and opted for flat shoes, instead of heals. As she changed, she phoned her mother, wanting to let her know she was fine, and they had reached their hotel on the island of Martinique. Her mother was suddenly upset, saying there was a bad hurricane moving in that direction. Milly calmed her down, saying how Drew had selected a very good hotel that had strong walls and he said it could withstand a hurricane easily.

Her father got on the phone with her then, telling her to keep track of the storm if she could and to evacuate if things got bad. "Right now, it's only Category One, but it's projected to get stronger," Ned said. "It's only about seven hundred miles away but that's the eye. It's getting large, so keep your phone with you and if it gets bad, I'll call you. And be careful."

This news left her a little shaken, but she decided there was still time to listen to Drew's proposition, since the storm was still seven hundred miles away and moving around fifteen miles an hour. So, doing some quick calculations, she estimated it wouldn't arrive for two days and if she could get Drew to spill his secret early, she could try and convince him to leave by tomorrow, especially if the storm kept on its track. Walking out of the bathroom, she was shocked to see Drew dressed in a tux. "Is that what you're wearing?" He asked.

Milly, realizing she might have misjudged what Drew had in mind, decided to keep her suit on as she was growing more annoyed with him. Inside her head, a voice was screaming at her to just tell Drew they needed to leave now and with a few minutes to spare, she turned on the TV and looked at the storm which covered the screen. The announcer was of course speaking in French, but it appeared the projected course change had it missing the island and possibly tracking south. Not good for St Lucia, or Barbados, but possibly sparing Martinique.

Drew watched the news with her, and when he saw this, he smiled and turned off the TV. "See, nothing to worry about. My hunches are always right."

The voice in her head was still screaming, but she ignored it and agreed to accompany him to the restaurant. The two walked down the stairs and found almost total bedlam in the main lobby as dozens of guests were now clamoring at the check-out trying to cancel their stay and find rides to the airport.

"Damn fools don't realize the hurricane is moving off," Drew said with a silly smile on his face. "People see a little trouble and panic. Come on, let's enjoy this night."

With no cabs available, they opted to walk to the restaurant, allowing them to enjoy the night.

<p style="text-align:center">~~~</p>

Six hundred and seventy miles away, Hurricane Genova was gaining strength and speed with each passing mile. Its eye wall was formed, becoming more distinct, allowing astronauts on the International Space Station to see it as they passed over the Atlantic. They relayed this information on its size to ground personnel. What they noticed most was the size of this storm, it was rapidly becoming a monster and measuring almost four hundred miles in diameter and its speed was increasing slowly. It was now heading in an erratically west-southwest direction.

~~~

Milly and Drew entered the restaurant that Drew had chosen especially for this night. Located in the heart of Fort de-France Bay, he'd been told that was the most romantic restaurant in the city and he was pulling out all the stops. Milly began to realize this wasn't a job offer, seeing little clues that led her to believe he meant something more. The wink from the doorman at their hotel. The smile and nod from the Maître-d who knew both Drew and Milly's name. This on an island, Drew had admitted never having been on before. Warning bells began to ring in her head, not only from the dangerous storm that she could see on every television over the bar, but the way the night was going.

They were promptly seated off to one side and drinks appeared quickly on their table. Milly grabbed hers and took a long pull. She saw Drew smile and kept wondering what he was thinking, and it was beginning to bother her. "Look, I don't know what you're planning, but we need to concentrate on the hurricane," she said, pointing at the television screens near the bar. "Look at it. There is a possibility it will come at us here. We really need to think about leaving. The sooner the better."

Drew looked at her calmly and smiled. "We've already had this conversation. I would never put *our* lives in danger. Even if that hurricane does turn, all I need to do is call my mother and she'll have the company plane fly down here in a couple of hours. Now that we have that out of the way, I wanted to ask you something important, something that will affect both or our lives" Drew tried to say, but Milly ended his statement.

"I want to know something first," she said to him and waited until he nodded to continue. "Is this trip to let me know I will be handling the redesign of this hotel?"
~~~

Drew started to laugh a little. "No. What gave you that idea?" He asked.

"You, coming into my office, announcing our company had bought this hotel and you wanted my opinion. Opinion of what? To me, it sounded like you wanted me to accompany you to let you know what I thought about the hotel, whether it was worth the cost, or something," she answered now getting miffed at his constant smile. "If it's not about the hotel, then why did you drag me out here when you knew I was worried about this approaching hurricane?"

"I wanted you to come here to ask you to marry me," Drew responded, now miffed himself.

Milly opened her mouth in shock. Never in a million years would she have guessed this, and she didn't want it. Didn't want him. She just wanted to leave this dangerous area. "Drew, we've only been dating for a few months and then there's this big acquisition. If I said yes to you now, people would think I agreed to marry you to get promoted. Your own mother might even think that. I'm sorry, this is the worst time to ask me, and now we're facing a hurricane. Were you serious about getting a plane in here to evacuate us?"

Drew was out of his element here. He had planned this trip down to the last item and only rushed it along when he had seen Andy. Now, Milly had said no, and he was wondering if it was because of him. It had to be. That bastard was ruining everything. "Are you telling me you don't want to get married now because it's too soon, or because you saw your old boyfriend?"

Milly's mouth opened. "Andy? What has this got to do with Andy?" She stared at him for a moment waiting for him to reply.

"Never mind, I thought you were thinking about him and not us. I realize your concern about the storm is probably clouding your thoughts, so I'll call right now and order that plane. With luck, it will be here in less than three hours," Drew said as he began to dial. A few seconds later, he was talking to someone on the other end and ended with, "That will be fine. Yes. The main airport here. We'll be waiting," he said, ending the call and looking at Milly.

"Are you happy? The office said the storm is probably heading this way, but it won't be here for at least thirty hours and by then, you and I will be safely back in Charleston."

Milly smiled at him. "I know this wasn't the kind of night you wanted, but you must understand. We have a dangerous storm coming at us and we're in the middle of a new acquisition. If I'm correct it will be the first international purchase for our company. Right?"

Drew didn't seem as happy as before. He finished off the last of his drink and just replied, "Yes."

"Give me time, Drew. I have too many issues in my life now."

"One of them being Andy," he said smugly.

"Andy? What the heck are you talking about? It has nothing to do with Andy. I haven't talked with him since the party and you made it pretty clear then that you didn't like me doing that, so I haven't had any contact with him since then," she responded, getting angry now.

"And his being," he stopped here for a second. She obviously hadn't seen him and if he mentioned that he did, she would get even angrier, so he took a second and changed the topic. "Never mind about him then, as far as I'm concerned, he doesn't matter to us."

"Why do you keep talking about him then? Let's just drop it and start getting ready for the plane," she responded. She tried not to let on that she wasn't interested in becoming his wife, in case he decided to leave her here and fly home alone. No, best to keep him thinking there was a chance and once they were safely back to Charleston, she would tell him it was over.

Ending dinner abruptly, they luckily found a taxi and headed to the hotel, and they both noticed the sky filling with clouds. They quickly collected and packed their belongings and as they began to head back to the lobby to check out, Drew's phone rang and when he answered it, his face fell. He looked at Milly for a second before hanging up and telling her that the plane had a mechanical problem and would be delayed until 9 a.m. tomorrow.

Milly got that creepy feeling up her spine. She had only come on this trip because she thought she was going to be given the chance to prove herself, and now they would have to put off their return until the morning. The storm was still out at sea, but if it increased its speed or changed course toward them, their departure might be cutting it close. Milly returned to their room and turned on the TV. The storm was now Category Two and expected to intensify, and Milly's fears were realized, as the track had changed once again, now moving toward the central Caribbean. It was expected to make landfall in Martinique on Tuesday.

"Maybe we should try and book a different plane out of here," Milly said. "Just in case."

"No, why? Our plane will be here tomorrow morning. Relax, I know the captain, he's a reliable man. I've flown with him before. Let's just make the best of it here and we'll leave plenty early tomorrow morning, a whole day before the storm hits. I promise."

Milly didn't know what to think. Her first instinct was to just run to the airport and try to get out on the first flight she could find. Drew could see this and did his best to calm her down. He took her down to the lobby where they spoke to the hotel manager. The manager didn't seem upset and said this old building had survived several hurricanes, one a Category Three and they had come out alright. Then Drew took her to the barroom where they again met with Odome, standing behind the bar.

She sat with them as the bar was almost empty, most people having fled the island, or were busy preparing to leave. Milly attempted to calm down, to try believing that Drew was correct, but that damn voice was in her head, only now it was saying to call Andy, ask him what she should do. She pushed that voice down, but told herself, if one more thing went wrong, she would call him.

Drew did what he could to relax her, still confident that they would depart the island before the storm, which was now heading once more toward Martinique. Odome had asked if she could join them at their table, even if it was against hotel rules. No one had come to the bar in hours, so was sure the hotel staff would not see her. She related to them both that several of the hotel staff had not reported to work today, obviously making plans to flee, or trying to prepare their homes for what was going to be a difficult couple of days, at best.

Odome admitted she also was growing concerned. Living alone in a small apartment near the beach she knew if the hurricane hit, her home might be lost, so she brought her most important possessions to the hotel for safe keeping. What bothered her most was the attitude of the locals, how they feared the coming storm, something she hadn't expected. And their fear had transferred to her, only she was stuck here not having enough money to buy a place ticket out.

Drew told her about the company plane coming in the morning and if she wanted, he would call her to fly out with them. That seemed to help her mood a bit, and she offered the two of them any drinks they wanted, on the house. Drew of course accepted and though Milly was still worried, the two of them pressured her to accept as well. Milly and Drew finished their drinks and Odome kept them coming, the alcohol slowly diminishing their fears. When it grew late, Odome suggested they head to their room to get some sleep, and the two groggy patrons agreed.

On their way to their room, Drew had to help Milly negotiate the stairs, and when they reached their room, he collapsed on their bed. Milly watched him fall asleep, but before she fell asleep herself, she made her way to the balcony and stared at the sky, which was now overcast. She so wanted to see the stars, feeling if she could see them, it might have calmed her down. At that point, she looked up the heavens and asked Andy to help her.

~~~

After having arrived at the Dominican Republic, Andy did what he could to make his guests' trip through customs as easy as possible when they departed the Munck. The customs people in the city were gracious, knowing that they would soon encounter a huge flood of people fleeing the hurricane. Now, with his guests on their way, Andy told his crew that he planned on remaining in the area, though he couldn't say exactly why he felt it was necessary, just that it was.

Yoates and Yolette didn't question his feelings, he was the captain and would do what he thought best. They convinced him to join them for dinner and all three sat watching TV at a small seaside café about the hurricane which was continuing to gain strength and heading right at Martinique. Andy suddenly looked at Yoates, who was sitting beside him. "What?" He asked.

Yoates looked at him. "I didn't say anything." They looked at Yolette and she just shook her head.

"I could swear I just heard someone say my name," Andy replied. He stood up and looked around seeing no one, which gave him the creeps. Then he grabbed his phone and called his parents, his father answering almost immediately.

"Hey, Dad," Andy started. "How are things with everyone there?"

"We're okay. What about you?" His father asked.

"We just arrived in the Dominican Republic," Andy replied.

"Are you still coming up to see us?"

"Not sure. I've been thinking I should stick around for some reason."

"Some reason, huh? Is Milly with you?" His father asked and Andy's face fell.
~~~

"No, why? Where is she?"

"Oh, I'm sure she's fine. Just that she called her mom the other day and said she was flying to the Caribbean. Not sure what island, but her mother said she was okay. That was before this storm. Her mother said she isn't answering now, but it could be because of the hurricane."

Andy knew. It was Milly's voice he had heard. "Dad, do me a favor. Try to find out where she is and if she's safe, then let me know," Andy said.

"I will, Andy. You be safe and stay away from that storm," his father said, but Andy wasn't listening.

"Guys let's make ready to sail," he told them.

"We don't have many provisions on board," Yolette said. "Where are we going?"

"Not one hundred percent sure, but I'd say Martinique," he replied.

Chapter Twenty-Five
Monster

The fishermen know that the sea is dangerous and the storm terrible, but they have never found these dangers sufficient reason for remaining ashore—Vincent Van Gogh

MONDAY 27 SEPTEMBER: Early Morning

The Munck was currently east of San Juan, Puerto Rico, having left the Dominican just after midnight, the rising sun greatly highlighting the cloudy sky. As he piloted his boat, he remembered an adage he had heard as a child, *red sky at morning, sailor take warning'*. Yeah, it was clearly a warning of a monster storm. He relayed to his crew his belief that Milly was somewhere in the Caribbean, and how he had a hunch she was on Martinique and needed help.

Yolette said that was romantic, Yoates just shrugged and said he was ready. The wind was mostly against them, forcing Andy to use his sails carefully, supplementing it with the outboard at times. He wasn't sure what he would do when, and if, he found her, it was just that Finn's words kept coming back to him, 'find her and marry her'. The only problem was the island itself. If she was on Martinique, where would she be, or how would he find her. Yoates told him he had only visited portions of the island a few times, mostly the casinos and bars; Yolette visited even less, so it would be up to Andy to try and find someone who could lead them around the island.

He put these thoughts away for the moment and concentrated on the challenges facing him, not only reaching Martinique but avoiding the hurricane and dangerous conditions it would create. He was sitting there wishing for his phone to ring as he waited for the call, and when it came, he almost jumped. Using his satellite phone, Andy picked it up, hoping it was Milly. Instead, it was his father.

"Just wanted to let you know, I talked with Milly's parents. They're a little nervous since they haven't been able to reach her. Not sure why. When they do, they know to ask her where she is and how she's doing. I'll relay that information to you, when I get it. Where are you?"

"A bit east of Puerto Rico and we're moving that way, but the winds are making it difficult. The weather here is overcast, obviously because of the hurricane, but as soon as it clears, we'll head southeast, check on my crew's home and assess any damage, then see what help we can offer people."

"Well, remember, be safe and don't take chances," his father said. Andy agreed and hung up as he looked up at the sky. "Come on, Milly, let me know where you are," he said quietly to himself.

~~~

Milly woke up to someone pounding on their door and looked at the clock. "Shit, the power's out," she shouted. Quickly, she rolled over and realized Drew was still sleeping in his clothes. She dug her phone from her luggage, noticing that it was turned off. She had been too drunk last night to notice it. She turned it on and watched as the phone displayed the information she wanted. It was 8:27 a.m., Martinique time, and then all the missed messages from her parents. She shook Drew awake, cursing herself for drinking so much. If she hadn't, she would have seen the messages and they would have been at the airport by now even if they had been forced to walk. They needed to get moving, now.

"Hey, we overslept. Get up. The plane will be here soon," she said, as she moved off the bed and grabbed her luggage. Drew got up and looked at his phone. "I can't believe we overslept," he said, holding his throbbing head. He agreed with Milly that he didn't want to spend another night here, especially with the storm now possibly hitting them. There was more pounding on their door, but by the time they got there, no one was around.

"Might have been Odome, but she's not here now," Drew said when he opened the door. Milly looked out and walked past him toward the stairs. The two headed quickly down the steps and found the lobby deserted. That was disturbing, but what bothered Milly most was there no staff at all. Not one person was on duty. She looked at Drew and they hurried outside, finding the streets deserted as well and now it was raining heavily.
~~~

"How are we going to get to the airport?" she demanded.

Drew tried to act cool, suggesting it would be easy to get a taxi now, but after a minute or two of waiting, not one vehicle passed their hotel. While Drew called the airport, Milly called her mother back, her parents picking up on the first ring.

"Mom, it's me."

"Oh, Milly," her mother said, almost in tears. "Where are you now?"

"We're on the island of Martinique. Drew insisted we wait for the company plane. It's supposed to be landing here soon. He's talking to someone now about it. Have you heard about the storm at all? "There's no one in the hotel to ask," even as Milly said this, she knew things were bad. The rain was coming down in sheets and the wind seemed to have a strange forcefulness. It scared her.

"Oh, Milly. The hurricane is now Category Five and it's moving faster. It's supposed to hit your island sometime later today. You must get out of there now."

Milly looked at Drew, he had this stupid scared look on his face, staring at his phone. "What is it?"

"The airport, the plane went down. Some rescue crews are trying to reach the spot now, but the waves are incredible. It's too dangerous to leave the island now. We're being told to shelter in place," he said.

Milly swore at him before talking to her parents again. "Mom, Drew says we're stuck here. I'll keep in contact with you as long as possible. Say a prayer for me. Drew said the hotel was strongly built and it should stand up to almost anything."

Milly's dad got on the phone now. "Milly, find what shelter you can. This hurricane is a monster and will do a lot of damage. Remember, it's not only the winds but the storm surge. How high up is this hotel?"

Milly knew that one, having learned it from the bartender last night. "It's on one of the highest spots in the city, say about sixty feet above sea level and our room is on the second floor."

"Good," her father said. "That will have to do, but if you see water around the hotel, get to a higher floor. How many floors are there?"

"Drew said there were five."

"Good, I wish you hadn't turned your phone off, we've been going crazy trying to reach you."

"I didn't, but I have an idea of what happened. Look, we've got to get to shelter, I'll call you back when we're safe," she said, before grabbing Drew and dragging him inside. Once there, she grabbed her phone and held it to his face. "Did you turn my phone off?"

He babbled a reply. "Yes. I'm sorry. I didn't want that guy Andy calling you when we were at dinner. I just forgot to turn it back on."

"Andy? Why do you keep bringing up Andy?" She looked at him for a moment, even though they were both dripping wet, she suddenly realized Drew was obsessed with Andy, but why?

"He keeps showing up, keeps interfering in our lives," Drew responded, extremely angry.

"What are you talking about?" Milly demanded, totally confused and angry herself.

"You're saying you didn't see him yesterday in the city?" Drew stopped and looked at her with angry eyes. "Or his poster in the casino?" Still angry. "I also heard you mention his name in your sleep. Is he the real reason why you said no to my proposal?"

Milly looked at Drew like he was crazy. "Andy's here? On this island?"

"Yeah, his picture's in the casino. Guess, he's got something to do with security."

"Don't you understand," she stopped talking when a large surge of air pushed in one of the patio doors. They both moved over and closed it, pushing the couch in front of the door to keep it closed and the rain out. "If Andy's here, he might have a way out for us."

"I hadn't thought of that," Drew said. "Call him."

"I don't have his number anymore, remember? You made me erase it. I'll call my parents and have them get it for me."

There was a tremendous flash of lighting, and the hotel shook as if hit by something. The air itself feeling electric. Milly tried her phone, it had power, but wouldn't connect to any numbers. "Shit, I don't have any service. I think that blast knocked out the cell towers," Milly said.

Drew tried his phone; it wouldn't connect either. Now, cut off from any outside assistance, the two could only hunker down while Hurricane Genova, a Category Five storm, moved toward their island. The main portion of the storm was still many hours away but the amount of rain and wind it caused forced everyone to seek what shelter they could.

The Munck was in trouble as well, when a larger ship, named the Jasmine, came out of the fog and rain right at them. Yoates saw the boat coming at them first and hit the emergency klaxon, sending out a high-pitched whine alarm out. The Jasmine's skipper heard the alarm and spun his wheel, but instead of turning it to port, which was the accepted course for ships about to collide, the approaching ship, for unknown reasons, turned to starboard and collided with the Munck, slicing into the side of the smaller Munck near the bow. The much larger metal ship did not even attempt to slow down as it cut the bow off the Munck causing catastrophic damage.

Instantly, the Munck began to fill with water, giving Andy little time to grab a few items and assist Yolette who had been thrown to the deck when the Jasmine sliced into the side of the Munck, just forward of the spot where she was sitting monitoring the weather system. Suffering cuts and bruises, as well as a badly wrenched ankle, she was barely able to get up the steps as the galley started filling with water and she needed help getting in the life raft which Yoates had inflated and thrown over the side, holding it steady while his friends climbed onto it. Then he grabbed their emergency electric outboard and handed it to Andy before climbing aboard as well. To their utter amazement, the Jasmine, only slightly damaged, pulled away, leaving the three of them stranded in rough seas and heavy rain.

Yoates screamed to the skipper of the Jasmine, whom they could barely make out on the bridge that he had better find a deep hole because he was going to find and make him pay. That captain just threw the finger. Andy looked at him. "Feel better?"

"Not really," Yoates replied.

"Administer some aid to Yolette while I make a call," he said, pulling at his old backpack, reaching down and pulling small items out. Finally, Yoates saw him pull out a small notebook from the pack and begin going through it. "Here it is," he said quietly, while grabbing his satellite phone from the water-proof case he had grabbed before helping Yolette onto the life raft.

"I was wondering why you were so calm, considering that bastard just left us stranded in the middle of the Atlantic," Yoates spoke loudly to be heard above the storm around them. "Facing a fucking hurricane."

"Shit, this battery is almost drained. I probably won't get more than a couple of calls before its dead. I'll make only one call, save the battery in case we need it later," Andy said.

"Good idea. Who you callin', the Coast Guard?" Yolette asked, as Yoates attempted to apply ointment to her cuts which was difficult in the rough seas.

"No, someone much worse. I've had this number for a long time and swore I would never use it unless hell froze over."

"Well, I guess this means that hurricane is hell," Yoates said loud enough for him to hear, as Andy worked his satellite phone.

It was difficult, holding the pad tightly with his left hand and using his pinky finger to push the buttons as he held the phone in his right. He let out a 'Yes' when he successfully placed the call. A second later, the line was answered. "Finn. Where the hell are you right now?" He asked, as they all watched the Munck slowly turn on its side, even as the waves continued to batter it, then the boat pointed its crushed bow to the sky and sank beneath the waves.

Chapter Twenty-Six
Danger

The purpose of life is not to be happy. It is to be useful, to be honorable, to be compassionate, to have it make some difference that you have lived and lived well—Ralph Waldo Emerson

Andy managed to use the small electric outboard to pilot them to the closest land, an island called Outer Brass in the British Virgins which they could just barely make out in the rain. Uninhabited for the most part, the raft was tossed and almost collided with rocks until Andy was able to get them into more calm waters along Rover Point. Landing on a tiny beach, they huddled together in the open as wind and rain tore at them until Finn arrived almost four hours later in a larger powered boat, having left the harbor at Roosevelt Roads and when he showed up, Andy was almost ready to kiss the old fool since their phone had died as he was giving Finn his exact coordinates, allowing him to find them.

Finn shot a line out to them which Yoates grabbed, and they pulled themselves along it to the boat, which caused Andy to smile a bit when he saw the name, Munck Too. As he climbed up the metal ladder along the side, he guessed that this was why he had just given Andy the Munck. *Sneaky bastard,* he thought. When he got up on deck, he gave Finn a hug and the three filled in what had happened. He also said he needed to check with home and find out about Milly.

"That the girl you and I talked about the last time I saw you?" When Andy nodded, Finn gave him his phone. "This is fully charged. Just hit star 2, that's your mom's number. I just talked to her earlier."

"You've been talking to my mom?" Andy asked. "What about all that stuff about staying out of her life and all?" Andy asked, not sure if he was impressed or pissed off.

"Easy, slugger. I only called her when this hurricane came around. Don't know why, but somehow, I just knew it would affect you in some way."

Andy smiled at that then called home. His mother picked it up. "Finn?"

"No, Mom, it's me," Andy replied, wondering what she was thinking when he heard only silence.

"I guess Finn found you," she said, more of a statement than a question. "How is he doing?" He could hear the nervousness in her voice, which made him wonder if Finn had been telling the truth about talking to her only about the storm.

"Yeah, we're okay, but we lost the Munck," Andy told her.

"Finn told us after he heard from you. I had no idea he was near you. He said everyone is okay. Are you coming back home now?" She asked.

"Depends. Do you know if Milly is alright?"

"No dear, I'm sorry. The last we heard from her mother she was staying in some hotel on that island. Something to do with redesigning it. They haven't had any contact since. If we hear something, we'll let you know, but what will you do? You've lost your boat," his mother was so concerned for him. "How would you help her if she's so far away?"

"No idea, Mom. But she's a pretty tough girl. Keep in touch with me. I guess Finn is taking us back to Puerto Rico and we'll regroup there, decide what to do. I'll talk to you later, Mom. Bye," Andy finished his conversation then joined his friends and Finn.

"Last my mom heard, Milly was somewhere on Martinique, but it's a big island and she might have gotten evacuated, so we'll just let it go and deal with our own problems. Speaking of which, how are you holding up, Yolette?"

"It's sore, but I'll live," she answered. "Ben says it's bruised, but I can walk on it, if need be," she responded using Yoates first name, meaning she was more concerned than she was displaying.

"Finn, think you can sail east a bit more, get us closer to Martinique if she needs help?" Andy asked.

"Aye, Aye, Captain," Finn said, turning the wheel slightly and plotting a course north of Anguilla.

~~~
~~~

TUESDAY 28 SEPTEMBER: Late Afternoon

The past twenty-four hours had been terrible for Milly and Drew. Even before the storm wall passed over, a small coconut tree had been torn from the soil by the winds and was sent crashing through the window on their balcony, allowing rain and colder air to invade their room. They ended up spending most of the storm huddled in the bathtub with blankets and could only listen as the storm grew in intensity and tore the hotel apart. With no electricity, or Wi-Fi, they had no way of charging their phones or of contacting anyone. Worse yet, at one point, Drew had walked down to the main lobby looking for someone to talk to, or some food. When he spotted water from the bay being pushed down the street in front of the hotel, he knew this storm was unlike any other to hit the island.

Thankfully, the water had receded after the eye passed over the southern portion of the island that evening. While looking for food once again, Milly discovered a flashlight and they could move around a bit without groping in the darkness, but neither of them could find any food. Finally, as the storm abated, they moved quietly downstairs to see if any hotel staff would show, but once again, it was silent, except the bar. There was a lot of commotion coming from there, some yelling and what sounded like a nasty fight. They decided to avoid it and wondered where Odome was. At this point, Milly explained to Drew that they needed to find food somewhere, even if it meant venturing from the safety of their room and walking around the outside of the hotel. Drew didn't want to do this, but then realized Milly was right, there was no telling how long it would be before help came and they would need food.

They ventured outside the hotel, seeing the devastation all around them as the sun finally rose above the carnage. Pieces of furniture, boxes, toys, and mud, everywhere there was mud. It made walking difficult. Many times, they slipped, Milly even fell in a mud puddle. All they could do was stand under rain gutters and let the dripping water clean them off. It didn't help much, but they were soon in the area they had been this morning; the place was devastated, it was hard to even determine what some buildings were, let alone what they might have sold. In spots, there were just piles of scattered rocks with other items mixed in. It was as they stood in this destruction that they heard their first gunshot.

Milly dropped and took cover, Drew did as well, trying somewhat to protect her. They were both scared when someone began screaming and then a loud BANG, and silence. Quickly and as quietly as they could, they got up and headed back toward the hotel trying desperately to gain a purchase on the road, so they could walk faster, but the damn mud made each step hard. Milly pumped her legs until she thought she would collapse and suddenly there was the hotel. It looked better than some of the buildings they had been to, and Drew had been right, Milly realized. The stone walls of the hotel had withstood the hurricane, but they discovered part of the interior was in shambles as they entered the hotel through a different door.

Here, they saw how the huge glass dome in one hotel hallway had shattered inward, collapsing three chandeliers into a sitting area, crushing plants and decorations beneath them and allowed the rain to create huge puddles. They hadn't seen that when they exited earlier. As they made their way back to their room, they had to walk though almost a foot of contaminated water filled with all sorts of debris. Not good for Milly since she was wearing open toe shoes. In their room, they tried the faucets and some water dribbled out allowing them to wash their faces before resting on their luggage.

As Milly opened her bag looking for a clean shirt, she found an unopened bottle of water and they were able to slake their thirst. Milly then put on a clean shirt and wiped the mud from her feet before putting on her only pair of sneakers. She was still hungry, and she needed food, they both did. Once more, they decided to look, but they would stay inside the hotel this time. They didn't want to go outside again and face the madness. Drew followed Milly down the stairs, though his heart wasn't in it. They checked the lobby office and rummaging through several drawers, Milly found three candy bars. Drew made out even better, finding a half empty bottle of Rum and a box of crackers. Grabbing these treasures, they retreated to their room and sat down to enjoy the first food they had had since finding some fruit the day before.

As they sat there, Drew suggested checking the staff lounge. If any staff were around, they might have gone there. Milly agreed and together they slipped down the wet and slimy stairs once more, turning off toward the lounge which was before the lobby. They had almost reached it, when Odome came sneaking out, having seen them, and signaled at them to be quiet, then quickly joined them.

"Where were you this morning?" She whispered when she reached them.

"We'll talk in the room," Milly replied. "Do you have any food?"

Odome held up a small cloth bag and told them it would be safer to return to their room. The three made it back safely and once there, she collapsed on the floor. "Stay away from the bar. Bad people there, really bad. I'm glad they didn't see me. I knocked on your door yesterday and you weren't here. I thought you left without me."

Milly looked at Drew. "We kind of overslept and then we found out our plane crashed. We've been around the hotel and into the city. It's bad there as well," she said.

"I can believe that" Odome replied. "I left the hotel as soon as the storm slowed down. My apartment is gone. I mean there's only water there now. Glad I didn't try to ride out the storm there. I'd be dead."

"We heard shooting," Drew said. "People yelling and then shooting."

"I saw more than that. I saw men rob and assault people, also what looked like a young woman being raped." She then explained how she made her way to the staff lounge where she found some cheese and a bottle of wine. She handed them over. "Go easy on them. It's all I could find," she finished.

Milly looked at her phone. "If we could just make a call."

"Wi-Fi is out, but what about the communications room?" Odome said.

Both Drew and Milly looked at her. "What?" They asked in unison.

"The Communications Room, it has power and closed Wi-Fi, but it's a blocked system. Some security thing, only the hotel phones will work on it. Who could you call?"

Drew looked at Milly though he didn't say anything. She just looked back at him for a second before turning to Odome. "I have a friend who might be close. Don't know for sure. I don't have his number, but my mom might."

"What are we waiting for? Let's go," Odome said.

The girls left the room while Drew agreed to remain behind to keep the door closed until the girls returned. They had to move quietly as there were now more people venturing out since the storm had passed and the sun was up. Twice they ducked and let individuals pass them until they reached the room and Milly was able to find a working phone. She grabbed it and they were about to leave when there was some shouting and three quick gunshots somewhere near in the hotel. They both cowered behind a counter for a minute, then moved past the lobby, seeing a fresh body on the ground.

"He was a guest from New Zealand, if I remember correctly," Odome said, looking at the body. "He was a nice guy. We have to get out of here," she stated as she led the way, stopping only when they saw strange people standing near the stairs.

"They aren't guests?" Milly asked.

"They could be, I just don't want to take chances," she replied as they moved to a portion of the hotel Milly had never been in before. Odome seemed to know all the twists and turns of this old building and as they rounded a corner, they bumped into two men emerging from the stairs leading to the maintenance areas area under the building.

"Hey, what's your hurry?" One of the men asked, with a major French accent.

"Sorry, our friends are waiting for us," Odome said, trying to get by them, but the man reached out to grab her, as the other tried to grab Milly. Without thinking, she reacted, her Karate training as a child taking over. 'Girls have more strength with your legs, so don't be afraid to use them', the instructor's voice came back to her and she followed the advice, lashing out with her foot into the man's groin and as he moved to cover himself, swinging around with a foot kick and sending him to floor.

The other man paused a second, allowing Odome to grab a ceramic vase near the stairs and slam it over his head, dropping him next to his partner. The two girls raced up the steps then, stopping when they reached the second floor. Here they found two more people, a man and woman, who seemed to cower in fear as they approached.

"These are guests," Odome said, reaching down and touching the man. "Hey, Gerald. It's me and this is Milly. She's an American."

The man looked up, relief washing over his face. He grabbed the girl kneeling beside him who was so afraid she was shaking. When she saw Milly, she stood up. "Oh, thank God," she said with a slight Spanish accent. "There were men chasing us. We came up here and Gerald saw someone in the hallway, so we just kind of hid here."

"Was one of them a fat guy with a heavy French accent?" Odome asked.

"Yeah," Gerald said. "And the other guy was skinnier, dark complexion."

"We bumped into them," Milly answered. "Don't worry, they aren't going anywhere for a while."

"Gracias," the woman said. "I am Angelica. We have a room on the fourth floor but came down here trying to get some food. We didn't find any but saw a lot of people on the first floor. They didn't look like guests, so we were trying to get back to our room, when we ran into those two men and hid here."

Odome looked at Milly and shrugged, as if to say it was her call as to what to do with them.

Milly didn't want the added responsibility for them but it was obvious if she didn't help, they would be in serious trouble. "Come with us. My room is down the hall," she said, as she moved to the floor entrance door and looked out. This part of the hallway was clear, so the four rushed to her room and Milly had to bang on the door several times and call out to Drew before he opened it.

"Brave hero," Odome said quietly to Milly as they slipped into the room.

"What the hell, Drew?" Milly said after they had entered and shut the door behind them.

"What took you so long?" He asked. "While you were out, someone banged on the door and tried to get in. I had to yell at them to leave. I thought you were them coming back sooner, and who are these people?"

"Gerald and Angelica. They were being chased and we found them in the stairwell, hiding," Milly answered curtly. "This place isn't safe anymore."

Milly grabbed the phone they had taken and walked into the bathroom where it would be quieter, to call her parents, her father answering after a couple of rings. He was a bit gruff, thinking it was some spam call but when he heard his daughter's voice, he called the wife into the room. Suddenly, they could all hear banging on their door, and someone testing the lock.

"Go away," both men called, almost without thinking. "Good," Drew said. "Make them think we're only guys in here." Gerald nodded and began helping Drew pile more items against the door.

"Milly, are you alright?" Her mother almost screamed into the phone.

Milly let her parents know that things were not going well, that there were now more people in her room on the second floor and they were piling furniture against the door to keep anyone out. Her father told her to remain calm and do whatever she needed to for them to remain safe and that he would try and get her some help.

Milly explained how things had gone from bad to worse so quickly and that they had joined with other guests in her room for safety. He told her he would do what he could and to try calling back in about an hour for an update.

She agreed and hung up the phone, joining the others in deciding what their next action should be.

Immediately, after the call, Ned Richards called the US State Department while Mary called the US Coast Guard. Both were told that Martinique was a French Sovereign territory, and hence there was very little the US government could do. Both were told that they should contact the State Department or try and American Consulate there, but the area had just recently undergone major damage from Hurricane Genova, and it wasn't expected there would be much anyone could do for the time being. They were advised to tell their daughter to seek shelter and do what she could to book passage off the island. There was no sympathy for her plight, nor any good advice and finally Ned slammed the phone back in its cradle after an hour of no help.

He dreaded when Milly called back again, which she did about five minutes later, he had to relay the bad news. Milly said she understood and knew it was a long shot. What she needed now was the cavalry to come charging over the hill.

Ned asked his daughter to say that again, and when she did, he said she had given him another idea. When she hung up, he left the house and headed quickly to Andy's parents, his wife in tow having left their youngest with Tyler, Milly's younger brother.

The two held a quick conference with Samantha and Mark, explaining the problems and that they were desperate.

"What I need is to know if you're in contact with Andy, and where he might be?"

Mark lowered his head. "We are in contact, but there was an accident, the Munck sunk and Andy and some friends barely got off before it went under. They lost all their stuff. Why?"

"That was my last chance to help Milly. I thought if anyone could help rescue her from that island, it would be him," he said, lowering his own head and starting to weep. "She's in trouble and I'm afraid what could happen."

That was all Mark had to hear. "Hold on. Let me call Andy and see if he knows of someone who might be able to help get to her."

<p style="text-align:center">~~~</p>

Ten minutes later, Andy hung up the phone and looked at Finn. "Look, that girl you told me to grab onto and marry is in a lot of danger. The state department said they can't do anything and there is no one else to help. I know it's a lot to ask of you, Finn, but can I convince you somehow to help me rescue a woman who means more to me than my own family?"

Finn looked at him for a long moment before answering. "You know, Andy, I'm a little pissed that you would think you have to convince me to help her. Far as I'm concerned, we're wasting time. Oh, and when we find her, you better tell her how you feel, or I'll ask your big ugly friend to tell her. How would that go over?"

"You're an asshole, Finn. But thank you. I need to ask my friends to go along with me now," Andy said, walking down below where he found the two lovers sitting at a small bar that was on Finn's boat. They were holding hands. "Ben," Andy stated, again using the first name of his fellow SEAL.

"I told you, I hate that name," Yoates said. "What?"

He told the two about the danger Milly was in and that Finn had agreed to take him to the island to find her, explaining that his father had been told where she was. "Guess what?" He added. "She's staying in the hotel that's attached to our casino. How is that for coincidence?"

"Frigging awesome," Ben Yoates answered. They both looked at Yolette, knowing her ankle was swollen and obviously painful. She just waved their concern away.

"Who am I to stand in the way of true love? I'll be fine. Especially since we've found Finn's alcohol stash. Let's go and rescue her."

"Wish we had some weapons, hell even a pea shooter," Yoates said, sitting next to her. "I lost all my cool stuff when the Munck went down. Bet that doctor would shit a fit if he knew he helped me carry a lot of illegal weapons on board back in the islands."

Finn came into the galley then. "You want weapons. How about these?" He said, pulling back a small wooden board and removing two twelve-gauge pump shotguns, and two pistols, both.45 Caliber which packed a significant punch. "Think that's enough?" He asked, letting the men inspect the weapons. "I've also got enough ammo to start another brush war."

"These will work just fine," Andy said, then put a call in to Milly. The phone rang for some time before someone picked it up. "Who is this?" The strange voice demanded.

"I'm looking for my friend. Andrew. Is he there?" The phone instantly hung up.

"What was that about?" Yolette asked.

"That was the number my dad gave me. When she didn't answer, I figured she lost her phone," Andy said.

"Or that she was hiding and someone else found it. No sense giving the person reason to start looking for a girl, especially if things are as bad as Andy feared," Yoates finished the statement. "How long till we reach Martinique?"

Finn looked at his watch. "About four or five hours. It'll be getting dark by then. Let's just hope your lady friend can stay safe until we get there," he said. "I've got the engine full open."

Andy looked out of the ocean. "SEALs operate best at night."

Chapter Twenty-Seven
Rescue

Life is inherently risky. There is only one big risk you should avoid at all costs, and that is the risk of doing nothing—Denis Waitley

Just moments after talking with her parents, there was another knock at the door and this time whoever it was on the other side didn't back off when the men called out to leave. Instead, it sounded like someone was kicking the door. Odome looked at the balcony and moved quickly to it. Seeing no one outside, she got Milly's attention mentioning that the balcony was only about seven feet off the ground, they could jump to the ground and make their way upstairs through a service door that she had keys to. With no other option, Milly got everyone's attention and pointed to the balcony just as Odome dropped off the edge.

Milly grabbed Angelica who was using the satellite phone trying to reach her family and dragged her along. The guys were right behind them and quickly they all clambered over the railing and dropped to the ground. "Oh no," Angelica cried. "I dropped the phone."

"Too late to worry about it," Drew said as they all heard the door being smashed open.

Odome raced ahead of the others reaching and opening the service door, then waved to them to hurry. The four ran as fast as they could, oblivious to the shouts of the men now on their balcony. Once they were inside, Odome slammed it shut, informing them the door was reinforced and the men chasing them couldn't get in, before leading them up a service stairwell stopping at the fourth floor.

Checking the hallway again, they found it empty, and Angelica led them to her room, 442, which was in a little better shape. Odome explained how she had learned from the maids that this floor was empty except for a few rooms.

Milly looked out the patio door at the interior courtyard which was almost directly across from her old room. The men who had broken in were still there and were shining a flashlight around probably looking for things they could steal. As she watched, the beam illuminated the balcony where she saw the satellite phone laying there, her lifeline to the world, but it might as well be a hundred miles away. Worse yet, one of the men reached down and picked the phone up.

Drew had volunteered to try and go back to their room and retrieve the phone but now it was too late. Milly didn't even know he was standing beside her until he turned and went back to the door, helping Gerald pile items against it, just like before. They were too high up to jump off the balcony, so they were effectively trapped if they were found. All they could do now was wait as Milly wondered what her father would think when she didn't call back. *Damn, if only Andy were here, I wouldn't be in this mess*, she thought, and the tears finally came.

They would just have to stay where they were and hope her father had found the cavalry.

<div align="center">~~~</div>

Almost four hours later, the Munck Too anchored less than a half mile off Fort de-France Bay and Andy was ready to move to the island. Though injured, Yolette could still operate the boat, as Finn, Yoates, and Andy took the life raft they used when the Munck sank, to make the short trip to the island. Leaving Yolette with a pistol, the men took the remaining weapons after covering their faces with grease and put the raft in the water. To ensure Yolette was safe, the men worked out a signal, they would flash their light three times when they were on the water again, whereupon she would turn on the navigational lights to allow them to find the boat quickly.

"You ready for this, Finn?" Andy asked.

Finn just smiled. "I never told you, Andy, but your grandfather and I once did a land rescue of two pilots who went down off Panama. The two of us volunteered to rescue them as they were both injured and couldn't move very quickly. Enemy forces were actively looking for the pilots, but we got to them first and then all hell broke loose when we were heading to the raft, your grandfather got shot. I had to drag all of them back to the raft, administer first air and then paddle away from the shore. Panamanian military forces sighted us about a hundred yards out, but our destroyer opened fire at them with everything it had, and I got everyone back to the ship safely. That's why your grandfather and I were such friends."

"Damn, Finn, you sure are a complicated guy," Andy said, now watching the shore. "This shouldn't be as difficult, but we'll still have to be careful. Milly's room is 214, so when we get to the hotel, we'll assess the situation and decide what to do. Got it."

Both men agreed as they shoved off from the boat. On the way in, Yoates brought up some information. "This raft can only take six people off at a time, so we may have to relay them out. Don't want to swim in these waters, too many sharks out here," he added.

Andy looked back at his darkened form. "Great, sharks. Okay, we don't want to try swimming with them around. We'll try the relay."

The men weren't worried about making noise, since their life raft was painted a bright orange yellow, the idea behind this color scheme is to give someone in the raft a better chance of being spotted on the open ocean, and with no way to camouflage it, they just paddled as fast as they could saving the small engine in case they had to leave in a hurry. Andy paddled on the starboard side, taking in the complete devastation the hurricane had caused. There were large trees in the bay and even in the darkness, he could feel the change; mosquitoes no longer attracted to the lights were attacking all three men in the raft.

Suddenly, Yoates felt something hit his paddle and looked at the water. "Body," he said quietly, seeing that it was floating face down.

A sudden gunshot to their left caused all three men to pull their weapons but with no further shots, they pushed on and a few minutes later, reached the shore on edge of the city. They all saw the damage the hurricane created. Fires in several locations of the city gave off just enough light to make the place almost unrecognizable with the collapsed buildings, and Andy had to rely on the GPS he took from Finn's boat. What surprised him most was the darkness. On his first visit, the city was brightly lit at night, so it was immensely strange to see only shades of darkness, with only an occasional torch or flashlight briefly illuminating a section. Even without night vision equipment, the SEALs had been trained to use the darkness to their advantage.

Once on shore, they covered the raft under a blue tarp and placed some broken palm branches over that. It wasn't hidden well but was better than nothing, and in the darkness, they hoped it wouldn't be noticed until they got back from the hotel, hopefully with Milly. Finn and Yoates carried the shotguns, leaving Andy the pistol and all three carried the largest knives Finn could locate on the boat. Yoates complained a bit, saying he wished they had better weapons, but Andy just ignored the concern. Milly was in trouble, and he was willing to venture through hell itself to save her, following the SEALs mantra, 'never leave anyone behind'.

Less than fifty yards from the raft, gunfire and screaming off to their left made the men pause. Andy was satisfied with Finn's capabilities when he saw the man drop and scan the area, just as the SEALs did. Milly's parents were right, things were bad already and the hurricane had just come through the night before. Without the use of Finn's GPS which showed the streets as they were marked, it would have taken them a lot longer to locate the hotel. Andy led the way inside, finding the main lobby wrecked and seeing a dead body on the floor. Yoates did a quick check of the man's vitals and shook his head to signify he was beyond help. The three then moved cautiously into the hotel doing their best to avoid the items littering the floors, which wasn't easy in the darkness. They finally located the main stairwell and climbed to the second floor where they suddenly came under fire. As Yoates and Finn fired their shotguns, Andy dropped to the floor and returned fire at two men until they turned and ran down one of the hallways.

"Why the hell did they shoot at us?" Finn asked.

"I don…don't know," Yoates stammered as he slid to the floor, and in the emergency lighting, Andy could see the blood. He had taken a large caliber round to this right calf. Instantly, Andy started dressing the wound, using the small first aid kit they took off the boat.

"Man, you've got to learn to duck, big guy," Andy said as he finished with the bandage.

"I wou…would've, but I was covering your ass," Yoates said. He was stuttering, a sign he was excited.

"How bad is it?" Finn asked.

"Could be worse. It's through and through. Might need a transfusion later, but you'll probably be fine. Think you can walk?"

"Takes more than one bullet to stop a Sasquatch," Yoates replied with a strained smile.

"I agree," Andy replied, before walking to the corner and looking around. No one was in sight. He used his flashlight to shine on the room doors. "Hey, this one here is room 205. Milly's just down the hall," Andy said.

Yoates staggered up to him, the rear being covered by Finn. "Which way, right or left?"

The short corridor they were in had corridors to either side as well forming a T. He shone the light to the right seeing room 203. "I guess to the left." The three moved as quickly as they could, Yoates now in the rear and struggling to keep up. Andy paused for only a second at each of the open doorways and swept each room quickly, signaling the others each room was clear until they reached Milly's room. Andy held up his hand in a closed fist at one point and the other two stopped and got low, seeing how the door, like most of the others, had been smashed off the hinges and was now part of the carnage that was strewn about the floor.

Carefully, he peeked around the corner, using the flashlight sparingly. Seeing no movement, he stepped inside, softly calling out to Milly. Suddenly someone hit him on the side, pushing him to the floor. Afraid it might be one of the people Milly had in his room, he yelled, "US Military, stand down!" However, his attacker ignored this and knocked the pistol and flashlight from his hands and as he went to grab it, there was a single blast, his assailant flying to the side.

Andy looked at the entrance and saw Finn standing there, his shotgun smoking. "This Milly's room?"

For some reason, Andy didn't expect that question, but nodded in response as he heard Yoates calling from the hallway. The big man's leg was bleeding too much, and he had to slide to the floor once more. "Andy, you guys okay in there?"

"I'm good, buddy, just getting rid of some trash," Andy replied. There was no other movement in the room and Andy began checking for anyone else, or bodies, finding none, he dragged Yoates into the room. "She's not here," Andy said to Yoates. "Finn, check the balcony."

Finn moved carefully to the balcony and, finding it empty, walked out and looked around, but could see no one. He walked back into the room to check on Yoates and see what ideas Andy had.

On the fourth floor, Milly was kneeling on the balcony, almost directly across the courtyard from her old room. Things had been quiet in their new quarters for some time, and she had wandered onto the balcony to monitor the courtyard. Her position offering her a view of her old balcony and she could watch any developments without being seen by anyone outside and she kept watching the enclosed courtyard, for any movement.

After the men who broke their door left, she had seen a couple more people walking around the room looking for things. The balcony door of her old room had also been shattered during the hurricane, so she could see partially into the room. Then she heard gunfire inside her old room, and someone fell to the floor causing her to duck lower. Then she saw a man she didn't recognize walk out onto her old balcony and get low as he surveyed the courtyard. Even in the sparse light from the partial moon, she didn't recognize him but was certain it wasn't Andy, he was too pudgy.

Then from somewhere inside the hotel, she heard another gunshot. Things were getting even worse, the gunfire happening more frequently now instead of occasionally. There were a few more shots and then silence. She moved closer to the balcony when she noticed the figure on her old balcony suddenly rise and charge into the room. There was yelling, she was too far away to make out what was said, and it just as suddenly ended with a gunshot and the man she had seen tumbled to the floor. She stood mesmerized to the spot, now seeing a flashlight pass around the room.

There was the sudden sound of fighting outside the door to room 442, the room they now occupied, and she heard Gerald emit a shush, knowing this was to make sure they were quiet. Milly stayed where she was, crouched down on the balcony, scared, and praying.

In room 214, Andy looked around the room with his flashlight, knowing Milly would have remained here unless she was either abducted or been forced to flee. He had no idea where to look now, the shattered room door made him think she used the balcony to escape, but to where had she fled? Finn said he hadn't seen anything, but Andy wanted to check for himself and as he studied the far end of the hotel, his eyes moved slowly as he scanned the yard looking for some sort of clue as to where Milly might have fled to. He noticed movement, a couple of figures moving in his direction, and he shone the light on two people moving toward his balcony.

Instantly, a bullet banged into the wall to his side, coating him with plaster as Andy returned fire with his pistol. He flashed his light toward the two, showing he had dropped both assailants. He stood there a moment, staring, mesmerized to the spot, his first kills and though he had tried to prepare for this mentally, but the now still bodies were still a shock to him.

Finn moved beside him. "Get your shit together, Andy. You came to rescue your girlfriend and you knew this might happen. You good?"

Andy nodded. "Yeah, I'm okay. I saw movement, thought she might be out there, but it wasn't her."

On the balcony, Milly heard the shots and when the light shone, she saw Andy! Her heart skipped a beat. Andy was here and only about fifty yards away, but the fighting in the hallway on her floor was getting intense and a body hit their door, then a gun shot. She needed to stay quiet, to scream out his name would only bring trouble down on them, yet she had to find a way to contact him before he left.

She searched for something to flash at him, a light, something to throw, when she spotted a broken lamp on the floor. It wasn't heavy but she knew it might attract attention. Grabbing it, she threw the lamp into the courtyard as far as she could, and it shattered as it hit the ground. Instantly, Andy turned his light on the lamp. Someone had thrown it on the ground for no other reason except to gain his attention and he was sure she was close by. This was exactly what Milly had been hoping for, but she saw someone looking out from a window on the floor above her old balcony, she got down and waved her arms, as she tried to quietly call out Andy's name.

Andy turned around when Yoates entered the room dragging his wounded leg. "I heard more gunfire. We need to exfil, buddy," Yoates said to him.

Andy quietly pointed to the courtyard and Yoates understood, someone was out there. Leaving Finn to cover the entrance, the two men scanned the grounds, seeing nothing. Yoates followed Andy's light as it moved up the side of the building. Sweeping the third floor and still nothing, then Andy moved up to the fourth floor. They both saw a woman on her stomach waving at them. The light wasn't bright enough to show who it is, but when he shined it at the figure, they both sow something sparkle.

"Is that her?" Yoates asks.

"Not sure." Whoever it is, is trying to get our attention in a big way. She's not yelling, so there may be bad guys in her room, or else there's some other danger.

"What's she holding?"

"Not sure, a light of some sort," Andy answered.

"It keeps changing colors," Yoates said, throwing another quick glance behind them.

"Holy shit!" The thing was changing colors. The necklace he gave Milly years ago at the carnival, the one with a small light inside. "It's her, it has to be!" Andy flashed his light twice more at her and turned it off. "We've got to check. You okay if we leave you here alone?"

"Go rescue your girl," Yoates said to him. He smiled when he said, but either Andy didn't see, or was too preoccupied to respond. Instead, he grabbed Finn, and pointed at the far side of the hotel and Finn understood. Quickly, the two headed out of the room.

Milly saw Andy blink his light at her and she knew he was on his way. Unable to contain her excitement, she entered the room and yelled he was coming. The others tried to shush her, but it was too late. Instantly, someone began banging on their door again, as Gerald and Drew stood and pushed against it with their bodies trying to keep the door from caving in.

That room was on the fourth floor and across the courtyard, Andy thought. The quickest way up was the staircase just down the hall. There might be people on it, but it didn't matter. He took the lead and climbed the steps two at a time, glad that Finn was keeping pace with him and both keeping their weapons at the ready. Just as they rounded the third floor, they ran into trouble. Andy was still in the lead, so he engaged first, Finn coming up behind him managed to fire his shotgun at the second guy and winged him with the buckshot. It was a tangle of bodies after this, Andy grabbed the first man and pushed him to the floor, pulling his knife and stabbing his attacker while Finn kicked the feet out from the second man and then slammed him over the head with his shotgun several times. Both men stopped moving after a few seconds.

Collecting themselves, the two warriors moved to the fourth floor and when they saw the floor was empty, headed quickly toward the end of the short hallway as one. They looked in a room where the door had been busted open seeing two bloody bodies, a man and woman. There was no time to check on their condition as they both heard a lot of screaming coming from another hallway ahead of them. To Andy, it sounded like Milly, so the two finished their run, turned the corner and came face to face with bedlam. Three men were fighting in the hallway, a fourth man, Andy didn't recognize lay on the floor, but it sounded like another struggle was happening in the darkened room to their right. Obviously, a fight was being waged.

Leaving Finn to handle the three hallway combatants, Andy entered the room and in the emergency lighting, saw one man reach back and punch an Oriental girl in the face, only to have another girl jump on him. To the side, another guy had punched a woman and pulled her head up by the hair, showing her face. It was Milly and without pause, Andy fired a single shot, hitting the man in the side, then turned his gun on the other man, who had tossed Angelica off him, and Andy put a bullet in him as well. As the two girls looked on in shock, Milly got to her feet and grabbed Andy around the waist, hugging and kissing him. "You came. I knew you would. I've missed you so."

"Oh damn, it's him," Gerald heard Drew say, as they reentered the room followed by Finn holding a shotgun on them.

When Andy saw Finn enter the room with two guys, he figured it was safe. Giving Milly a kiss again, he told the others to follow him, after Milly quickly said they were friends who needed help. Andy didn't have time to question this, he just had them form a single line with Finn bringing up the rear. "Listen," he said to them. "There are several bodies on the way down. Keep your eyes glued to the person in front of you and follow me. We'll stop on the second floor; we have an injured friend there. When we collect him, we'll head to the ocean. Any questions?"

There were none, so Andy took the lead and led his charges down the hall. Just because he had cleared the way before, didn't mean their route was still clear. He knew others could have arrived and might be waiting, so he had to be careful, especially careful now that he had Milly with him. He stopped at the first turn, checking to see if anyone was there and spotted a couple at the end of the hall who had ventured out of their room. They were elderly and obviously nervous as Andy stopped when he reached them.

"Are you okay?" he asked quickly. "Do you want to leave this island?" He realized the absurdity of his question. These two elderly people were looking at him with fear; he didn't even know if they spoke English. However, the man said he was an American and he and his wife had become trapped. He asked Andy where he was going.

"I've got a boat, and we're heading for it. There is room for you to come along, if you want. We're heading to Florida, for a start, any takers?"

The man looked at his wife and nodded. "Let me get our luggage and we'll come along," he said, as his wife looked at him like she was mortified.

"No time for luggage. Just grab your important papers and we're out of here," Andy replied.

The man replied that they had their passports and money and wanted to come. So, Andy put them in the middle of the line. "Same instructions I just gave. This isn't a sightseeing tour. Keep your eyes on the person in front of you and don't stop unless I say so."

With that he led them to the stairwell, stepping over the bodies on the third floor. "Sorry, forgot about them. They attacked us on the way up. Ignore them," he said quickly as he continued down the stairs to the second floor, where he stopped. "You two guys at the end. Come with me. The rest of you, that man at the end is in charge. Stay here. We'll be right back," he said and headed down the hall followed by the two men had had chosen, Gerald and Drew.

Minutes later, the group saw him emerge with the two helping another injured man, a man dressed like Andy with a darkened face. When they rejoined the group, Andy led them down the stairs, stopping just at the bottom floor where three more men were standing. None of them was armed, and the group watched as Andy spoke to them, offering the same terms, but the men declined.

Finn took the lead, Yoates, helped by the two guys, was next followed by the rest. Andy took up the rear of the procession, keeping Milly by his side, the two holding hands. The group had to move quickly out of the building, but it was difficult with all the debris, and it took longer than he liked, the older couple having great difficulty in the dark. Outside, he could see more people moving around as they made their way down the ravaged streets. Andy tried to urge them to keep moving quickly, but it was impossible with all the debris and darkness. The two men holding Yoates were having difficulty as Yoates was now unconscious and they were carrying him. The elderly couple was out of breath and close to exhaustion, so he had them stop when they reached a cleared area to let them all take a break and catch their breath.

As the group dropped to the ground, Andy checked on Yoates. He was bleeding again, the bandage was saturated, and Andy knew the trip, even with the help of the two guys, was causing so much movement that the wound started to bleed more. Leaving Finn in charge, Andy told everyone to follow Finn's orders while he scouted the route ahead. It was still dark and unfortunately, the stars were now shining brightly, their soft light bathing the area meaning they would have trouble staying out of sight as more people had now emerged from their homes and other buildings. Andy wasn't worried about them, but rather the other kind, those who would use the clear night to pray on their fellow man.

He moved to a small cluster of buildings, some of which were damaged and found what he was looking for. The main door on one structure had been almost wrenched off its frame. Putting his pistol away, Andy began pulling and twisting at it, until he managed to pull it free from the building. He made more noise than he'd wanted and stopped to scan the area, but no one bothered to investigate the noise. When he was sure it was safe, he grabbed the door and made his way as quickly as possible back to his group, the darkness making it hard to see though he did find a ripped tarp on the ground and cut a large line of frayed rope attached to a grommet and then a second, shoving them into his pocket before continuing. He had only gone a short distance when he spotted the group, sitting where he left them. He handed the door to Gerald and Drew. "We're going to put Sasquatch on this," he told them.

Drew looked at him. "Sasquatch?"

"His SEAL team name. Here, I found some rope as well. We'll wrap this under the door and use it to carry him out."

Gerald took the rope. "This'll work, but we'll need two more people to help carry the door."

"I'll do it," Milly said, followed almost immediately by Angelica.

Andy waited till they were set. "We're close to our raft. Only about thirty yards or so. When we reach the water, you'll be transported to our boat in groups."

There was a gunshot close by. Then another and another. "Take off," Andy ordered, as he fired at some men with Yoates' shotgun, watching as the men scattered. Spurred on by the shooting, the group moved quickly, though several times they stumbled and at one point, Angelica dropped the rope she was holding and the stretcher with Yoates hit the ground just as they reached the spot where the boat was hidden. Milly checked on him when she realized he hadn't made a sound. Andy's friend was still unconscious from blood loss.

When Andy caught up, he started to apply his last bandage when shots rang out and one of the girls screamed.

Finn stood and began firing back, directing Odome and Gerald to uncover the boat and pull it to the water, while Andy finished his bandaging, he turned and in the gun flashes, saw Milly laying on the ground, blood flowing from her arm and rolling around crying in agony. He was out of bandages, so he grabbed his belt and decided to use it as a tourniquet until they were safely on the boat.

"My arm, Andy. It hurts," Milly said through her tears, clutching her left arm which was now bleeding heavily.

"The belt needs to be tight. I'll take it off once we all get on board," he told her. He knew, even in the darkness, that that amount of blood from an arm wound was serious and he needed to get her to the boat so he could dress would properly. Quickly, he picked her up and placed her in the boat with Yoates placed beside her, still unconscious. "You'll be okay," he said, trying hard to believe his own words.

She smiled at him. "I knew you would come for me. I knew it,"

"Milly. I was a fool. I'm not letting you go again. Do you hear me? You're going to make it through this and then we're talking more. You hear me? Don't die on me, girl. Do you hear me? Don't die. I need you. I love you."

Milly had closed her eyes, concentrating on the pain, but she opened her eyes when he said this. "I'm holding you to your words," she said with a smile. "And I love you too," she replied, then looked at Drew. "Sorry, Drew, I didn't want to hurt you, but Andy and I were meant to be."

Off to the side, Drew sat there listening. "Fuck 'em both. I don't need her. All I did for her and she tosses me aside," he said to himself, but loud enough for Andy to hear.

Once they were on the raft, Finn grabbed Gerald, Odome, and Drew and put them in the boat as well, telling them he needed help getting the wounded on board and he would return for the rest. When everyone was on board, Andy had the rest get low as they waited for Finn to return. Thankfully, the gunfire had tapered off and it was almost quiet. He peered carefully at the surrounding area, keeping alert for anything, but there was no further movement.

Ten minutes later, they could hear the raft engine. It was Finn returning for the rest of them.

Chapter Twenty-Eight
Rescue

You cannot swim for new horizons until you have courage to lose sight of the shore—William Faulkner

As soon as the inflatable hit the shore, Andy rushed the remainder of his group onto the raft, but as they climbed on, he spotted several more people heading their way, obviously attracted to the noise of the boat engine. Andy knew that if these new people were armed, it could be a difficult trip back to the Munck Too. He threw a quick look at the raft and saw it move back quietly, Finn obviously using the oars to push back but then it stopped, and Andy knew he had to do something.

He looked in their direction and said loudly, "Danger close, get out of here!" He was relieved when he saw the raft motor crank to full power and pull away, then he pointed the shotgun at the approaching people, some of whom were now running toward him. As he feared, a shot erupted from the crowd, obviously aimed at the raft and though Andy couldn't see who fired, he raised his shotgun and fired into the air causing the group to stop, some of them dropping to the ground.

"This is a US Navy rescue operation. Do not approach or you will be fired upon," he said loudly.

He was greeted by a series of shouts, like 'We need help as well', or 'Bring that boat back you ass, we need to get out of here', and his favorite, 'Damn tourist are more important than us'. That helped him decide the people were probably residents of this island.

He wanted to help them, but the shooting and shouts were attracting more people, more than they could possibly help and he had to make a decision now before half the island showed up. *Damn the sharks*, he thought, as he moved backward, watching the crowd.

"If this is a rescue mission, where are the rest of you?" a voice asked. Then another voice, "We should get to the water and grab the boat when it comes in."

Andy knew what he had to do now, and backed more quickly into the bay, almost relaxing a bit when he felt the water swirl around his sneaker and soak his good foot. Then he kept moving backward, his shotgun up and ready. When he felt the water reach his knees, he turned and began moving into the bay, relieved that there were no more shots. A few seconds later, the water was deep enough for him to start swimming, the shouts from the beach now getting louder and more numerous.

For some reason, he didn't worry about sharks, just getting into the water felt like he was back in the SEALs and holding the shotgun above the water as best he could, he used one hand and his legs to propel him through the water, which was warmer than his days during Hell Week, where the water was much colder. He kept swimming, soon hearing the raft motor getting closer. Seconds later he could see the brightly colored raft as it pulled close.

"Hey Swabbie, I saw you splashing around and thought you might like to ride the rest of the way to my boat," Finn said.

Even tired, Andy had to smile at the words from his friend. "'Bout time, you old gizzard," he replied, as the raft pulled alongside, and he pulled himself aboard.

"Weren't you worried about the sharks?" Finn asked, as Andy pulled his prosthetic leg out of the water.

"I didn't see any sharks here, probably too close to the shore."

"Really? What do you call that?" Finn asked, shining a red light at the water.

Andy looked and could just make out the tip of a shark fin in the water very close to the raft. He sat there staring for a moment. "Son of a…" he didn't finish the statement as he felt the squiggly feeling move up his spine. "How are Yoates and Milly?"

"We'll be there in a minute or two and you can see for yourself."

Finn guided the raft alongside the boat and Andy scrambled aboard, not an easy chore as the sea was still a bit choppy this close to the open ocean and the raft bobbed a bit. Still, he managed to get a purchase and climbed into the boat. There were only a few dim lights on as he moved quickly to the cabin, passing by the older couple who were standing to the side of the boat, watching him as he entered the Fly bridge. Without a word, both simply pointed to the galley.

Andy nodded and headed inside and down the steps seeing both Yoates and then Milly stretched out on the galley benches. Yolette was working on Yoates, so he turned toward his love. She had her eyes open and when he walked in, she smiled. Since the windows were covered with screens, the lights were on, and he could clearly see her wound and the blood. Instantly, he went into action, his training as a SEAL now came into play as he looked at her arm.

"I could really use a drink now. You know, to help with the pain," she said to him, but Andy refused.

"I'm sorry, my love, but it would thin your blood and only complicated things. Let me see your wound. Now, this might hurt a bit, so let's get it done, fast."

It had only been less than ten minutes since he applied the tourniquet to her arm and prepared to remove it. Moving back to Yolette, he asked for gauze and tape. She just grunted a bit, working hard to stem the bleeding in Yoates would and simply pushed the box to him. Andy grabbed the tape and gauze, there were still a few packets and headed to Milly. He released his belt from her arm and immediately her wound began bleeding heavily, but Andy was ready. He pulled out gauze and pressed it against the wound, relieved somewhat when the gauze stemmed the flow of blood. Milly cried out at this and closed her eyes, Andy knowing that the pain had caused her to pass out, which he expected.

Now, the hard part. Andy walked back to the box and removed the suture and needle, then he began to stitch her arm. Even in her sleep, Milly groaned as he pushed the needle through her skin but kept working to close the jagged portion of the bullet exit wound. It took him longer to do this, but he didn't stop, knowing time was critical. In a few minutes, he finished and with the bleeding now reduced, he covered the entry wound, which was much smaller, with gauze and wrapped it with medical tape. Finished, he checked her vitals as she started to come around.

"Andy, my arm hurts worse now," she said through clenched teeth. "What did you do?"

"I sewed up your wound. I'll get you something for the pain," he replied quietly. After getting some Tylenol, he gave her the pills and offered her a glass of water, glad when Finn came into the galley.

"We're in open water now and I have that guy Gerald, steering the boat. He has a little experience with small craft. How's your patient?"

"I sewed up her arm and applied a dressing. She'll need a doctor quick, so I guess heading to Florida is out. Best to put into a closer port, one with a hospital," Andy replied.

"Already decided on that. I told Gerald to take us to the Virgin Islands. That hurricane turned southwest a bit after it passed Martinique, so the islands will be in good shape. Venezuela looks like the next land mass it'll hit."

"That's unusual, isn't it? A storm like that changing course after hitting an island."

Finn shrugged. "The water is warmer to the south and the hurricane has a mind of its own."

Andy nodded, now concerned about his fellow SEAL, "You keep an eye on Milly, I'll check on Yoates," he replied, as Finn moved over her.

To his surprise, Yoates was awake and looking at him as he came closer, he even looked better, well better than Milly. "Damn, big man, I thought you would be down for a bit."

"Can't keep a good SEAL down. Yolette said you did a good job of packing off my wound, kept me going into shock," Sasquatch said with a smile.

Andy looked at Yolette. "I didn't know you were trained in medicine," Andy said.

Yolette brushed her hair back with a bloody hand. "Yes, I was a paramedic in my former life, but the pace and hectic lifestyle almost broke me, so I came to the islands for some rest, that's how I met this big goofy fellow," she replied, squeezing Yoates hand and giving him a kiss.

When they broke the kiss, Yoates looked at Andy. "I came upon Yolette when a couple of jerks, get this, Italian sailors, were giving her a hard time on the islands a few weeks after I got here. I was just hanging out, taking in the local atmosphere…"

He was cut off by Andy here, "You mean you were bar hopping."

"Well, yeah. Anyway, I had just left one place when I saw Yolette walking down the street and saw three local goofballs giving her a hard time. They were bugging her, and I saw the look of anger in her eyes. She was trying to get away from them when one of those goofs put his hand on her ass and pinched her. She turned around and slapped him and when the guy grabbed her arm and pulled her back, I stepped up, and let's just say, let them know they couldn't do that."

Yolette smiled at the memory. "He didn't just stop them, he picked up that one tough and threw him into the other two. Then the police showed up and put a stop to things. They let us go and I bought him a drink at a local pub to say thanks. I knew by his demeanor that he was the man I wanted to spend my life with, especially when I called my family and told them what happened, and my cousin was the one who convinced me to stay with him. We've been together ever since."

"I wondered about that," Andy replied. "Well, he looks like he's in good hands. I'll leave you two love birds in peace and go check on Milly."

"You'd better marry that girl," Yoates said, "after all we've been through."

"I plan to do just that. Finn said we're heading back to the islands, and when we get there, I plan on getting a ring for her. Maybe you can help me pick one out, Yolette."

"I'd be honored," she replied.

Chapter Twenty-Nine
Family

Pearls don't lie on the seashore. If you want one, you must dive for it—Chinese Proverb

Realizing how badly both Milly and Yoates needed medical attention, Finn convinced their passengers that they had to change plans and would make arrangements to get them safely back to the United States, he pushed the Munck Too, as fast as the boat would go, getting the two injured people to the island where he knew they would need immediate medical care, arriving there on the last bit of fuel in the motor, while Yolette contacted the local authorities about their emergency and arranged to have medical personnel waiting as they pulled into the harbor there.

Worried about Milly especially, Andy was greatly relieved to see an ambulance waiting near the dock and made a final check of her arm, greatly relieved to see that the color had returned a little and she was able to move it a bit, even though it was still extremely painful. As the boat came to a stop on the dock near the ambulance, Andy grabbed her hand and told her she would be fine, then helped the medical team bring their gurney onto the boat and led them to where she was.

Andy stopped the paramedics for a second, as they were ready to escort Milly down the gangplank after Yoates had already been taken since his injury was more serious. "Kind of a change, me standing here and you heading to the hospital," he said to her. After doing what he could to apply medical attention to her wound, he had applied a bandage.

"Don't get used to it, Sailor," Milly replied.

"Only when the kids come," he replied.

"Oh, it takes me getting trapped in a deadly hurricane and then getting shot to get you to finally come around to my way of thinking," Milly said, gauging his response carefully. "I should have done this sooner."

"What getting shot?" Finn said, intruding on the conversation. "Don't give him any ideas, Milly," he told her with a smile. "Now, get off my boat and see a doctor. Your parents told me to take care of you two and I mean to do it. When you're released, we're sailing for Aurora."

"I'll meet you at the hospital as soon as I get a car," Andy said, before he gave her a kiss. "Brings back some really good memories," he said as he touched her necklace. "Really good memories." Then the paramedics pushed her down the gangplank.

That night, Andy and Yolette waited in the hospital while Finn worked to get the other passengers safely on their way, explaining that the two wounded meant a change of plans as they could not sail to Florida like they had hoped. When they were gone, he joined them at the hospital and the three waited in silence for a bit until Yoates' doctor came out. The smile he had, let them know he would survive, though he would be off his feet for some time as the wound and the trek across the island had taken a toll on the man.

An hour later, Milly's doctor came out. He didn't smile and Andy's heart fell, until the doctor told him she would survive, just that it would take months of physical therapy and maybe more surgeries before she would regain most of the use of her arm. The news that she would survive and not lose her arm was like music to his ears, knowing the pain and anguish of losing a limb. It would take several days before she was well enough to travel.

Andy almost burst into tears with this news, comforted by his friends. Yolette told him to get Milly home and she would stay and take care of Yoates, promising to keep him updated and that they would visit them both as soon as they could.

~~~

The Munck Too departed the islands just a week later and after a trip through calm seas, docked at the Aurora Marina, having left St. Thomas just the day before. Standing on the bow as the boat moved into the Mariana, was Andy holding Milly's good hand and smiling, as Finn stood at the helm and steered the boat to anchorage.
~~~

Milly led the way down the gangplank and into the waiting arms of her parents and siblings. Andy came closely along behind her, and like Milly, was swarmed by both his family and hers. Samantha pulling him aside and telling him what a great job he had done and how proud they all were of him. Milly's father thanked him but in a more subdued manner. However, it was as Milly was being hugged again by her family for the second time that her mother noticed the ring.

Because of her sling, the diamond ring on her left hand had gone unnoticed, that plus her arm was still bandaged and hurting, so she kept it close to her body as she headed into the throng. Mary pushed her daughter back a moment and looked down, while Milly slowly brought up her left hand and held it out for her mother to see. "You're, you're..." she couldn't get the word out for a few seconds, just stood there in shock as she looked at her daughter and Andy who came over to stand behind Milly and placed his arms around her.

"Yes, Mom, we're engaged," Milly answered, which started a whole new round of congratulations and hugs from the families.

When things had quieted down enough to be safe, Finn slowly came down the gangplank and was intercepted by Mark. "Finn," he started. "Thanks for saving Andy and rescuing Milly. I know, we've never been friends, but I'm man enough to stand here and to offer my thanks. You did a good job," Mark said, putting his hand out for Finn to shake.

Finn looked him in the eye for a second before shaking it. "I've been away from this area for too long. I did so out of respect for both you and Sam. I'd like to stick around a bit, but I won't unless you tell me you're okay with it. Oh, and I promise, I'll never do anything in the future to cause you to regret allowing me to stay here," Finn said cautiously. "I mean that," he said, finally accepting the shake.

Mark looked at him and then at his wife, Samantha, who was busy hugging the happy couple. "Okay, I owe you that. Andy told me how you got him off that rock after his boat sank, then how you joined him getting the others to safety. Way I see it, we're even. No more late-night strolls with my wife or taking her out on your boat alone though. Okay?"

"Fine," Finn said, shaking Mark's hand, as Samantha came over to them and both men looked at her.

"Why do I feel like I'm being talked about?"

"Never mind, Sam. It's all good," Finn answered, but Sam kept looking at the two of them strangely. "Besides, we've got a wedding to plan."

Andy stood off to the side after the family had enjoyed a great meal back at the Thompson home. Thankfully, being raised in North Carolina meant that this early-October day was still mild, and the family had been able to enjoy a huge luncheon outside on the grass. Milly was standing beside him, her head on his shoulder. This was almost exactly the way she had dreamed this day would be like as a child. She suddenly raised her head and pointed out two figures approaching from off to the side. "Who is that?"

Andy looked but didn't recognize the man standing with an older woman. "I'm not sure. Looks like they're joining the party. Wait, my parents are seeing who they are," Andy said, pointing as both his parents walked over to this couple. He watched them carefully, when suddenly his mother hugged the woman while his father hugged the man.

"Are they old friends of your parents?" Milly asked.

"I don't know," Andy replied, as they both walked over. It was only when they reached the group that Andy realized who the couple was.

"Hey, Andy and Milly. Just heard you got engaged. About time," the man said.

Milly saw Andy smile and shake the man's hand, before he looked at her and smiled. "Figured it out yet?"

That was when she recognized Nathan and the woman was probably his mother, which led to even more hugging for all of them, but as Andy pulled back from Nathan for a bit, he asked him a question. "How did you know we got engaged?"

"After you left the Navy, I became a SEAL, and SEALs keep in touch. Sasquatch didn't tell you?"

"No, that SOB never let on that he knew you," Andy replied, a huge smile on his face.

"Who do you think told Yolette he was a great guy after she bumped into him in the Virgin Islands? "She's my cousin," Nathan said. "She told me all about helping you choose that ring and that you were coming home today, so I convinced mom to come with me and see the old neighborhood. Hope you remember to invite me to the wedding," Nathan said.

After more hugs, they of course invited Nathan and his mother to the party, and later, as they were standing off by themselves once more, Andy looked around their old neighborhood. "You know, Milly, this neighborhood holds such good memories," he told her.

"I agree, but what about your seeing the world?"

"I've seen enough, for now. How about we get married and live here, but we vacation around the world?" Andy replied.

"I could live with that. Took you long enough to realize that all you need to be happy, is already here," she said smiling.

Andy smiled back. "When you smile, it always makes me feel happy, ever since we were kids," he responded, placing his arm around her and kissing her again.

Epilog

The truth of the matter is that you always know the right thing to do. The hard part is doing it—Norman Schwarzkopf

The jukebox was blasting off some loud, foul mouthed, song, *what passed for a love ballad these days*, Yoates thought, as he sat nearby and watched the patrons, especially one guy in who was really drinking heavily and getting loud, battling with the jukebox for most obnoxious noise in the bar. Already the bartender told the man to calm down, or he would be kicked out. The man just looked at him, put his finger up to his lips and made an obnoxious noise like he was blowing farts.

"What an ass you are," Yoates, now recovered fully from his leg wound, said to the man.

The man turned around and looked him in the eye. "Do you know who I am? Don't mess with me, man, I'm the captain of a large cruise boat, the Jasmine, and I could own your ass. You know what happens when people piss me off? They get pissed on," the man laughed loudly at his antics.

"Wow, funny. I thought, since you're the captain of the Jasmine, all you did was ram people's boats and leave them to die in the ocean," Yoates responded.

That comment got the man's attention. "Fuck you. Were you on that little piece of shit boat? The one that doesn't know the rules of the sea?"

"Are you the asshole that rams others and leaves them to die?" Yoates asked. He looked around the room. "Your fucking drunk ass buddy here did just that. And yes, we know the rules of the sea. When approaching another boat, veer to port, or left for your information. Asshole." Yoates responded, before he reached out, grabbed the man by his shirt and pulled him into his fist which was rushing to meet him anyway. The man's nose exploded, and he fell to the floor, the blood gushing out. "I was coming here to beat the shit out of you. But you're not worth the effort."

"I will say this, if I ever hear anyone tell me, you rammed another boat and left without trying to help, I'll find you and kill you," Yoates stated as he stepped over the man and headed for the door. Not one person tried to stop him, but the captain of the Jasmine, still lying on the floor, received many a dangerous stare. His antics would be spread around the entire island by the end of the week, and no one would probably sail with him again.

THE END